THE PENNY-DEEP WITCH MURDERS

Charlie Stickman

W and S Books

Best Wishes
Charlie.
Stickman

ISBN-13: 978 1 914243 00 4

Cover design by: More Visual

I would like to thank the following.

My Parents Joyce and Lewis.

My Partner Louise for all her love and support

Phil Sokell (a very close friend of Professor Kip Lo'Shell) and Patricia Sokell for all their support.

Stephen Frost for his advice and guidance.

And a very special thank you to the magical Liz whose kind words and inspiration are the reason for this book being written.

I would also like to extend a big thank you to Annie Jenkinson, Copy Editor who went above and beyond. Annie can be found at Just Copyeditors.

Thank you also to More Visual Ltd for the book cover creation.

Chapter 1

"We are all born to be magic – but from that time onwards, we are conditioned to forget."

The town of Penny-Deep had been in existence, in some shape or form, longer than any written records—and certainly longer than anyone could remember. As a settlement, it had somehow managed to survive without any name at all for many hundreds of years.

But as the settlement slowly expanded to become a village and then, over time, into a town, the name Penny-Deep had eventually become attached to it.

Nowadays, not many people knew the name's origins, and no one even seemed to give it any thought. But some—just a few—believed they did know.

The town itself was stuck out on a far-reaching limb of the county it inhabited, surrounded for many miles by both moorland and dense forest. The first settlements had been located at the top of two adjoining hills, and one of these pagan sites had long been used as a place of worship. But by the fourth century, old beliefs practised there had been forced to give way to Christianity. Thus, the site of worship had also quickly shifted from pagan to Christian, a small church then having been built on the hill. By the eleventh century, a large Norman church was occupying the site and the addition of a bell tower would be made to it some five hundred years later.

And this building still stood to this day: the Church of St Augustine, Penny-Deep.

The pagan settlement at the top of the *other* hill had also long since vanished in the mists of time, but most people around now did not know what lay at the top of it.

They only knew the land there was privately owned and trespassers were unwelcome, but in truth, what kept folk away were the many stories of much strangeness associated with the land. There were tales of ghosts and demons, goblins and fairy-folk, and of course witches, while some even spoke of people simply vanishing into thin air up at the top of that hill.

However, no one could ever come up with specific names or definitive facts. That said, there did exist some historical documentation relating to a witch trial sometime in the seventeenth century, but few now knew the details of this story either. Fewer still could produce the name of the witch.

But some—just a few—thought they remembered that too.

Most locals were more than happy to take no interest in the story; after all, it had happened so long ago. And anyway, most townsfolk in Penny-Deep would tell you they disbelieved in such things as real witches, content to write such things off as the superstitions of a bygone age.

Oddly though, despite all that, no one ever ventured to the top of that hill. The closest anyone would go was to visit Mrs Chattox who lived on what had been a smallholding, on land positioned halfway to the top. Even then, Mrs Chattox had few visitors after dark, and what's more, the old barn opposite her farmhouse had been converted into a dwelling and had been up for rent for the longest time. And even though the barn was described very favourably by all the letting agents, no one ever seemed inclined to move in, certainly nobody from around those parts.

What was now the town of Penny-Deep had mainly settled around the base of those two hills, producing a small town by anyone's standards, but pretty, with stone-built houses and shops, and on some of the narrower lanes, the old cobbles lay still intact.

Visitors could be forgiven for thinking they had stepped into the pages of a Dickensian novel.

The town had always been reasonably self-sufficient, most employment in the area coming from local farming. However, over the past fifty or so years, farming had become less labour-intensive, and many of the original families had moved out to seek employment and a new life elsewhere. This, in turn, had given rise to an influx of incomers, mostly business types with enough money to purchase a piece of this picturesque rural idyll and who didn't mind a lengthy commute.

That was if they weren't already retired, of course. Penny-Deep was an ideal spot for that.

The O'Neil family had lived in the Manor House ever since its construction in the mid-1500s, yet Archibald—'Archie'—O'Neil was still considered an incomer despite having lived on his family's ancestral estate on the outskirts of Penny-Deep for the past twenty years.

He had been next in line to inherit the estate and the family money, though, by then, he had also amassed significant wealth of his own through property development. A bumptious man who had little to do with the townsfolk, it's fair to say he was disliked by all who had dealings with him.

Little more could be said about Penny-Deep when describing it in general terms, except—perhaps one of the town's most unusual features because of the surrounding dense woodland—it had only one road leading in and out. This meant that anyone using this road had to cross the river Lethe via the shallow crossing point situated at the next village, Stony Ford.

Chapter 2

The small red car travelled along the winding grey tarmac road to Penny-Deep like a single red corpuscle making its way along a vein. The day had reached its final quarter, and the evening sky was the colour of lead, looking twice as heavy. It had been threatening rain most of the day, but so far, the threats had not been followed through. The clouds hung darkened and ominous.

The only occupants of the car were father and daughter, and both sat silent, lost in a world of their own. Sophia Cadman was eight years old and small for her age, a pale and sullen child with big mournful brown eyes and shoulder-length dark-brown hair. As she watched the country-side pass by, she wondered what her new life in her new home would be like.

Most children Sophia's age would have been filled with a mixture of excitement and discomfort at moving on to such an adventurous experience, though they might also be filled with feelings of regret and isolation at leaving behind old friends. But Sophia felt none of these things.

She was just indifferent to the situation in which she now found herself.

It had been just over a year now since Sophia's mother had died from something called cancer, and she missed her every day. She tried to put on a brave face, and the teachers at her school had all been very nice but the other children, even those she had once called friends, had all started acting mean towards her, particularly the girls. Her mother's death had weakened her, and her vulnerability had shown, making her easy prey for the other children.

They had teased her and said all manner of horrible, ugly and mean things.

But without a doubt, the worst came from three girls who had once been her closest friends.

These girls claimed that because Sophia's mother had only been young when she'd died of cancer, little Sophia was bound to die young also. These spiteful comments seemed to stick with her, haunting her thoughts, hanging over her like a dark shadow.

She could not sleep some nights, while during the daytimes, nothing could interest her.

The ominous and horrible words constantly flitted through her mind like a cloud of angry bees buzzing around her head. And it was at times like these that a little girl most needed her mum.

Sophia was glad to see the end of the school term and the beginning of summer break.

Many were the times she wished she could talk to her father about what scared her so much, but ever since her mother's death, he had also seemed so quiet and withdrawn, with a saddened look.

Sophia could tell he was hurting but didn't know what to say to make him feel better, and she certainly didn't want to add to his pain with her own fears and upset.

One worry that became a constant companion was, if she did die young, who would look after her father then? He needed her, and she couldn't bear the thought of deserting him.

Sophia studied her father's face secretly from the corner of her eye. He was still a young man, tall and well-built with a crop of short black hair that, on very close inspection, was now showing the odd sprinkle of silver. Sophia knew she had inherited her mother's eyes, as her father's own were clear blue, and in happier times, they had seemed to light up and dance when he talked with her. Now though, they seemed to have faded, the dancing permanently at an end.

Adam Cadman, Sophia's dad, was driving on mental auto-pilot, wondering how different this move to Penny-Deep would have been if Diana, his wife, had been still alive.

Perhaps if she had still been with them, they wouldn't have had to move in the first place?

He had met Diana while still in the army; he had been on a stopover in Gibraltar, after a deployment in the Middle East. The then beautiful young Diana had been on a holiday there, and they had met one evening in a bar, falling in love quickly and deeply. Following a whirlwind romance, he managed to leave the army with only a week to spare before their wedding.

Once back in England, Adam had managed to find employment by joining the police, adapting to civilian life quickly and enjoying the challenge of his new career. After two years of beat work, he had become a detective, and in the two years following, he'd gained promotion to the rank of Detective Sergeant. During this time, Sophia had been born, making life just seem better by the day. He and Diana purchased a new home, and by the time Sophia had reached three years of age, he had been promoted yet again, this time to Detective Inspector.

They dared to dream about the future and set about making plans.

Just four years later, though, Diana had been diagnosed with an aggressive form of breast cancer, already stage IV, and it spread so rapidly that she died only months after her diagnosis.

Adam Cadman had always been considered —both by himself and those around him—as a tough, practical individual. But the death of his wife had shattered him, and he was the first to admit it. Now no longer able to live in the home he and Diana had built together, Adam sold the property, father and daughter moving together into a small, rented house.

In a desperate bid to cope, he threw himself headlong into his work, leaving Sophia in the care of schoolteachers and childminders. His fierce commitment to work gave him an enviable reputation as a top Detective Inspector who had cleared up five murder cases, a large international sex-trafficking ring, and several other large cases involving organised crime.

But as Adam began to slowly rise from his depression, he realised he had not been there for Sophia. She too must have been grieving, and he had done nothing to help her.

Now, it was weighing upon his mind and heart.

Lately, Sophia had become quiet and withdrawn, and her teachers had told him that she was being bullied at school, though she would never talk about it to either them or him. Now, while driving to Penny-Deep, he recalled the pain he felt living in their old home without Diana. But too late now, he realised how selfish he had been in selling the property without consulting Sophia. It was the only home Sophia had known and filled with the memories of her mother.

Adam knew he'd been a terrible father over the past twelve months and that he had to make amends with Sophia. She was all that he had left that was truly a part of Diana. He also knew that Diana would be horrified at how he had neglected their daughter, even though he had not done so consciously, but due to battling with his own grief and depression.

As soon as he could after this realisation,

Adam met with his Chief Superintendent and tended his resignation. He cited that he needed to spend more time with his daughter after the death of his wife. Of course, all his colleagues understood but he still knew it was the worst possible time, and that his swift departure would be leaving his team in the lurch. The city teams were all under pressure investigating three separate disappearances of young women over the past two months. But from now on, Sophia would *always* come first.

Fortunately, his Chief considered him a far too valuable asset to lose permanently, and so proposed an alternative solution. The inspector at Penny-Deep Police Station was retiring and needed a replacement. It was an ostensibly uniform role, Adam was told, but surely still a better option than leaving altogether. Also, the place was out in the middle of nowhere, and nothing of any note ever happened there, so he could work the hours that best suited his and his daughter's needs, and work in either uniform or plain clothes, as the need arose.

In addition to this, Chief Superintendent Wise stated that Adam could continue his career at Penny-Deep until his daughter was older and the time was right for him to return to the fold.

Suddenly, all thoughts of past events cleared out of Adam's head.

They had reached the tiny village of Stony Ford, and Adam changed down into low gear as he steered the little Vauxhall Corsa down the slope towards the river. Here, he knew they would meet the shallow crossing point that would be the only way into Penny-Deep.

As they crossed the River Lethe, Adam noticed Sophia looking out of the side window with some concern; he saw, too, that she had lifted her feet high onto the backseat of the car, presumably to prevent them getting wet, though there was little chance of that.

The crossing point was nothing but a wide and stony track covered by no more than an inch of water. It had been formed hundreds of years ago, if not earlier, to facilitate the crossing of horse-drawn carts, giving rise to the village name of Stony Ford.

Once across the river and back on solid tarmac, Sophia seemed more at ease, and Adam smiled to himself. It was just a couple more miles to Penny-Deep, and suddenly, for some reason, he felt a huge weight lifting from him, and the cares of the world were all forgotten.

As they passed through the tiny and quaint town, the shopkeepers were turning on the lights in the pretty little shops, and the bow windows all shone like lanterns in the fading evening.

It was a different world from what he was used to, but he hoped that given time, he and Sophia would enjoy it, even to become a part of it.

Eventually, Adam Cadman found the turning

that took them up a small track leading off to their new home. Pulling into the yard of Old Anna Farm, Adam turned to Sophie.

"What do think, sweetheart? Do you think you will enjoy living here?"

Sophia just shrugged, but Adam knew he had done well.

The converted barn was newly modernised and looked idyllic. When he'd first viewed the property, he had been convinced it would be well out of his price range, but the agents said that the place had been empty since its renovation and the owner was keen for it to be rented.

He was, therefore, asking just a nominal rent, something Adam had barely been able to believe. At last, his luck was turning and with the little barn, he had struck gold. He inquired about the owner, but the estate agent said he couldn't help him. Apparently, the owner wished to remain anonymous, and all dealings were to be carried out by a firm of solicitors based in London. Adam had simply shrugged. *Each to his own,* as the saying went.

"Let's go in, and I'll show you around, "Adam said to Sophia. "You can pick a bedroom before we begin to unpack." And with that, they both climbed from the car.

Their arrival had not gone unnoticed. Mrs Chattox watched with interest from behind the pristine white net curtains of her home, tweaking and twitching the flimsy voile and standing on tiptoes to get a better view.

***

Hours later, Old Anna Farm stood quietly at the intersection of night and day, and a mist had swirled down into the yard and surrounded the old farmhouse and the converted barn. Standing at the entrance to the yard was a young woman with long dark hair, wearing a sweeping black dress that fitted close to the curves of her slim body. The woman held her ground for a while as if deep in contemplation. Then she walked slowly and silently into the farmyard, watched by no one.

The woman walked around the red Vauxhall Corsa parked outside the Old Barn, peering in through the car's windows, and tracing a single fingertip over the vehicle's paintwork.

Then she turned her attention to the converted barn, studying every minuscule detail before walking between the two drystone walls and along the path to the front of the building.

Once at the front door, the woman first pressed her right cheek against it, seemingly unbothered by the coldness it must have emanated. Then she laid the palms of both hands over its surface, the way a doctor might gently feel for a pulse on a newborn child.

In truth, she was waiting to feel the vibrating soul of the barn, to detect any tiny and subtle change in the energies emitting from the building. It was there! She could feel it, and it pleased her.

The woman turned and silently walked back down the path, stopping at the gateway in the drystone wall. She crouched down by the wall on her left side, inspecting the stones till she found the one she was looking for, and then gently removed it.

The removal of the rock revealed a hollow space with flat sides forming a small compartment. The woman took a small leather bag from her belt and untied its long drawstrings.

Reaching into the bag, she now removed what looked like a little pouch of bouquet garni, a bundle of plants and herbs bound with a fine string. But this bundle was not to be added to a cooking pot. The plants wrapped in this delicate bouquet were mint, calamus and High John the Conqueror root and the young woman placed the bundle of plants into the stone compartment and then replaced the stone that concealed it.

The young woman walked back through the farmyard, and the mist seemed to part before her as she went, making away for her. Like a ghost, the woman walked out onto the track that led to the farm and beyond. She stopped and looked back at the old barn before turning right and heading up the trail towards the dark woods.

Chapter 3

Victoria Timperley wasn't beautiful, but neither was she ugly. She was what could best be described as plain. Victoria was lean and had a good figure, but her face lacked eyes that could captivate or lips that would draw a man in for a kiss. Her cheekbones failed to make any sort of an appearance, while her nose, she thought, was just a little too straight. But Victoria had learned that with brushes and make-up, it was possible to paint beauty onto the blank, unremarkable canvas that was her face.

Her mousy, shoulder-length hair was dyed and highlighted in shades of blonde, and as she walked into the city centre wine bar that Friday night, more than one male head turned and looked her over in appreciation. Even Clive something or other, whom she recognised from school, looked approvingly at her—and he had apparently gone off to be a church curate or something of the sort!

It was early evening, and the gang had all arranged to meet in Genevieve's wine bar, due to its proximity to the insurance company where they all worked. The night was organised as a send-off for Bill Walters in middle management, who was now leaving to set up his own business.

Well, as Victoria didn't really know Bill Walters, this certainly wasn't her idea of a good night out. But she had recently split from Sean, her feckless boyfriend, so at least this would be something to help pass the time. Sean had failed to commit to anything, and in particular, he had spectacularly failed to commit to *her.* Victoria had been with Sean for three years, but he was no different now than when she had first met him. Yes, the man was roguishly good looking, but also very immature. Sean lacked any sort of ambition, and though he'd had four jobs during the time they were together, none had ever lasted more than a few months.

The majority of the last three years he had spent shamefully unemployed.

Alas, she had hoped he would mature with time, but he didn't, and three years was all she could afford to invest in him.

Victoria had always possessed a vision of how her future would be, with an adoring husband who had a good job, who could provide a well-appointed home in the suburbs where she could spend her time raising their two children and hosting coffee mornings.

Of course, it would help if her husband was also handsome, but that really wasn't a deal-breaker just as long as he could provide the lifestyle and the children.

So, the object of this night at Genevieve's wasn't to have a good time with friends and colleagues, but to find a replacement for Sean. She had a feeling that several of the younger, single, junior-managers from the company would be in attendance, and that should provide a decent pool of potential candidates. Victoria scanned the room, looking for her clique of friends.

While doing so, she noticed with delight and anticipation that she was right about the number of young single managers in attendance.

They were out in droves, and to Victoria, it wasn't hard to guess why.

Their primary motivation for coming out was not to wish Bill Walters good luck and farewell either, but rather to use the informal setting as an opportunity to network and jockey their positions in the firm's hierarchy. Victoria would normally have taken a cynical view, but tonight, that would have been a little hypocritical seeing as she had attended with her own agenda in mind, in which Bill Walters didn't feature either.

Pushing through the crowd, Victoria purchased a gin spritzer from the bar. She then made her way to join Jill, Fran, Julie and Debbie. As usual, office gossip was the order of the day and Victoria made a mental note of anything useful about the young male prospects from the firm, if and when such nuggets cropped up in the conversation.

As the evening passed, Victoria downed a couple more gin spritzers, chatted with the girls and watched the potentials. She was delighted by the occasional glance and smile that came her way. One young man, in particular, caught her eye. She didn't know him and wasn't sure if he actually worked at the firm, but Debbie assured her that he did, and said his name was Simon.

He was, in fact, a new employee and had only joined them in the last month or so, during which time he had been away on courses to get him up to speed with the firm's working practices.

Victoria estimated Simon's age to be around twenty-five, a couple of years older than herself. He was tall and slim in an expensive suit and sporting a good tan, and, what's more, he was a bit of a looker. Simon had noticed her, too; she knew he had. During the time she watched him, he had looked over several times and smiled. On one occasion, he had even nodded!

Victoria nodded back. Simon was looking promising, she thought. Sitting her drink down on the corner of the bar, she made her way to the toilets to carry out a make-up inspection.

The mirror in the ladies' room assured Victoria that her artwork was intact, and after the application of a little more lip gloss, she was ready to make the acquaintance of Simon.

Walking back into the bar, Victoria collected her drink and downed the contents of the glass for a little boost of courage. The drink tasted strange, and for a moment, she thought she had picked up the wrong glass. But if that really was the case, it was too late.

Victoria decided she would have to order another; after all, she couldn't wander over to Simon empty-handed. That would have looked presumptuous, and just feel awkward.

Victoria spent what seemed like an age trying to catch the bartender's eye, but in actual fact, it was only a couple of minutes. She turned her head to check that Simon was still where she had last seen him in the crowd. Suddenly, the whole room carried on turning, though her head had stopped moving. She felt unbalanced and grabbed the edge of the bar to stop herself falling backwards.

Fran, who noticed her clinging to the bar for dear life, came over and asked if she was alright. Victoria managed to stand up straight and hoped whatever was wrong with her had passed. She assured Fran that she was okay, though her eyesight was now a little blurry. But she knew she couldn't afford to create any kind of a fuss, not with Simon nearby and almost on the hook.

The noise in the bar now seemed deafening, and she decided to make her way back to the ladies' toilets to compose herself. As she walked down the narrow corridor towards the toilets, Victoria was forced to lean against the wall with her left shoulder in order to keep upright.

Now, she was feeling hot and decided to bypass the toilets; she needed fresh air instead, and quickly, so she exited the building by a fire door at the end of the corridor.

It led to a small alley that ran down the side of the wine bar.

Once outside, the cool evening air hit her, and she felt slightly better. She leaned back, resting against the brickwork. What the hell was wrong with her? She hadn't drunk enough to be feeling this way. She knew her limits, and she was nowhere near intoxicated. Had she picked up some sort of a bug, she wondered? Bloody typical, tonight of all nights!

Suddenly, Victoria felt an overwhelming tiredness. Perhaps if she closed her eyes for a couple of minutes, it would pass, and she could go back into the bar. She shut them tight, and immediately fell into a vast black void.

Chapter 4

Sophia Cadman woke early. It wasn't the sound of the raucous cockerel somewhere outside that woke her, since on this occasion, it seemed she had beaten the noisy bird by a full ten minutes. The truth was that Sophia was keen to explore her new home and surroundings. Her bedroom had come fully furnished, and the double bed she slept in was much larger than the one she had been used to in her old home. The bed and bedding were luxuriously soft, with a faint smell of lavender that gave her the best night's sleep she'd had in a long time.

Her father, as promised, had let her pick her room, so she made the obvious choice, the bedroom with the en-suite bathroom. On exiting her bed, Sophia was in such a hurry to try the walk-in power shower that she nearly stepped in still wearing her nightdress. Once inside, the force of the water almost battered her to the floor, until she managed to adjust the water flow.

The shower was so warm and inviting she stayed in there for a good five minutes longer than she needed. The whole experience made her feel very grown-up.

Then, once out and dressed, she made her way downstairs to the kitchen where sunlight streamed in through the windows, casting a yellowy glow and a warmth across the room.

Locating a bowl in the kitchen cupboard, Sophia poured herself some breakfast cereal. She added milk from a large carton that someone had thoughtfully left in the fridge for them to use, and pulling out a stool, she climbed up and sat at the kitchen's central island unit. All of these things she tried to do as quietly as possible so as not to disturb her father, who was still in bed.

Sophia had been devouring her cereal for a couple of minutes when she had the strangest feeling that someone was watching her. Then, from the corner of her eye, Sophia saw a large black shadow sweep over the surface of the central island. Instinctively, she turned to look out of the kitchen window just in time to see a ghostly, silvery-white shape move to one side and out of sight. Sophie was startled, but curiosity gained the upper hand, and she quickly made her way to the kitchen door.

Adam Cadman had given up any hope of catching a few extra minutes of sleep.

Somewhere outside, there was a bloody cockerel making an enormous racket.

But it wasn't this that had woken him; it was the sound of his daughter leaping out of bed with all the grace of a baby elephant. Then had come what had sounded like a waterfall, crashing down in the next bedroom. Eventually, this sound was replaced by the baby elephant stomping downstairs and into the kitchen, where a particularly bad juggling act sounded to be taking place.

Adam had just become resigned to his fate and pulled himself out of bed when he heard the kitchen door open and Sophia speaking to someone.

With growing concern, Adam quickly pulled on a pair of jeans and a tee-shirt and ran downstairs to the kitchen. On nearing the door to it, he could clearly hear Sophia asking someone what their name was. Snatching at the handle, he flung the door open. His mind was playing numerous images of what was happening outside, from the benign to the downright terrifying.

But none of these images prepared him for the spectacle that greeted him.

Sophia was standing in the garden, talking to a large white horse. It nuzzled into her chest, and she wrapped her arms around its large head and hugged it.

Occasionally, the horse nudged her gently and made her laugh.

Adam realised that it was the first time he had seen his daughter laugh, or even smile, for a long time. He couldn't recall the last time it had happened; she certainly hadn't done so since her mother had died. He thought back for a moment, trying to pinpoint the last time a smile had graced her beautiful face. Sophia suddenly looked at him, quizzically.

"Daddy, does he come with the house?" she said, still hugging the horse.

"No, I'm afraid not, sweetheart, and I think you'll find that he is a she!"

"Oh," said Sophia, laughing, as the horse nudged her once more.

A friendly but unfamiliar voice suddenly spoke up.

"She lives somewhere up the track at the back of your house, dear. It looks like she's popped down to introduce herself."

Both Adam and Sophia turned to see a stout, elderly woman with a warm, welcoming smile and wearing a long floral apron. "Hello to you both," she said, "I'm Annie Chattox, and I live in the old farmhouse over there, opposite you."

Adam introduced himself and Sophia, though Sophia was still too wrapped up playing with her new friend. "Here you are dear," said Mrs Chattox, pulling out a handful of carrots from her apron pocket. "Give her these, and she'll be your friend for life."

Sophia, still smiling from ear to ear, took the carrots and began feeding them to the horse, which gently took them one by one. The horse chewed each carrot thoroughly, before nudging Sophia, to tell her that it was ready for another one.

“Thank you,” said Sophia, graciously. “Do you know her name?"

"No, dear," said Mrs Chattox. "All I know is she lives somewhere further up the hill and pops down occasionally to see if there are any carrots on offer. I always have a supply in ready if you ever need some for her."

"Oh, thank you!" said Sophia, beaming the broadest smile.

Turning to Adam, Mrs Chattox inquired if they had settled in alright. Adam said that they had and Mrs Chattox continued, "It'll be nice to have neighbours after all this time. Since my own daughter's grown up and moved on, it tends to be ever so quiet up here."

She nodded towards Sophia.

"And it'll be nice to have a young one running around the place again. I love to hear the sounds of children playing, and this place is a real adventure land for kiddies."

Adam took an immediate liking to Mrs Chattox.

She had a very homely, motherly way about her that made him feel at ease. While Sophia was still feeding her friend, Adam and Mrs Chattox talked, getting to know each other a little better.

During their conversation, Adam uncharacteristically confided to the neighbour about the death of Diana and how he had made the decision to move out to Penny-Deep for Sophia's sake.

While he spoke to Mrs Chattox about his

reasons for moving to Penny-Deep, Adam realised that he was seeking reassurance about doing the right thing in moving his daughter away from her old school and out into this isolated part of the county. Somewhere during their conversation, Mrs Chattox rested her hand on his arm, saying, "She'll do just fine here, don't you worry about that. If you ever need a hand with anything, just knock on my door. You know where I am."

That gave him the reassurance he so badly needed.

"Oh, you poor soul," she went on, "You and that young lass have been through the wringer good and proper. But you're here now, and you've done the right thing. Life will get better for you both. You'll soon see!"

"Did I mention I'm a policeman?" said Adam. "I've also transferred here to work at the police station in Penny-Deep." Then he said more thoughtfully, "It's strange, but a year ago, this would not have been something I would have planned to do."

Mrs Chattox smiled a comforting smile.

"Well, I'd heard you were a policeman," she said. "In a small place like Penny-Deep, word soon gets around and you'll find that out soon enough. As for not planning to move here, I always find people rarely end up where they planned to be, but always end up where they are supposed to be! Don't you think? You should give that some thought. You'll soon understand it, Adam."

With that, Mrs Chattox gave Adam a wink and made her way off towards her home, calling out yet again to tell him to let her know if there was anything at all he or Sophia needed.

By this time, the horse had gently devoured its way through all the carrots that Sophia had, and giving her one last nudge, the horse turned and walked off across the farmyard, turning right towards the track at the rear of the house.

Returning indoors to the kitchen, Sophia climbed back up on her stool and began chattering on excitedly about all things horse-related, including whether they could be adopted or not? It was good to see her so animated and excited, and Adam just let her go on. It was good to see his little girl so animated again after so long. He interjected when needed, but for the most part, he just listened to Sophia, enjoying her company, letting her ramble on, enthused.

After a while, Sophia turned her attention back to her breakfast cereal, and once the conversation had lulled a little, Adam turned on the small counter-top radio for a little background music. He made himself a black coffee, and that was all.

During the time it took to finish breakfast, they made a plan of action for the rest of the morning. But as he did so, Adam thought about the words the old lady had used—about how things rarely turned out as planned but went the way they simply were supposed to.

The plan, such as it was, boiled down to making a start on unpacking the suitcases and cardboard boxes containing their worldly goods which, by any one's standards, were not many things at all. Sophia insisted that she was grown-up enough to do her own unpacking, and with that, they both made their way upstairs, Adam carrying two of their three suitcases.

Sophia was soon occupied with unpacking and sorting out her own clothes, putting them onto hangers and into the slim little wardrobe in the corner of her room. Adam decided to head up to the bathroom and took the opportunity for a quick shower.

The water was hot and relaxing, and as steam filled the shower cubicle, he breathed in deeply, twisting and stretching his body under the warm downpour from the shower head.

Once out of the shower, Adam towelled off and mixed a bowl of shaving cream with a badger-hair shaving brush that had seen better days. The scruffy old thing was starting to moult at an alarming rate, but the stainless steel safety razor was holding a new blade and made short work of the shadowy black stubble shading his face. Stepping back from the mirror, he cast an appraising eye over his body. He had an athletic build and had only put on a pound or two since his army days. That said, his body felt a little baggy somehow, and seemed to have lost some of its once muscular tone. Perhaps now, he would have a bit more time to exercise before he descended too far down the slippery slope of comfortable living, he thought.

Adam dressed and made a quick check on Sophia, who was making an excellent job of unpacking and putting away her clothes. He couldn't help noticing that many of her things had also seen better days and could really do with being replaced. This used to be a mother and daughter undertaking, something that both Diana and Sophia had enjoyed doing together.

Now though, the task was going to have to fall to him. He knew that taking his young daughter clothes shopping was going to be as awkward as it was unavoidable. Adam said nothing and left Sophia to her chores whilst he began his own unpacking.

By midday, they had gone on to unpack the few meagre household items they had brought with them, the most priceless being several framed photographs of them all during happier times with Diana. Adam watched Sophia gazing lovingly at each picture, no doubt lost in her memories.

Adam was correct in his assumption, at least in part.

Sophia missed her mother terribly and would give anything to have her back. But what Adam couldn't know was Sophia's mental anguish as she remembered what the girls at her last school had said. Her mum had been beautiful, something plain to see in each photograph.

It was also plain to see that her mum had only been young when she'd died, and Sophia wondered how many years she would even have left with her father.

As time passed, the excitement and joy of exploring their new home had slowly descended into silence. But then the silence, alongside their thoughts, was suddenly interrupted by a loud knock at the kitchen door. Mrs Chattox suddenly burst in, sporting oven mitts and carrying a large orange-coloured Le Creuset casserole pot.

"Sorry to barge in like this," she said. "But this is heavy! I thought you two might be hungry so I've done you a nice bit of lamb stew. "

She set the pot down on the stove. Adam began thanking her, but she waved him off with her left arm and said. "Come and get it while it's still hot. I'll pop back for the pot in an hour or two, and don't you dare try washing it. I'll sort it out later."

Mrs Chattox then bustled off through the door, leaving them to eat.

The lamb stew had been divine, and they both cleared their plates.

Sophia decided she wanted to reorganise some of her clothes and so trooped off upstairs whilst Adam defied orders and washed the casserole pot.

True to her word, Mrs Chattox returned at about the time she said she would. Adam finally managed to thank her, but she insisted it was she who should be thankful.

"Living up here on my own, I never bother making myself proper meals. Cooking a hearty meal for one seems such a waste of time, but cooking this stew knowing you two can share it —well, it gives me a good excuse to cook something tasty, and besides, I love to cook," she said, adding, “There is plenty more where that came from if you liked it.”

Adam complimented the elderly neighbour on her cooking skills but said they wouldn't want to impose on her good nature. Again, Mrs Chattox dismissed his words with a wave of her arms.

Adam decided that whilst Sophia was out of earshot, now might be a good time to pick their neighbour's brain. What he desperately needed was a little local knowledge.

Adam asked Mrs Chattox if she knew of anyone in Penny-Deep who did childminding.

He explained that he would have to report into work at Penny-Deep police station soon, and he would need someone to mind Sophia, particularly during the summer school break.

Mrs Chattox listened carefully as Adam told her what he had paid the childminders back in the city. Then he said, "The problem is, I will have to work some night shifts. Do you know of anyone in Penny-Deep who might be willing to take on a similar arrangement?"

Mrs Chattox looked thoughtful. Then said, "I'm sure you'd find someone in town, but you know, I raised my own daughter and worked as a teacher in the primary school before I retired. What about if I looked after her? I'd always be close at hand for emergencies, and it would cut out any messing about with travelling."

She paused before continuing. "I'd be willing to do it just for the company, but if you insist on paying me, then I insist on providing the both of you with a couple of decent meals a day."

Adam couldn't believe his ears or his luck.

"That would be great! But are you absolutely sure? I've not mentioned anything to Sophia yet, so..."

Mrs Chattox interrupted. "Tell you what. Why don't you make an excuse to leave her with me tomorrow? Just for a couple of hours, say, to see how we get on."

"That's a good idea," said Adam. "What about ten a.m. tomorrow? Would that be okay with you?"

"That would be perfect. I'll see you both then."

***

Annie Chattox stomped across the farmyard like a woman on a mission. Her life now had a purpose once again. After her daughter had married and moved away, her life had taken on a dull routine, with nothing to look forward to but sitting alone in a house of memories.

She had been widowed for ten years now, and still missed her John every day. Teaching at the local primary school had been a happy distraction, but retirement had come three years ago and with it, the realisation that her home was now an empty nest. It was during her darkest hours that Katherine Dee had come into her life, and although Katherine was far younger, she realised that they had much in common, including a deep appreciation for the 'old ways.'

In truth, Annie had no ability when it came to the 'old ways', but she had been told all the stories as a child by her grandmother, who had lived in the very same house where she now resided. She had never been afraid of living on the hill with all its legends and mysteries, but then she had also never foreseen a day when she would be lonely. Being alone was the only thing that frightened Annie Chattox. But now, things were beginning to change for her, as Katherine had always said they would.

Pushing her way in through the door of her home, Annie Chattox made her way over to the telephone and began dialling. Within three rings, the call was answered.

"It's me, Annie!" she said, breathless with excitement. "Yes, I've made contact, and they seem to be settling in, I've even volunteered my services to childmind the little one." She listened a little and then continued. "Yes, she's a bright little button, but there's a sadness that hangs about her."

She listened again. “Him! Oh yes, I think he'll do nicely for what you need, not to mention he's a handsome thing," she said, smiling to herself as she listened. "Yes, I will. Don't worry. Okay bye!" And with that, Annie Chattox put down the phone’s receiver.

***

After Mrs Chattox left, Adam walked through to the living room and sat back on the sofa, looking up at the exposed oak beams. Finding someone nice to mind Sophia whilst he worked had always been problematic in the past. He had envisioned that finding someone in Penny-Deep was going to be a nightmare, and he couldn't believe how easily things were working out. Penny-Deep was proving to be a marvellous place to bring up Sophia, and he couldn't help feeling somewhat enamoured with it. But at the same time, Adam knew he was going to miss the excitement of working in the city's CID unit. Penny-Deep was going to be a completely different way of life but working here might well end up being death by boredom.

And maybe it was the very thought of that

impending boredom that caused him to slip into a light sleep. It had been a busy couple of days.

The kitchen had now fallen back to near silence, the only sound being that of the radio playing away to itself. The music was interrupted for a local news bulletin.

"News is just coming in that another local woman has been reported missing this morning. The family of Victoria Timperley state that she went out last night to meet work colleagues at a bar in the city centre. Having failed to return home this morning, her family contacted the police, who are currently making enquiries. Currently, this is still being treated as a missing persons' case, but no one denies that Victoria Timperley not showing up at home is out of character.

"The police ask that if anyone knows the whereabouts of Victoria Timperley, or has any information at all, they should please contact them immediately." The newsreader went on to say in a stern tone. "And in case anyone needs reminding, Victoria Timperley is the fourth young woman to go missing in our area, in the past two months."

With that, the radio returned to the music.

Chapter 5

Victoria Timperley opened her eyes. It was dark, and she was disorientated.

Eventually, she became aware that she was lying on the cold, hard ground, and reasoned that she must have passed out in the alleyway outside the bar. In fact, she still felt a little queasy, and her head was throbbing. Victoria didn't know how long she had been lying in the alley, but she knew that if she could just make it back inside the wine bar, she could get help.

Slowly lifting her head, Victoria looked around, though her vision was still a little blurry.

She immediately knew something was very wrong; she was no longer outside in the alley, and the only thing she could see was a flickering light just above the ground. Rubbing her eyes, Victoria could now make out that it was coming from a large candle seated in some sort of a holder. Victoria pulled herself across the rough floor, which seemed to be made of large stone flagstones.

Reaching for the candle, she sat up and raised the flickering flame, moving it around to try and illuminate her surroundings.

Fear welled up from the pit of Victoria's stomach, and her arms and legs began to shake uncontrollably. Her mouth was dry and her voice hoarse, but she still managed to call out, "Help! Can anyone hear me?" There was no reply, so she tried again and again.

After a while, Victoria gave up on calling out. It was apparent there was no one around, or if there was, they weren't interested in either her or her wellbeing.

Still holding the candle, she unsteadily climbed to her feet, now realising that she was barefoot and her stiletto-heeled shoes were missing. Looking down, she saw in the dim candlelight that some of her other clothing was also gone, including her belt. Victoria scurried around, looking at the floor, but couldn't see her missing clothing or handbag anywhere.

Victoria followed a stone wall into the corner. Then she followed the second wall for a few feet till she came to a large wooden door, which she took the time to inspect in the dim candlelight. It was large and solid-looking, arching to form a point at the top.

Midway down, she saw a handle with a large iron ring attached. Putting the candle down, she first tried to pull and turn the ring, but the door seemed to be locked. Victoria began pounding on it with both fists and resumed her cry for help, but still there was no reply. What's more, the door was so solid that her pounding on it barely made a sound, though she bashed on it with all her might.

But in the end, her only achievement was bruised hands.

Victoria continued to edge around the rough, cold stone walls, trying to get a sense of the room's dimensions as the candle was too dim to get a view of the room in its entirety.

While walking by the third wall, she came upon a plastic bucket and a toilet roll, and next to them a plastic, litre bottle of water. By the time Victoria had edged along the fourth wall, she had estimated the room to be about twenty feet in length by about twelve feet in width.

She held the candle aloft and saw that the ceiling was also made of stone, forming an arch only around ten feet high at its tallest point. Whatever this place was, it put her in mind of a wine cellar, though it was empty except for the few items left for her comfort.

Victoria sat down on the cold stone floor in a corner near the large wooden door. She wondered how long she had been locked in the room and who could have put her there.

She felt her left wrist, searching for her watch, but it wasn't there.

It had been taken, along with the phone that had been inside her handbag.

With no daylight, it was impossible for her to work out what time of day it was in here.

Victoria tried to make sense of it all. Had it only been a few hours, or a whole day?

Was the farewell party still in full swing at

the wine bar, and were any of her friends wondering where she was? What if she had been missing longer? Had her family noticed she had not returned home? Her mother would be worried frantic by now, surely.

Suddenly, the tears came, and Victoria began to sob. Who would do this to her? Why would they do it? Then she remembered hearing something on the local news about other girls who had gone missing recently. Victoria hadn't taken much notice of the news stories; why would she?

But now she desperately tried to think back to what had been said in those news items, searching her memory for any detail that might help her. What proved most horrifying of all was that as far as she could remember, none of those girls had ever been found.

Was that a good thing or bad? Did that mean the girls were still alive or not?

Then just by chance, something caught her eye as the candlelight washed the surface of the wall next to her. She moved the candle closer and saw words roughly scratched into the stonework. The letters were uneven and of different sizes, but still, the message was plain to see:

MILLY CANARY HELP ME PLEASE

Reading the words, Victoria realised that the message had more meaning than the words alone conveyed. It was the strangeness of the name that struck her first, sounding whimsical, like the name of an old music hall performer. That was what made the name stand out and jogged her memory. Milly Canary. She knew she had heard that name before.

She was sure of it. According to the local news, Amelia Canary was one of the girls reported missing. But where was she now? Victoria's mind rapidly reached a most horrifying conclusion.

Victoria thought about her parents and her younger sister.

She loved them so much, and now, in this instant, she wanted to tell them.

Victoria realised that she probably wouldn't see them again, and a scream of anguish suddenly rose from her as she threw herself headlong onto the hard floor, crying hysterically.

Victoria cried until she couldn't cry any more.

When the tears finally subsided, she remained face down on the ground and hoped that sleep would come and put a stop to the horrific thoughts that raced around her head.

Perhaps if she fell asleep, she would wake in her bed at home, and this would all have been a nightmare. Eventually, sleep mercifully found her, softly taking her terror away.

Hours passed but then there came a sound, barely perceptible at first, but Victoria thought that she might have imagined it. However, she heard it again and again, the intervals between the sounds decreasing each time until eventually, the noise became constant, steadily growing louder.

It was a rustling that brought to mind thousands of cockroaches scurrying across the floor. Victoria sat upright. The sound seemed to be coming from the farthest corner of the room.

Raising the candle, Victoria tried to see what was making the noise, but still that corner was shrouded in shadow. The sound only grew louder, then suddenly, caught in the flickering light, something moved towards her from out of the dark. It was barely definable at first, but as it inched towards her, it took form. It was tall and thin, the body draped in what looked like long black clothing, with elongated, draping sleeves. There was something pale where a face should be, but Victoria couldn't make out any features, and the thing's odd pallor seemed to be framed with long black hair hanging down below the shoulders.

The figure frightened Victoria but she forced herself to speak.

"Hello. Who are you? Can you help me?"

The room fell silent, and even the rustling had stopped. Victoria tried again.

"Can you help me? Where am I?"

The dark figure made no reply, and Victoria slowly climbed to her feet. Holding the candle out at arm's length, Victoria crept forward. But as soon as she did, the rustling sound started up again, the creepy figure withdrawing back into the shadows.

Victoria darted forwards trying to catch hold of the figure but missed.

She reached into the shadow with the candle, but all it illuminated was the corner of two walls. Victoria banged her hands against the stonework, finding it depressingly solid. There was no figure there, and no doorway. Victoria thought she must have been hallucinating. Now she sat back in that corner dumbfounded and exhausted.

The apparition had looked so real!

Then a thought crossed her mind.

What if *that thing* had been the ghost of Amelia Canary?

Chapter 6

The following morning, Adam managed to sleep through the raucous calling of the local cockerel and catch a little extra sleep. By the time he did manage to pull himself from his bed, he could hear Sophia already up and about downstairs.

Adam had decided he would kill two—or even three—birds with one stone that morning.

First, he would go for a run. Lord knew he needed the exercise, and he had already made his mind up that he was going to regain some of his former fitness while working at Penny-Deep, and today was a good time to start! Second, he had also decided that while out running, he would call into Penny-Deep Police Station and look the place over.

Adam was keenly aware that his leave of absence couldn't go on forever, and that he would have to give some indication of when he was returning to duty.

But the third thing he would do, and really the main reason behind this morning's sudden urge to run, was to use it as an excuse to see how Sophia felt about being minded by Mrs Chattox.

Though Mrs Chattox made an excellent candidate for minding Sophia, she was very different from any of the childminders Sophia had known before.

The previous minders back in the city had been much younger, with children of their own around Sophia's age; these childminders, therefore, had given Sophia someone with whom she could play. What was more, many of her former minders had been friends of her mother, and they'd had that as a kind of bond. Adam prayed to God that it would work out with Mrs Chattox since it would make his life a whole lot simpler if it did.

But this was all about Sophia, and he knew now that she had to come first in all future decisions.

Adam dressed, quickly putting on his running gear that consisted of black tracksuit bottoms, a black tee-shirt and a pair of running shoes that had seen better days.

Sophia was in the kitchen buttering a doorstep-sized slice of toast when Adam arrived downstairs. She turned and thoughtfully asked if he wanted a slice.

“No, thank you, sweetheart. I'm going to go for a bit of a run this morning like I used to. Remember?”

Sophia nodded her head, looking a little confused. Then Adam said, "I thought you could visit Mrs Chattox and she could keep an eye on you. How do you feel about that?"

"Okay," Sophia said, shrugging her shoulders nonchalantly.

It was difficult for Adam to try and work out

what Sophia was really thinking. He would have given anything to know what was going on in her head. Was she okay with being left with Mrs Chattox, or was she just going along with it for his sake? He really couldn't tell.

The time sped by quickly, and at ten o'clock, Adam walked Sophia over to Mrs Chattox' house and knocked at the door. Mrs Chattox greeted them both with a huge smile, and Adam asked if she could watch Sophia for a short time while he went out for a run. The old woman beamed an even broader smile, saying she would be delighted and glad of the company.

Of course, the exchange was all staged for Sophia's sake, having made arrangements the previous night. Mrs Chattox reached behind the door and produced a considerable-sized bunch of carrots, handing them immediately to Sophia. "Looks like you have a job to do first though, Sophia. Your big furry friend has come down for breakfast."

Both Sophia and Adam turned to see the white horse appearing from the track at the far side of their house. Sophia's face immediately lit up, and off she ran.

She began feeding carrots to the horse, which gently dipped its head towards Sophia and seemed genuinely pleased to see both her and its delightfully crunchy, favourite food.

Adam noted that the horse never snatched at the offerings, but took each carrot carefully, never taking another even if offered until she had thoroughly chewed and swallowed the one before. It seemed this giant beast had more table manners than most humans! Sophia giggled to herself.

Adam and Mrs Chattox exchanged slips of paper with their respective phone numbers on each one. Adam would keep his mobile with him on his run, just in case, and asked Mrs Chattox to contact him if there were any problems whatsoever. Between them, they decided around two hours would be about the right amount of time for him to leave Sophia and see how she took to both his absence and the company of Mrs Chattox.

With everything decided, it was time for Adam to go, but he couldn't help feeling a pang of guilt at leaving Sophia in someone else's care once again. Adam told himself that it was unavoidable and that he would soon need to return to work, so they would both have to get used to it again.

But nothing made him feel any better as he steeled himself and began jogging across the farmyard. Adam shouted to Sophia and waved, but his daughter was too engrossed in feeding her new best friend. The first ten minutes of the run were torture; Adam's muscles were stiff, and he struggled to get into a regular breathing pattern. But from then on, his body began to loosen as it warmed up, and his breathing settled down. Reaching the bottom of the lane, Adam turned left.

He was now at the main road, striding out towards Penny-Deep town.

The first four miles were wooded countryside, but eventually, there came the odd one or two houses and other buildings, gradually growing in number till he reached the edge of Penny-Deep town. Several times while running, he checked his phone to make sure he hadn't switched it to silent or turned it off by mistake. He hadn't, of course. But there had been no calls, and he was almost wishing there were. He was just a little unsettled about leaving Sophia, and on more than one occasion, almost turned around to run back to see her, on the pretext of some half-baked excuse.

But as the time ticked by, Adam began to feel more at ease, and after about thirty minutes, he began climbing the hill towards the town centre. Adam slowed to a brisk walk as he reached the High Street. It was his first real look at the town, other than the time he had driven by when he and Sophia had first arrived. This time, he took advantage of being on foot and paid attention to some of the sights. There was a greengrocer's store, its supplies spilling out onto the wide pavement in open boxes and cartons, all on display under a canvas canopy which provided shade.

Next to the grocers' was a post office and then a butcher's shop.

A small bookshop came next, then several clothing stores of varying kinds, the sight of which reminded him that he needed to buy Sophia some new clothes.

Across the road, several other small shops lined the High Street, selling all manner of things.

One shop that particularly stood out, even from across the road, was called *Changes,* displaying an array of brightly coloured materials and prints in its window. Then, across the way, Adam saw Penny-Deep Church with its tall bell tower. Situated roughly in the centre of the town, the church had been built on top of a small hilly mound, from which—over the surrounding stone wall—Adam could see two large men digging what appeared to be an old grave in the churchyard.

A short distance along, Adam came to a side street called Snig Hill Lane, and turning down the steep, narrow road, he saw Penny-Deep Police Station set back from the road. As an austere building built of stone and brick, Adam estimated that the police station must have been constructed during the Victorian era, judging by the architecture.

Reaching the gate in the outer stone wall, he climbed a few steps and then carefully followed the path over the neatly trimmed lawn to the police station.

Entering the foyer, Adam found himself in the enquiry desk area, which was surprisingly modern, with glass screening and a smartly dressed civilian desk clerk.

Adam suddenly realised that he had forgotten his warrant card, but on introducing himself, the clerk just smiled and told him not to worry. She introduced herself as Angela and asked him to take a seat while she marched off into the back office. A short time later, Angela returned and told him that the station inspector was on his way down to meet him.

The wait was a little longer than Adam envisaged, and he and Angela exchange pleasantries whilst he waited. On commenting on the strange name of the lane where the station stood, Angela informed him that it came from bygone days, when the drivers of horse-drawn carts had to put wedges or 'snigs' under the wheels, to stop the carts rolling backwards when parked on the steeply inclined lane.

Inspector Brian Winter finally emerged from a door at the side of the enquiry desk.

He was a tall, well-built man with gunmetal grey hair and an even greyer complexion.

His face was broad and flat with a boxer's nose and two dark, deep-set eyes that stared coldly at Adam before he strode over towards him.

"So you're my replacement," Winter said without a trace of warmth or humour.

They shook hands, and Adam introduced himself, though the pleasantry evidently wasn't reciprocated. But Adam already knew about

Brian Winter. He had taken the time to do a little digging before arriving in Penny-Deep and found out that Winter was a thirty-year police veteran who seemingly had carved out a career by doing very little.

This sort of thing wasn't unheard of if you had the right friends or belonged to the right golf club, but fortunately, these days, it had grown increasingly rare. Winter had risen through the ranks with surprising speed, showing little or no talent before transferring out to Penny-Deep where he'd whiled away the majority of his career in quiet seclusion. Inspector Winter would probably have stayed on past his thirty years if it weren't for the Chief Superintendent virtually shoehorning him out and pressuring him to retire. Adam thought this was perhaps the reason for his icy reception. However, Winter didn't look to be the warm, cuddly type under any circumstances.

Brian Winter led Adam up to his office, where the atmosphere didn't improve any.

"I've heard about you! Of course, I have!" said Winter, sitting behind his large desk. "You've carved out quite a career for yourself as a big city detective, so I must say, I'm a little puzzled that you agreed to take over my spot. It's a sleepy little town, and the folks here like it that way. Nothing of interest happens, certainly no crime to speak of, so I imagine you will find it quite boring, not to mention a career-killer."

Adam became aware that Winter's eyes were continually scanning him, looking for any reaction or cue that might give away what he might be thinking. Adam told Winter that he saw the posting as only temporary and that he was there due to family circumstances but didn't embellish any further.

Winter went on to give a brief, but all too scant, an outline of his duties at Penny-Deep, so dull he even seemed to be boring himself. In fact, Winter only appeared to come alive and take an interest when he mentioned the local landed gentry Archibald O'Neil, of whom he spoke in such glowing terms that Adam concluded there might be some sort of acquaintance or even friendship between the two men. It wouldn't have surprised Adam one bit; it struck him that Winter could, in all probability, be quite sycophantic around someone like O'Neil.

"Oh yes, Archibald O'Neil is a splendid chap, a real pillar of the community, and a philanthropist," Winter went on.

"Though he does like to keep himself to himself. Apart from the parties he throws for his friends from out of town, that is. You know, people that move in the same circles."

Adam just nodded. "When would be most convenient for me to take up my duties here?"

Winter didn't even consider the question. With a sardonic smile, he raised both arms in the air and said, "You can start whenever you like.

This is my last day, and then I'm off. I don't give a monkey's! Now if you don't mind, I have my desk to clear before I go, so I must press on."

Adam felt as though he was being dismissed, so he stood up and walked out of the office without uttering a word. *Damn the man and his rudeness,* he thought.

Once downstairs, Adam made a quick call to Mrs Chattox to ask how things were going with Sophia. "Oh, we're getting along like a house on fire," said the elderly neighbour. "We're just baking some bread and a chocolate cake, made with beetroot!"

Chocolate cake made with beetroot? Adam had never heard of such a thing, and it sounded bizarre to him, but at least Sophia appeared to be enjoying herself. Mrs Chattox went on to confide that Sophia seemed to be comfortable with the arrangement, and Adam then had a quick chat with his daughter, who did seem genuinely happy.

Speaking once again to Mrs Chattox, Adam asked, "If it's alright with you, and of course Sophia, do you think you could look after her tomorrow so I could work an afternoon shift, from four till midnight?"

"Of course, dearie. We'll be fine. You're going to have to start back to work sometime so it might as well be tomorrow."

Over the phone, Adam could hear the neighbour asking Sophia if she would like to stay with her again and help her whilst her dad was at work.

Then Sophia's voice resounded, saying, "Yes!" excitedly.

With childminding arrangements made to everyone's satisfaction, Adam decided to have a brief look around the rest of the police station. A tall thin, gangling youth, in a constable's uniform introduced himself as PC Jason Newman. The young constable seemed happy to meet him and offered to show him around. During the short tour, Adam learned that Jason had been in the job just shy of two years and had ambitions to become a detective once out of his probationary period. Working at Penny-Deep really wasn't what he wanted, but he had been posted there because he lived in the town. While chatting further, Adam got the impression that Jason was pleased Inspector Winter was retiring and looking forward to having a new inspector running the sub-division.

The tour of the police station didn't take long. The inspector's office was upstairs along with the sergeant's office, while downstairs was the reception area, a report-writing room and an interview room. Also on the ground floor were a kitchen and dining area.

In the cellar were two, still functional, detention cells, and at the rear of the station was a large carpark. PC Newman answered all Adam's questions regarding the station and the area it policed. Winter had been right; there wasn't any crime, and the only occasional problems were public-order-related, mainly attributable to two local brothers, the Armstrongs. By all accounts, they had grown up in the area and weren't the sharpest knives in the knife drawer.

PC Newman described them both as being a little bit 'country', which Adam took to mean that they were inbred and a bit simple, due to coming from a limited gene pool as sometimes used to happen in remote rural locations. According to Newman, they took occasional work on local farms and would do a bit of grave digging when required. Adam cast his mind back to the two large men he had seen in the churchyard. PC Newman went on to inform Adam that the station's full complement of personnel consisted of twelve constables covering a three-shift rota and rest days. Three sergeants who were flexible with their hours also ensured the best cover, depending on demand, and Angela, the desk clerk worked nine till five on weekdays only.

Eventually, Adam had seen all he wanted to see of Penny-Deep Police Station and had gained a pretty good idea of its workings. He turned to PC Newman, asking, "Who will be working tomorrow?" That was when he intended to start work. The young officer's face lit up.

"PC Scott, PC Lilly and yours truly—meaning me," Newman replied.

"Right then young PC Newman!" Adam announced. "I will see you tomorrow afternoon, and you can show me around the district. Our first foray together!"

"Yes, Sir!" said the young police officer with conviction.

Adam left the police station and began to briskly retrace his steps to the edge of the town, where once again, he eased into a steady paced run. The air was cool and fresh, and he soon became lost in his thoughts. On reaching the farmyard at Old Anna Farm, Adam checked his watch and realised he had only been out for an hour and forty minutes, so he decided to push on up the track at the side of his house, to see where it led. The rough bridleway had trees on either side with a couple of areas of grass meadow to the right. After the second meadow, the track became quite steep and was nothing more than a single clay path. The steepness of the climb tore into Adam's lungs and leg muscles, but the farther he went, the more his curiosity grew as to what lay ahead.

The woodland was quite beautiful, and all he could hear was his own heavy breath and the birds singing in the trees.

Suddenly, a roe deer shot across the path and startled him, quickly disappearing into the thicket.

On he ran until he eventually heard the rumbling of fast-flowing water.

On nearing the top of the hill, the trees to Adam's right gave way to a view down onto a large pond. The water looked deep but crystal clear and was surrounded by a rocky limestone outcrop. At the far end of the pond was a waterfall fed by a beck above. He estimated it to be in the region of a thirty-foot drop and was responsible for providing the sound of the fast-flowing water he'd heard on his approach. Adam looked down, admiring the scene.

It was a charming, tranquil spot, natural and unspoilt. But then something moved, catching Adam's eye, something behind the waterfall. Strangely parting the falling curtain of water at the base of the cascade, the figure of a naked woman emerged. Even from where he was standing, Adam could see the woman was stunningly beautiful with long black hair that was wet and shiny hanging down around her shoulders and over her large breasts. Suddenly, the young woman dived headlong into the pool of clear water, and Adam watched as she swam under the surface, till she emerged and strolled out onto the shallow shore at the opposite end of the pool.

The woman reached down and picked up a towel from some rocks, beginning to towel her hair dry. Then a large black dog suddenly ran up beside her. Some kind of mastiff, it stood about the size of a Shetland Pony. Adam had never seen a dog so huge, and it proceeded to sit beside the woman like some canine bodyguard. As Adam continued to watch the scene below, the dog suddenly shot its gaze up towards him, as though it had suddenly become aware of his presence.

The woman, too, seemed to sense him and stopped towelling her hair, looking in his direction. Adam immediately felt uncomfortable and embarrassed. Surely, the woman couldn't have seen him through the trees and foliage? No, he was sure she couldn't have seen him, but he stepped back all the same. Adam slowly moved his head to take another look.

The woman's eyes seemed to be staring straight back into his, and he could feel them burning like lasers. Adam turned away and began running back down the track, feeling a little like a dirty Peeping Tom. But at the same time, he couldn't help but feel a tinge of excitement.

The woman, whoever she was, had to be one of the most alluring he had ever seen.

On reaching Old Anna Farm, Adam made his way directly to Mrs Chattox' house where he was greeted by an overly excited Sophia, who was extolling the virtues of home baking and adding that Mrs Chattox had shown her how to make bread and a chocolate cake with beetroot.

Adam internally winced at the thought of the cake being made with beetroot, not a vegetable of which he was a fan, but Sophia cut him a large slice. She watched him carefully as he bit into it. Of course, he was prepared to lie and say how good the cake was even if it tasted foul, but instead, he told the truth. The rich sponge tasted delicious with no taste of beetroot at all.

Adam realised he must have looked or sounded puzzled because Mrs Chattox interjected.

"The beetroot is to sweeten the cake, dear. It's better for you than all that white sugar."

Adam thanked Mrs Chattox for looking after Sophia and checked that everything had gone alright. Mrs Chattox smiled and said, “We had a nice time, didn't we, dear! We're both looking forward to tomorrow! We've got plans, we have."

Sophia nodded her head, smiling broadly.

"Well that looks like it’s settled then," said Adam. "Are you sure it's alright with you, Sophia, if I start back to work tomorrow afternoon? Is that okay?"

Sophia, gathering up a large loaf of freshly baked bread, was full of enthusiasm, stating she would be okay and that Mrs Chattox was very clever, knowing all sorts of things such as how to bake with beetroot. And apparently, Mrs Chattox was also going to teach her how to bake and cook. Sophia then marched off across the farmyard, carrying the loaf back to their own house.

Adam was about to follow Sophia when he remembered the woman in the pond. Turning to Mrs Chattox, Adam asked if she knew the woman with the long black hair who was accompanied by a giant, black hound. Mrs Chattox simply looked away, busying herself, distractedly tidying the baking stuff. It was almost as if she had not heard the question.

"I haven't been up there in goodness knows how long!" she said. "Not many people venture up there, so it could have been anyone."

Adam nodded thoughtfully and didn't pursue the matter any further. He didn't want to upset his neighbour and new childminder, but it didn't escape his attention that his question had been expertly avoided, deflected rather than answered. Adam thanked Mrs Chattox and followed after Sophia. It was strange, but he had a distinct feeling that Mrs Chattox knew more than she was letting on.

In fact, quite a lot more...

Chapter 7

Despite the coldness of the hard stone floor, Victoria Timperley managed to drift in and out of sleep. After all, there was little else for her to do. She had long since given up on shouting for help and banging on the large wooden door. During the time Victoria was awake, her mind was engulfed in horrific thoughts revolving around what was going to happen to her.

She had thought of all the tormented anguish her family would be experiencing, and also about the life she had dreamed of but would probably never know. Sleep seemed to be the only thing that brought her any respite, and when she woke, she tried not to move. She clung on to the edges of slumber, trying to plunge back into its dark, peaceful depths.

This time when Victoria woke, it was because something had disturbed her, stirring her senses. At first, she became aware of the vibration in the stone floor, and of the sound of footsteps quickly accompanying this. Victoria swiftly pulled herself to her feet and began shouting for help.

The footsteps grew louder, and she could tell they belonged to more than one person.

It sounded like a crowd of people.

The footsteps stopped outside the wooden door, and Victoria stood up squarely, facing her only route of escape, in readiness. Perhaps this was the police coming to rescue her, she thought. But she knew that no matter how much she hoped that was true, it was improbable.

If it weren't the police or anyone else coming to save her, then this would probably be the same people who had brought her here and locked her away. Victoria was suddenly afraid of what these people might be going to do to her now that they had come to call. She desperately tried to think about what would be her best course of action. But all she could come up with was that perhaps she could catch them off guard, push by them and make a run for freedom.

Victoria heard the sound of the large lock turning. She readied herself, crouching low and standing on the balls of her feet, ready to sprint forward. The large wooden door swung inwards, just missing her, and the light blinded her. As she ran forward, two buckets of freezing cold water hit her hard and knocked her half a step back, stealing all the air from her lungs.

Before Victoria could recover, they were on her, two large men grabbing an arm each and pinning her back against the stone wall. Victoria tried for all she was worth, to struggle, but the men were far too strong. Several others crowded into the room, all wearing long black gowns with hoods that covered their heads and masked their faces in shadow. Some in the group carried flaming wooden torches which lit the room in a blaze of colourful light.

Victoria tried to reason with her captors, pleading to know what they wanted of her and begging for them to let her go. But she was answered only with a slap across her face.

The slap dazed her and brought tears to her eyes.

The hooded figure that had slapped her now spoke, and to her surprise, it was a woman's voice.

"Be quiet. If you make any more sound, I will be forced to hurt you," said the woman, who raised a large dagger-type knife in front of her. The woman stepped forward and began cutting and ripping at Victoria's clothes till they lay in a pile on the floor and she was totally naked.

Someone else in the crowd handed her a bar of carbolic soap, ordering her to wash thoroughly. Victoria was mindful of the dagger, the point of which hovered dangerously near to her.

Afraid of what might happen if she refused, Victoria washed as instructed, and in doing so, washed her painted beauty from her face. Several more buckets of water were then thrown over her before she was handed a towel and instructed to dry herself. Victoria stood there, cold and shivering. The woman holding the dagger then said, "You must be freezing, dear. Put this on."

Victoria was handed a long white robe made of thin cotton that would do little to keep her warm, but she slipped it on to hide her shame and embarrassment at being naked in front of so many strangers. The woman with the dagger then took a glass of red liquid from one of the others in the room and handed it to Victoria.

"Drink this, dear," she said, "This will warm you through."

The glass, when grasped, revealed itself to be plastic, and when Victoria sipped the contents, she recognised the taste of Port.

It was a large measure, and sure enough, Victoria felt the warmth of the alcohol as it passed down her throat. The woman with the dagger demanded Victoria drink down all the Port, and while complying, Victoria calmly asked again, "Why am I here? What are you going to do with me?"

The woman who had now lowered the dagger said in a soothing voice, "You are a special guest. All that we have arranged tonight is for you. It's such a great honour being bestowed upon you. You will never understand how great your service is."

"Oh," said Victoria. She didn't seem to mind anymore; she felt so relaxed and calm, as if she could float away. Her fear already had left her.

Victoria let her new friends lead her through the door and along a narrow stone corridor. Then suddenly, she was hoisted up and carried by the group that continued walking, holding her aloft. She was lying on her back with her arms outstretched. She felt so light. Perhaps she really was floating somewhere near the ceiling, and not being carried at all?

Victoria could hear music now, sounding like a Gregorian Chant and, as she floated along the corridor, the song grew louder. Suddenly, Victoria passed beneath an archway, and the narrow ceiling of the corridor gave way to a larger, more expansive one. Casting her eyes down, Victoria saw that she was in a large stone chamber containing twenty to thirty people all dressed in hooded robes, all pacing slowly around a stone slab in the centre of the room.

The circling crowd parted as Victoria was carried forward and placed down on the cold stone slab. The woman with the dagger stepped forward, and the thin cotton robe Victoria was wearing was cut from top to bottom, falling apart and leaving her naked once more. Then a figure in a purple robe stepped up and stood where the top of Victoria's head reached the end of the slab table. Victoria looked up as the figure removed its hood to reveal a large goat's head.

The figure reached out and took hold of her head with both hands, beginning to recite words in a language that she recognised from when she'd attended church as a child. It was Latin.

Victoria looked away from the hideous goat's head, and then looked down towards her feet.

Hands from both sides grabbed Victoria's ankles and pulled her legs apart.

She screamed in realisation and revulsion as someone to her left painted an inverted pentagram on her chest in what seemed to be thick, dark animal blood.

But the scream only seemed to excite the people gathered in the chamber.

The goat-headed figure held her head firmly, but as she felt a sharp pain sear through both arms, she momentarily broke free and saw both her wrists being cut. Her blood was being caught in two metal goblets, from which figures in the crowd were eagerly drinking.

The repulsive site of her own blood being consumed caused Victoria to lose consciousness.

***

She didn't know how long she lay out cold and unaware, but slowly, she regained her senses. Victoria was crying now, yet unable to make a sound. She silently prayed that was the worst of it, over. Whatever had been contained in the glass of Port had now worn off, and the terror that filled Victoria's body left her traumatised and unable to move. The figure with the goat's head began reciting in Latin once more as the crowd in the chamber started to walk around the stone table once again, anti-clockwise. Victoria stared up at the figure with the goat's head who had now let go of her. The entire crowd in the chamber now joined in the Latin chant as they walked faster and faster around her. The atmosphere in the room seemed to grow denser and denser.

A smell of some sort of incense pervaded the space, the excitement of the crowd palpable now.

Victoria became aware of a sudden movement above her head, and as she looked up, the goat-headed figure raised its arms. There, in the flickering light of the wall-mounted torches, she saw the glint of a dagger. Then in one swift movement, the blade plunged down with such force that it pierced her chest, right up to its brass hilt. Victoria didn't get a chance to scream.

The blow knocked all the air from her lungs, and when she tried to breathe in, she couldn't.

Just for a second, the dagger felt like an icicle, so cold, embedded in her chest. Then from the edges of her vision, darkness swept in, engulfing her.

Chapter 8

Both Adam and Sophia were up and about early. They had been awake a good hour before the cockerel began to crow in the new day, so Adam had risen early that morning because he had a plan to get certain jobs out of the way before he started work. Sophia was up early too, simply because she knew some of her father's, 'to do' list involved her, and she was excited at the prospect.

Adam had called the police station and informed them that he was going in to work at four p.m. till midnight. That would give him enough time, in the morning, to take Sophia on a much-needed clothes shopping expedition in the town.

It was clear that Sophia was a lot more enthusiastic about the shopping trip than he was. He just knew he was going to feel uncomfortable and awkward throughout.

The previous evening, Adam and Sophia had both conducted an inventory of the clothes that Sophia already had, then sorted out what still fitted her, and what didn't, what was serviceable and what was worn out. Eventually, they had come to a mutually agreed list of clothing items that Sophia needed. From that moment on, Sophia's excitement grew and grew at the prospect of buying new clothes. Adam couldn't remember the last time his daughter had received new clothing, and he immediately felt a familiar pang of guilt for neglecting her in this way.

Breakfast consisted of omelettes and coffee for Adam, and omelettes and fresh orange juice for Sophia. Adam was convinced his daughter was hyper enough that morning without adding caffeine to the mix. Then with the list of required clothing items securely tucked in his pocket, Adam told Sophia it was time to go, and she bounded from the house and into the car before he had the chance to put his jacket on. Adam had made a written list so as not to forget anything.

But during the drive into town, he realised that the list, in all probability, wasn't actually needed. Sophia chirped on regarding each item written on the scrap of paper in Adam's pocket. For someone so young, Sophia had definite ideas about what colour, style and material, she wanted the clothing to be. It was, Adam concluded, highly unlikely that Sophia would forget anything on the list. Adam listened patiently to Sophia as he drove, adding the odd, timely comment when required.

***

Once in the centre of town, Adam found a parking space and decided to throw himself into the shopping trip at the deep end and get the most awkward part of it out of the way first.

On finding what appeared to be a suitable shop on the High Street, father and daughter entered.

Once inside, Sophia suddenly went very quiet, and Adam realised that he must have looked awkward and out of place because he noticed an attractive young woman wearing a sales assistant's badge watching him with obvious amusement. Eventually, the assistant came over and asked if she could help. Adam explained that his daughter needed a complete set of new underwear, tights, socks and *whatever else*. He left the vagueness of the 'whatever else' hanging in the air, hoping that the young woman would fill in any blanks from his list.

Fortunately, for Adam, she seemed to understand his predicament and took pity on him. After introducing herself to Sophia, she told Adam he could take a seat over near the counter, if he wished, whilst she and Sophia took care of trying on and sorting out the required items. Adam took a seat, more than happy with his non-involvement.

Shopping for girls' clothing, as Adam found out, was a lengthy process, but in due course, he and Sophia emerged from the first shop, bags in hands. Next, they set about buying a couple of school uniforms in the green livery of the local school. Shopping for uniform was easy enough as there was a shop stocking seemingly endless supplies of school wear in all shapes and sizes. After this, Adam let her run riot buying three pairs of jeans, a couple of pairs of shorts, and several tee shirts and blouses. These purchases took in several shops, and Adam cast a critical eye over Sophia's choices, but couldn't find fault with anything his daughter chose since everything seemed serviceable and appropriate for a girl her age.

The problems arose when they began looking for what Sophia called *best dresses*. Adam had promised her she could have two best dresses, but hadn't realised, at the time, what he was letting himself in for. Sophia led him into every clothing shop in Penny-Deep, some of them twice. But try as she might, his daughter couldn't find anything she liked.

Several of the dresses she looked at seemed perfectly fine to Adam, but Sophia was resolute that none she saw were good enough to be her *best dresses*.

Eventually, all hope was abandoned, and they began to trudge back to the car. Adam could tell Sophia wasn't happy. But there seemed little else he could do. Then Sophia stopped and began staring in the window of *Changes* fabric shop and haberdashery.

"I like that material there, for a dress," said Sophia, pointing at a gold-coloured material in the window display. Adam had to agree that the material was eye-catching, but he also had to point out that it wasn't a dress, and he, for one, couldn't sew.

They were about to move on when someone spoke.

"Oh, it is lovely, isn't it! It's silk, you know, and end-of-line," said a voice from the doorway of the shop. It was a small woman with blond bobbed hair and wearing green-tinted spectacles that curved up on the corners, lending her face a feline appearance. Adam explained that it was actually a dress that his daughter was after. But the woman just smiled and said, "In that case, you came to the right place, come in and meet Saffron, our in-house design artist and dressmaker."

Before Adam could reply, Sophia had shot through the door of the shop, while the small feline-looking woman continued speaking to Adam.

"My name is Primula, but most people call me Prim," she said, smiling.

Once inside, they were greeted by a tall, young woman with long dark hair, wearing a long, floaty, lacy dress. Adam concluded this was Saffron, as she wafted about taking Sophia's measurements and showing her various pattern designs in a large book. Before long, Sophia had chosen a pattern that she liked, and expressed her wish for it to be made in the gold silk material.

Before Adam could ask about prices, Sophia

had picked out a second pattern, and Saffron was busily holding up different swatches of material against her as Sophia looked into a large mirror. This time, Sophia chose a brightly coloured floral print material.

Prim watched with an almost maternal interest, looking like the cat that had got the cream. Saffron showed the dress designs to Adam, asking if he approved. He had to admit, the designs were beautiful, but as for having the dresses made, he feared that was going to prove expensive.

He asked for a price, and Prim did a quick bit of mental arithmetic.

Much to Adam's surprise, the price for both dresses was very reasonable, far less than he was expecting, and well within his budget. Sophia asked, "When will my dresses be ready?"

"What do you think, Saffy?" said Prim

"I'll have them both done for you the day after tomorrow, around mid-morning."

Adam was equally surprised at how quickly the dresses would be made.

"That's amazing. I thought it would take much longer. Do you always make them so quickly?" Adam asked.

"Only for our special customers," Prim said, smiling at Sophia.

Before leaving the shop, Sophia made Adam promise that he would bring her to collect the dresses as soon as they were ready.

The journey home turned out to be no less quiet than the trip into town. This time, Sophia chatted on endlessly about having all her clothes made at Changes, and how Saffy and Prim regarded her has a special customer. Adam had to smile. When it came to sales promotion, the two ladies at Changes had certainly proved an instant hit with Sophia.

***

Mrs Chattox brought over a fish pie for their dinner, and Sophia revelled in telling their neighbour all about her new clothes. Then, with dinner eaten and the dishes out of the way, Mrs Chattox helped Sophia put her new purchases away whilst Adam changed into his uniform.

Adam had not worn a uniform for several years and had had to pick up several new items from the police stores before leaving the city. The uniform fitted well, and he looked smart, but he couldn't help feeling awkward. He had always enjoyed an informal working relationship with his colleagues in CID, despite his rank. But wearing an inspector's uniform always brought about a certain formality, drawing a distinct line between himself and the other officers at the station.

Before leaving for work, Adam had to pass an inspection from Sophia and Mrs Chattox.

Sophia looked him over carefully; it was the first time that she had seen him in a police uniform, and from the look on her face, it was also the first time that it had registered what her father did for a job. To Sophia, he now looked like a real policeman.

On arrival at Penny-Deep Police Station, Adam found the building quiet and deserted except for Angela, the front desk clerk, who was busily taking down details from someone on the phone. Adam gave her a friendly nod and then made his way upstairs to the inspector's office. He removed his tunic and hat, hanging them on a coat stand by the office door.

Then, sitting behind what was now his desk, he began checking the four desk drawers. They were empty, except for a few pens, a ruler and several paper clips. The same couldn't be said for the three admin trays, however, that were on top of his desk. They were full to overflowing with paperwork. So much for Winter clearing up his desk before he left.

It looked more as if the man hadn't done any clerical work for a month or more. The office phone rang, and it was Angela asking if he wanted a cup of tea.

Adam looked at the mountain of paperwork and decided coffee might be the better option.

Two hours later, Adam had finally read through the stack of memos and replied where necessary. Angela had left for home at five p.m., and, having seen more than enough paperwork for one day, Adam decided to have a snoop around the station, trying to find something that might take his interest. He failed miserably. Even the police radio channel had been quiet.

Adam decided it was time to take a look at the district for which he was now responsible.

Picking up the phone, he called the central communications room and asked if PC Newman could return to the station and collect him.

PC Newman arrived to collect his new inspector within ten minutes of the call going out.

The young constable appeared just as keen to impress as he had the day before.

Adam asked him to drive around the district and show him the boundaries so he could get a general feel for the place and the scope of the area.

They drove for hours, chatting all the while about various policing topics. Adam was interested in finding out about any problems involving crime in the area, but PC Newman couldn't think of any for the life of him. During their time together, PC Newman also politely interrogated Adam about his career and about being a city detective, a career path that he dreamed of taking too.

Adam could see the lad was desperate to pursue this avenue of police work and regaled him with several stories from his past cases. Adam took an instant liking to Newman and made up his mind to keep a close eye on his career progress. It was obvious that the young man was intelligent and keen, and Adam would try and assist him in achieving his dream in any way he could.

***

Adam and PC Newman had now been out for most of the evening, and the light began to fade before it quickly turned to total darkness. Adam checked his watch. It was ten-thirty p.m., and just as he was about to ask the constable to take him back to the station, a call came over the radio, asking them to attend one of the main routes leading into Penny-Deep since there had been a report of loose cattle in the road. Dealing with escaped cattle was going to be a first for Adam but he accompanied the young officer, assisting him in herding the cows back along the road and into the field from which they came. Then, with some effort, they managed to secure the gate to the area, once the last cow was inside. With this, his first real taste of rural policing under his belt, Adam asked to be taken back to the police station.

A mile ahead of Adam and PC Newman, a small green van joined the main road at speed, from a side lane. The van didn't stop or even slow as it joined the main road heading towards town.

The van was being driven recklessly and would have been a definite candidate for a stop check if it had been in sight of the officers. But sadly, it wasn't.

The occupants of the van, the driver and front-seat passenger, were in a desperate hurry to get rid of their cargo. These men were brutish and by no means fainthearted, but their load creeped both men out, though they would never admit it to themselves or each other.

The van swayed around the bends as the headlights splashed over the road surface and the surrounding hedgerows. The driver of the van was hunched over the steering wheel in concentration. Suddenly, something black shot up from the centre of the road in front of their vehicle. Whatever it was stood still and looked, in the brief glimpse afforded by the van's headlights, like a woman dressed all in black, with outstretched arms.

It was a knee-jerk reaction that made the van driver swerve the vehicle to the left. If his nerves had not been on edge to start with, he might have reacted better. Given their circumstances and their cargo, he would have been inclined to hit the figure and carry on regardless.

But his involuntary reaction sent the van careening across the road and into a drainage ditch. The front nearside wing of the vehicle suddenly lurched forward and down with a loud bang, before coming to a sudden stop.

The occupants of the van both climbed out, with the passenger immediately hurling abuse at the driver. "You idiot, I told you to take it easy! Now, look what you've gone and done. You moron."

The driver ran into the centre of the road, looking all around. "Where did she go?"

"Where did who go?"

"That stupid bitch who was standing in the middle of the road, that's who. I'm going to wring her scrawny neck when I get a hold of her."

The passenger looked bemused.

"You're starting to hallucinate. You need to lay off the booze and the whacky-baccy."

The driver continued to look around the roadside and in the hedges, whilst the passenger inspected the damage to the van. "Front nearside wheel's buckled. We're not going anywhere in this pile of shit. Now, what do we do? You gormless idiot!"

Suddenly, both men fell silent and looked up as they heard the sound of an approaching vehicle. Looking across the fields, they saw the headlights of the car travelling in their direction, approximately half a mile away. Both men felt a mild panic as they recognised the vehicle by its illuminated sign and the blue light mounted on the roof. It was a police car.

"Now, what do we do? We can't leave it like this," said the man who had been the passenger.

"Quick, get that thing out the back," the driver said. "There's some petrol in a can in there. Try and burn it."

The passenger opened both rear doors of the

van and climbed inside to look for the petrol container. He was careful to move around their cargo, touching it as little as possible.

Eventually, he found the plastic petrol carrier. It had barely any petrol left inside, but the small amount in the bottom would have to do.

Both men then reached into the rear of the van and pulled out their cargo.

The load slid out easily, and they let it fall to the ground where they began pouring petrol over it. There was only enough fuel to cover the legs and lower torso, and he hurled the empty container into the back of the van.

"Shit!" shouted the driver. "Light the bloody thing, will you?"

The other man lit a match and threw it onto the petrol-soaked legs of the body. Immediately, the legs and lower abdomen erupted in flames. Both men then ran across the road and leapt over the hedges, running into the woods beyond.

***

The sudden explosion of flames ahead illuminated the surrounding darkness, catching the attention of both officers. PC Newman put his foot down, and the police car accelerated along the lane towards the fire. As they neared, Adam could make out the back of the van in the flaming firelight. The vehicle looked to have left the road and tipped over into a ditch.

Whatever was burning on the ground at the

rear of the van was well ablaze.

But neither officer could make out what it was.

As soon as their car stopped, Adam grabbed the fire extinguisher from the seat well of the police car. Both officers alighted and ran over to the fire. However, neither Adam nor PC Newman expected the horror about to meet their eyes. There on the ground was the naked body of a young woman. The bottom half of the body was well ablaze, but the top half remained untouched by the flames, its features recognisable.

Adam released the catch on the fire extinguisher and let out a spray of carbon dioxide that smothered the roaring flames. The smell of burning flesh that met both men was unmistakable to Adam; he had experienced it previously, and on more than one occasion.

PC Newman, on the other hand, had not, and he promptly ran across the road, away from the immediate crime scene, where he threw up.

Adam searched around the van in case of any other injured parties, but there were none. He reached for his radio and called the communications room. After making a report and requesting back-up, Adam took out his phone and called Mrs Chattox.

He was going to be late home.

Chapter 9

Adam had arrived home just before three a.m. to find Mrs Chattox seated in the living room watching television and knitting. Sophia had made her way up to bed around nine p.m., Mrs Chattox informed him. Adam apologised profusely, though the elderly neighbour didn't seem to mind and was more interested in finding out precisely what had happened in her sleepy little town. Adam told Mrs Chattox a very edited version of the evening's events, informing her that a young woman had been found dead at the side of the road, and little else could be ascertained until a proper investigation was conducted. Though she seemed less than satisfied with the scant details, Mrs Chattox soon perked up when Adam told her that he was planning to go into work later that morning to check on the progress of the investigation.

Annie Chattox readily agreed to come over and mind Sophia at eleven a.m. Adam had to smile. He could see the old lady was visibly excited at the possibility of learning more of about what had happened to the dead woman and what the subsequent police investigation might reveal. It was obvious that Mrs Chattox believed her role, helping the inspector, made her an integral part of the police investigation team by proxy. For the elderly neighbour, this was all very exciting and quite unlike anything that had happened in Penny-Deep during her lifetime. Collecting her knitting together, Mrs Chattox bid Adam goodnight and made her way off across the farmyard to her own home, promising to return in time for Adam to leave for work.

***

Adam fell into a deep sleep and remained there through what was left of the night. He didn't stir until his alarm clock woke him at nine a.m. Even the cockerel hadn't disturbed him, though the damned bird must surely have been making its early morning racket at some point while he'd slept.

Adam lay motionless as the last vestiges of sleep backed away from his mind. From the sounds coming from downstairs, Adam took it that Sophia was already up, and Mrs Chattox already in attendance. He showered and dressed quickly, putting on a clean shirt and uniform. The one he had worn previously smelled of smoke and needed dry cleaning.

Much to Mrs Chattox' disdain, Adam's breakfast consisted only of a cup of black coffee. He explained to Sophia that something 'very important,' had happened at work and that he had to go in early to deal with it. Sophia was a little quiet but seemed to understand, though she sought reassurance that Adam would be taking her to collect her dresses the following morning. Once that was confirmed, Sophia appeared happy enough.

***

Penny-Deep Police Station was a hive of activity when Adam arrived, with several uniformed and plainclothes officers, brought in from elsewhere, milling around.

Adam made his way directly to his office only to find it occupied by Chief Superintendent Wise.

"Morning, Adam. Thought I'd hang around to brief you personally before heading back to HQ."

"Thank you, Sir," said Adam, surprised at the Chief Superintendent's presence. He would have thought someone might have warned him about the Chief's presence as he'd passed through the building. But no one had!

The Chief Superintendent seated at Adam's desk looked pale and tired, and Adam realised that he must have been there all night, heading up the investigation. Adam had called out Chief Superintendent Wise as soon as the body had been discovered. The Chief had taken over the crime scene with some detectives from the division, then—as soon as the major investigation team arrived and got to grips with the crime scene—the Chief had released Adam and PC Newman from duties concerning the incident. Much to Adam's annoyance.

The Chief began consulting some notes laid

out on the desk. "Well firstly, the crime scene is now being opened up, and the van has been taken down to a drying room at Headquarters for forensic examination," said the Chief Superintendent. "The registration plates came down to a van owned by a local plumber in the city. He was visited first thing this morning, and his van was present, minus its plates. Looks like they were stolen sometime during the night and the plumber himself has a solid alibi. He was at home all night with his wife and two children, so he's pretty much eliminated from inquiries. The body of the young woman has been taken down to the medico-legal centre for a post-mortem which is being carried out as we speak."

The Chief Superintendent took a sip of coffee from a mug and then continued.

"The scene and the surrounding area has been thoroughly searched. The grass on the opposite side of the road to the abandoned van was found to have been disturbed but the ground was too hard and dry to provide any footprints. We tried dogs, but they only tracked about three hundred yards into the woods, and then lost interest. And the truth is, we don't know if they were tracking anyone pertinent to the inquiry in the first place. Those woods are teeming with wildlife, so that aspect of the investigation has all boiled down to nothing."

The Chief Superintendent sat back and rubbed his eyes. He looked weary, and looking directly at Adam, he confided, "What I can tell you is we are pretty sure that the deceased young woman is Victoria Timperley. She was reported missing three days ago, after going out on a works do at some wine bar in the city centre. Obviously, we will have to get the body positively identified, but what's left of her does look very similar to the photo we have on file. If it is Victoria Timperley, she is one of four young women who have gone missing over the last few weeks from the city centre. As yet, we haven't found hide nor hair of the other three."

Adam realised that finding the body of the last girl to go missing had terrible implications for the wellbeing of the other three. But at the same time, Adam couldn't help but feel the familiar buzz of excitement, the same as he always felt at the beginning of a major incident investigation.

"Is there anything in particular that you want me to be looking at, Sir?"

Wise looked thoughtful and then said, "I've decided to keep the major incident team based down at division HQ. That's where the four girls were last seen, and that's where the van's registration plates were stolen from. I'm not ready to uproot the major incident room and move everything up here just yet. That said, a part of my reasoning is based on the fact that you are out here, Adam. If I'm honest, part of me does feel a little uneasy about not having at least some of the investigation team up here. But I've precious few detectives to spare, and I always regarded you as my best lead investigator, so if the body were going to be found anywhere outside the division, it's fortuitous that it's was found out here, where you are now based. I don't think there's much that can be done out here at the moment, but I'll keep you informed of any developments with the Major Incident team. I would appreciate it if you did a bit of digging around up here in Penny-Deep, just where you see fit. I'll expect you to contact me immediately if you turn up anything."

"Understood, Sir."

On concluding his briefing with Adam, the Chief Super rounded up all the additional officers he had brought from the divisional HQ and set off back to Headquarters. Adam couldn't help but feel a little deflated at not being in the thick of the major investigation. But he reminded himself why he had come out to Penny-Deep in the first place. Sophia had to come first, and he was just going to have to get used to being away from the excitement.

Shortly after the Chief had left, Adam sat down at his desk and began writing his statement regarding the discovery of the van and the burning body. He was interrupted by the ringing of the office phone. It was a Scene of Crime Officer asking for Chief Superintendent Wise.

Adam introduced himself and told the officer that the Chief Super had left twenty minutes earlier and was heading back to the divisional HQ. The man on the phone sounded a little deflated and said he had information for the Chief Super.

Adam asked, "Is the information regarding the body found at Penny-Deep? If so, I'm the officer in charge of the inquiry up here at the Penny-Deep end. If you would like to pass on the details, I will make sure the Chief Superintendent is fully updated."

"Well in that case," said the Scene of Crime Officer, sounding a little more cheerful. "We have found loads of fingerprints in the van, but there is smearing on the steering wheel and gear lever, indicating that the last person to drive it was probably wearing gloves. We have also managed to pull the chassis and vehicle index number from the van. Adam wrote down the details. Interestingly, the numbers, when checked, came down to a van registered to O'Neil Estate over at Penny-Deep."

Adam thanked the SOCO, then hung up. Next, he radioed the communications room and asked if PC Newman was on duty. When it was confirmed, Adam asked for the officer to be contacted and directed to return and collect him right away.

PC Newman had expressed a wish to a detective, thought Adam, so his training might as well start now. By being thrown in at the deep end, with a visit to Archibald O'Neil.

***

Archibald O'Neil's office looked more like a large decorative sitting room, with large settees and ornate furnishings. Only a large French desk with delicate inlays denoted the place as a workspace.

O'Neil marched back and forth in front of the desk, occasionally stopping and gazing out of the large floor-to-ceiling windows towards the driveway. He was expecting company, and as always in the build-up to business meetings, he was feeling a little anxious.

Once again, O'Neil marched over to the window and stood willing the arrival of his guests. But after a minute passed by with no sign, he turned on his heels to resume pacing. But then, before he took his first step, the distant sound of a car engine reached his ears.

The black Bentley Flying Spur glided effortlessly up to the front of the house. O'Neil watched as the rear doors opened and two figures alighted. One of the men was John Laitner, an accountant and financier with whom O'Neil had previously conducted several business deals.

But it was the second man who interested O'Neil more, Charles Dutton. Dutton was a wealthy man by anyone's standards, but unlike O'Neil and his friends, Dutton had risen from the dirty backstreets of the city. Dutton had educated and refined himself out of necessity as his wealth had grown and the circles he moved in had changed. Still, his early rise to power had been down to a natural animal cunning and absolute ruthlessness. A man such as Dutton interested O'Neil because he knew that Dutton was a closer fit to his own ancestral blueprint than he could ever be.

O'Neil knew that when his family had first come over to England from Ireland in the sixteenth century, they had been cut from precisely the same tough cloth as Charles Dutton.

Generations of privileged living had softened the O'Neil gene pool, and Archibald O'Neil understood that he was the end result. Small, rotund, and soft.

An expensive education had replaced the animal cunning, but the ruthlessness remained in some measure, and what the costly education and privileged upbringing had bestowed upon him were influential contacts, something that Dutton didn't have.

O'Neil watched both men approach the front steps of the house. Where Laitner walked with a stiff purposeful gait, Dutton prowled with animal grace, lithely springing up the steps three at a time. He was a tall man; O'Neil estimated him to be around 6 feet 3 inches, though he could be taller. He was slim with broad shoulders, accentuated in an exquisitely tailored, navy blue suit. The dark tan, black hair and chiselled cheekbones gave him a Mediterranean appearance, but there was nothing Mediterranean about the backstreets where Dutton had been raised. Everyone knew how Dutton had made his money, from drugs to pubs, and from pubs to nightclubs and casinos. He'd had one or two brushes with the law in the early days, but nothing ever stuck, mainly because witnesses had a habit of disappearing. O'Neil didn't mind any of this; after all, 'business was business'.

O'Neil sat at his desk and picked up a pen to give the impression he was hard at work. Eventually, there was a knock at the door, and O'Neil shouted "Enter!"

O'Neil's personal assistant, Ms Carfax, opened the doors and announced both men as they entered. O'Neil stood up and casually threw the pen onto the desk as he walked over and shook both men by the hand. He led them over to the settees where they sat to discuss arrangements.

John Laitner crossed one leg over the knee of the other and casually brushed an imaginary speck of dust from his trousers. "My client, Mr Dutton, and I would like to express our appreciation for the returns made on Mr Dutton's portfolio. I know I speak for both of us when I say that the returns were well above what we expected or hoped for," he said.

O'Neil was struck by Dutton's silence, becoming acutely aware that Dutton was studying him in much the same way he, himself, had studied Dutton. Close up, Dutton looked no less impressive, especially for a man in his forties. O'Neil detected a pale, hairline scar that ran down Dutton's tanned cheek, terminating at his jaw.

"We understand you may be undertaking another significant investment strategy, and my client would appreciate his portfolio withdrawn," said Laitner.

O'Neil sat back, contemplating what was said. Then breaking the silence, he replied, "I'm not sure how you came by this information but let me say that Mr Dutton's investment portfolio is in very safe hands and the returns will be enormous."

Charles Dutton sat forward; his clear blue eyes were like arctic pools that sent out a chill, reaching O'Neil's bones.

"Are you in some way saying that my money is not mine to do with as I please?" said Dutton.

"Not at all," replied O'Neil with a dry mouth. "But your portfolio is now worth in the region of fifty million pounds sterling, and it was understood by my fund managers and associates that your investments were with us for the long haul. You must understand that such a significant portfolio as yours helps form the foundation of our next investment strategy.

“Yes, there are risks, but these risks, though high, are matched by potential returns. The reason it's a closed group of investors is that all those selected understand the high-risk, high-return strategy involved, as well as the clear advantage of having all investments thoroughly laundered."

"I have always been a gambling man, Mr O'Neil. Over the years, I have learned a couple of things about gambling. First, if the risks are high, then the possible return must be equally high. Second, no one takes a high-risk gamble unless they think they can pull it off. Am I right?" said Dutton.

O'Neil couldn't fault the man's logic. "Yes, that is correct," he said with delight, hoping he had got through to Dutton's basic instinct for greed. After all, it was probably Dutton's advisor Laitner who was steering him on this prudent course to withdraw his portfolio.

"But don't mistake this gambling man for a fool," Dutton continued. "I stick to mathematical probability and play the averages. As well as you have done for me, I sense the tides are turning."

O'Neil fought the urge to argue with the man. How could he possibly tell him the truth? That mathematical probability just didn't apply.

"We both know that I can afford to make the investment," said Dutton. "The question is, can I afford to lose that amount of investment? Again. Yes, I can. So you can put your mind to rest on both those counts. But what should concern you is how I will feel if I lose that money, and what might be the consequences of those feelings."

O'Neil knew he was being threatened without even the pretence of a veil. Ordinarily, O'Neil would have been somewhere far to the north of worried. But he wasn't. O'Neil had a secret. Simply put, he couldn't lose on the upcoming investment strategy. Now it was his turn to sit forward and fix Dutton with an icy stare.

"Very well, I'll have your portfolio excluded from the next investment strategy. But it will take time to realise your investment into a readily accessible form."

"How long, exactly?" asked Dutton.

"I should be able to have something in place by the middle of next week," O'Neil replied.

Dutton looked over at Laitner who nodded in agreement, and a deal was struck. Once the finer details were agreed, all three men stood and shook hands. Dutton's hand was large and powerful, though he didn't over-exert his grip, childishly trying to make a point. O'Neil felt almost apologetic offering his small, puffy and clammy hand, but then he reasoned that it was Dutton who needed him more than the other way around. He was the one holding the real power in the relationship. After all, he had total control of Dutton's investments.

O'Neil walked both men to the front entrance and watched them drive away in the Bentley. He remained standing at the top of the stone steps leading to the great house, contemplating his next move. Of course, he should contact his friends and tell them about the late withdrawal from the investment pot, but that meant that his own return on the investment would be significantly down, as a good portion of his stake was really going to be Dutton's money.

But that wouldn't be a problem. He knew his friends wouldn't want details, and he had just bought himself time to use Dutton's capital before it had to be made available to him.

The fool! thought O'Neil. All Dutton had achieved with his posturing and petty intimidation was to lose out on the investment return whilst increasing his own exponentially.

Yes, it may have appeared there were risks, but with the help of the 'Twelve', he had transcended the world of chance where mere mortals played their games of give and take. For a moment, his thoughts drifted to the previous evening, to the dinner party he had held for his friends, and he thought how lucky he was to know such people.

As O'Neil continued to gaze absentmindedly out over the grounds, two large outside catering vans came down the driveway, no doubt coming to clear up after the previous night's festivities. O'Neil turned and walked back into the house; he didn't want to get caught up dealing with such people. Carfax could take care of that.

***

The journey to the O'Neil estate led Adam and PC Newman past the now vacated crime scene. The road had been reopened, and except for a few meters of police incident tape and a sign appealing for witnesses, there was very little to look at unless you knew exactly where to look.

Even then, all that could be seen was a patch of burnt grass and scorched earth.

Adam couldn't help staring as they drove by, and a shiver ran down his spine as memories of the burning body invaded his mind. He looked away and glanced at PC Newman who, he noted, kept his eyes fixed rigidly on the road ahead.

On passing through the gates of the O'Neil estate, they travelled down the driveway towards the very large, and very grand-looking manor house.

Parked in front of the house were two large vans. Adam watched a steady stream of people walking to and fro, loading the vehicles with items being brought from the house.

As they parked next to the vans, Adam noted that both vehicles carried a logo that read:

CREME BESPOKE OUTSIDE CATERING

The two officers walked over to the front of the house and began climbing the stone steps towards the entrance. But before Adam and PC Newman could reach the top step, they were confronted by a very austere middle-aged woman wearing horn-rimmed spectacles and a smart business suit. The woman was carrying a clipboard and introduced herself as Ms Carfax, Archibald O'Neil's personal assistant. She asked in a very condescending manner, "Do you have an appointment?"

"No, we are here on official police business regarding a very serious incident," replied Adam, who had taken an instant dislike to the woman. Ms Carfax made no attempt to move out of their path but instead took out a pen and readied herself to make notes on her clipboard.

"Now, can I ask what sort of incident?"

Adam found he had already had enough of this woman and in a harsh tone, replied, "The sort that doesn't need an appointment. Now I would like to speak to Mr O'Neil immediately."

Carfax could tell that her usual bullying demeanour didn't hold much sway with the Police inspector, and so led them through to an elegant drawing room and asked them to wait.

After a couple of minutes, the doors of the drawing room swung open. A squat, portly man with a head resembling a turnip marched in. He had thin, swept-back hair, overgrown eyebrows, and was wearing a tweed suit; he reminded Adam of Toad of Toad Hall, but there was no doubting that this was Archibald O'Neil. The man had a confident bearing about him as he stepped directly up to Adam and shook him by the hand.

"You must be our new Police inspector. The one who is replacing Carl Winter."

O'Neil's hand was soft and clammy, and Adam fought the impulse to wipe his own hand after disengaging. "Welcome!" he announced loudly. "Good to have you aboard. Now how can I help you two fine officers? Ms Carfax said something about a serious incident?"

"Indeed, yes. We are looking into an incident that took place last night involving a van which is registered to this estate," said Adam.

"Oh, dear! It's not speeding, is it? I keep telling the chaps who work for me to slow down on these country lanes. But do they listen?"

Adam explained that the incident was much more serious than speeding but gave no further detail. He handed O'Neil a slip of paper with the van's registration number. He then asked, "Would it be possible to find out who was the last person to have access to this vehicle?"

"Oh, yes, of course. Each of our vehicles has its own logbook in which the driver enters the date, time, and nature of use, along with their name. Now if you will bear with me, I'll call the yard foreman's office and get you the details straight away."

O'Neil strode over to a nearby desk and, picking up the phone, made a call. He gave the registration number of the van to the person at the other end and asked who was recorded as having driven it last. O'Neil suddenly sounded surprised, spluttering, "When was this? Are you sure? But how can that be?" O'Neil put the phone down and turned to face Adam.

"I'm sorry, gentlemen. I won't be able to help you, after all. It seems the Yard Office was broken into last night and the van keys and the van were stolen!"

"Have you any idea when the theft occurred?"

"Haven't a clue. It's the first I've heard of it. I was hosting a dinner party last night for a gathering of friends and business acquaintances. I haven't been down to the yard since yesterday morning," said O'Neil.

O'Neil obligingly took Adam and PC Newman down to the estate yard to inspect the scene of the theft. The yard was located approximately five hundred yards from the main house, consisting of a large, cobbled area with stables on both sides. A little farther up was garaging for several of the estate's vehicles and farm machinery. Tucked away in one corner was the estate's office.

The two police officers followed O'Neil into the office, where he introduced them to Maltravers, the estate foreman. Maltravers was a tall man in his late forties, with a hawkish face and sharp eyes.

When questioned, Maltravers told them that he himself had used the van around mid-morning the previous day and had hung the keys in the office. As far as he was aware, no one else had used the vehicle and the office had been locked and left secure at six p.m. The yard foreman went on to state that he had discovered the theft on arriving for work at the yard that morning and had been just about to report the theft to the police when Mr O'Neil rang him.

Adam asked how the office had been entered, and Maltravers pointed to an open window with a broken glass pane by the catch. Adam inspected the damage.

O'Neil, who had been standing silently listening to all that was being said, asked, "Has the vehicle been found? I can send someone to collect it if necessary."

Adam informed O'Neil that the vehicle appeared to have been used for transporting a dead body. The inspector studied O'Neil's face for a reaction, and sure enough, the man looked shocked and somewhat disbelieving. The van was currently impounded, said Adam to O'Neil, whilst forensics went over it with a fine-toothed comb. O'Neil dropped himself onto an office chair, looking as though he'd had all the air knocked out of him.

"Dead body?" he gasped, turning to look at Maltravers. The yard foreman took a step back and protested, "Don't look at me! I don't know anything about any dead body. We don't have any dead bodies around here."

"Quite right!" said O'Neil. Then he added, "Keep the van as long as you want. I'm not sure we want it back after finding out what it's been used for."

Adam informed Maltravers that he would have Scenes of Crime attend as soon as possible to photograph and fingerprint the office and its window. He asked that the office be closed until that could be done. Adam also asked for the details of all estate employees so that the appropriate checks could be carried out. Maltravers began to protest but Archie O'Neil assured Adam that Ms Carfax would forward the details as soon as possible.

Adam was satisfied nothing more could be done for the moment.

He gave both O'Neil and Maltravers his card, asking them to contact him if they discovered anything else missing or suspicious.

***

Back at Penny-Deep Police Station, Adam made straight for his office and phoned Chief Superintendent Wise. The phone rang a while, and Adam was just wondering if maybe Wise had gone home when the Chief answered.

Adam updated him on the van and the break-in at the O'Neil estate.

"Does the break-in seem genuine?" asked Wise.

"There's nothing to make me feel otherwise, Sir."

"Very good," said Wise. Then he continued,

"Well, I've just got the preliminary post-mortem report. You had better sit down for this one!"

Adam listened carefully to what was said.

"The girl's body was positively identified as Victoria Timperley by her parents. We are still waiting for toxicology," the Chief Superintendent went on. "But what I can tell you at this moment is that the poor girl was dead long before her body was set alight."

"Had she been subjected to sexual assault?" Adam asked.

"It can't be ruled out, but there's little actual evidence due to the damage caused by the fire."

"Cause of death?" Adam asked.

Wise paused before answering. "They couldn't give a definitive cause at this time. But I can tell you that the poor girl's heart is missing."

"Oh, my God," gasped Adam.

"It gets stranger," said the Chief Superintendent. "Victoria Timperley's left hand is also missing."

Chapter 10

Adam Cadman sat in his office, silently contemplating the events of the past twelve hours. Only a week ago, he would have had his team of detectives crawling all over this case, picking it apart, looking for avenues of investigation. He would have had witnesses to interview, forensic evidence to consider, and would have steadily constructed a timeline of events and hopefully found some pattern, or conversely, some anomaly that would break the case open. But now he sat in his sparse office wearing his uniform, envying the city detectives involved in this investigation.

Adam had to agree with Chief Superintendent Wise's logic in keeping the investigation centred in the city, and he appreciated the Chief's sentiments that he could investigate any links between the abduction and murder and Penny-Deep.

But something made him feel more than a little uncomfortable. He couldn't put it into words; he couldn't even put it into thoughts. It was just a feeling, the strangest thing!

Thinking about the preliminary post-mortem report, Adam concluded that it threw up more questions than it answered. He could understand all the reasons someone might have for abducting a young woman, and he could understand why someone might burn the body as a way of destroying forensic evidence. But why on earth remove her left hand and her heart?

One theory the Major Incident Team was looking at was the organ trade—the theft of bodily organs to sell on to wealthy individuals in need.

Although once considered just an urban legend, several reported cases from around the world added some credibility to these stories. But that still didn't explain the missing left hand.

After theorising in ever-decreasing circles, Adam sought distraction by reading through PC Newman's statement of evidence for the previous night's events.

Adam was impressed. For someone of little experience, the officer had put together a well-written statement laying out the facts in a detailed, chronological order.

Adam spent the following hour typing up his own statement of evidence along with a covering report for the major incident team. During this time, he was interrupted only once, by Angela bringing him a cup of coffee and reminding him that he had a regular monthly appointment at the church to discuss local policing matters with the church group and the Women's Institute.

This kind of thing wasn't what Adam had been used to, and despite his reluctance, he knew this was exactly the sort of activity his new role would involve. Having no previous experience, he asked Angela what was usually discussed at the meetings. But Angela too was at a loss.

Apparently, Inspector Winter had used it as more of social event and a useful pit stop for tea and biscuits. *Oh well,* thought Adam, he'd just have to play this one by ear.

Having completed his statement and covering report, Adam hoped for a miracle to save him from the church meeting. He even went so far as to phone the communications room to check on the current status of all things Penny-Deep, just in case he had missed some emergency that would necessitate his urgent attendance and drag him away from the church meeting.

But it was not to be; fate had let him down like a cheap set of braces, and he reluctantly put on his tunic and cap, setting off to walk up to St Augustine's Church.

On arriving at St Augustine's, he was met by the local vicar.

Father Fenton Akers was a small, slight man with a thin face and angular features that gave the impression of two profiles stuck together. His small wire spectacles were barely balancing on the bridge of his nose, and his short red hair looked distinctly unkempt.

"Ah, you must be our new police inspector! So pleased to meet you," said the vicar in a high, reedy voice. "This way! We're all waiting for you."

Father Akers led the way into the nave and on to an area in the centre of the church transept, where Adam saw a group of ladies all sitting on small seats placed in a circle. A thin, gangly young man with a pasty complexion and a mop of black hair was crouched down, talking to two of the younger women who giggled away at something he said.

"Thank you, Clive!" said the vicar in a dismissive tone, causing the young man to skulk off. "Clive is my curate here at St Augustine's, a nice young man but I'm not sure being a curate is his true vocation," Akers confided.

Adam and the vicar sat on the last two empty chairs, and Father Akers introduced Adam as Penny-Deep's new police inspector.

Adam felt everyone's eyes turn towards him, and he decided the best way forward was to formally introduce himself and give a little information about his background and police service.

At the end of his introduction, a plump lady in her fifties commented on how young Adam was compared to Inspector Winter. The two far younger women either side of her were both blushing.

Adam couldn't decide if the comment was

meant as a compliment or a criticism, implying that his lack of age correlated with a lack of experience and knowledge.

Of course, nothing could have been further from the truth. Adam had a wealth of experience and knowledge, especially if making a direct comparison between Inspector Winter and himself.

But Adam decided to let the comment pass by without a reply.

"We hear there has been some excitement overnight. Inspector," said one of the blushing younger women.

Father Akers then piped up, "Yes! What can you tell us about this incident, and how the police investigation is progressing?"

Adam was mindful of giving as little information away as possible, particularly at this stage, and particularly as this investigation wasn't his to direct. Adam tactfully answered, "Very little, I'm afraid. The body of a young woman was found last night around ten p.m., by the side of the main road into Penny-Deep. Detectives based at district headquarters are carrying out the investigation, and unfortunately, I have been given no further information at this time."

His answer was evasive but basically true.

"Do you know if she was from Penny-Deep?" asked an elderly woman wearing a crumpled, grey, knitted hat that sat on her head like a melted plastic bucket.

"Inquiries are ongoing. But at this time, we have yet to find what, if any, ties the woman had with Penny-Deep," replied Adam.

"Do you think she was hit by a car?" asked someone else.

"It's possible," said Adam, conscious that the answer, again—though not strictly a lie—was unlikely in the extreme. Besides which, cars didn't usually perform major heart surgery, though the odd amputation had been known.

The questions regarding the dead young woman went on for another five minutes with Adam managing to bat them off without giving anything away.

Fortunately, proceedings were interrupted by the arrival of a stout-looking woman pushing a tea trolley, and everyone broke away to collect tea and biscuits.

By the time the circle reconvened, the topic had changed to preparations for an upcoming church fete. Adam relaxed and sat back, drinking his tea and idly looking around the church, paying little attention to the discussion at hand. He had never been a churchgoer, except for the odd Christening, wedding, or funeral—the old hatch, match, and dispatch. The truth was, Adam just wasn't a religious person. But for some strange reason, he did like churches.

There was something about them that felt calming.

He liked the architecture of churches too,

particularly the really old ones like St Augustine's. And he loved the large stained-glass windows with their various pictures and religious symbolism.

Just then, something occurred to him. It was symbolism. What if the removal of the heart and left hand from the woman's body was some kind of symbolism? After all, the same mutilation could have been carried out on all the other girls. None of their bodies had been found, so it was a possibility. But if that was the case, then the other bodies must be hidden, meaning the symbolic mutilation had probably not been done for public consumption. That would mean that any time and effort given to such symbolism was for the perpetrator's gratification only and had some significance to them as part of a ceremony or ritual.

Adam could only think of one circumstance in which such symbology might be relevant. Some kind of black magic, or devil worship! He'd heard of such things but had never before encountered it, either professionally or in his private life. Still, he was aware that on rare occasions, cases had come to light across the British Isles and to his mind, Penny-Deep certainly fit the geographic profile for where such things had been known to happen. An old, isolated town with the remnants of an old, isolated community. Country folk with strange country ways. Adam wondered who would be the best person to ask about such things in regard to Penny-Deep. It didn't take him long to realise that the most obvious candidate was sitting only a few feet away. Father Fenton!

Adam sat patiently until the end of the meeting. He then, good-naturedly, bid goodbye to several of the ladies who filed past on their way out.

Father Fenton was deep in conversation with a couple of his parishioners, and Adam stood nearby, waiting for their conversation to end before he approached the vicar.

"I wonder if I could have a word about something that may seem a little bizarre?" said Adam. "Also, I would prefer that what we discuss remains confidential."

Father Fenton looked surprised. But then his expression turned to one of intrigue.

"Of course, Inspector. If you think I can help. I can assure you that anything said between us will be treated in the strictest confidence."

Adam wasn't sure how to broach the subject. So, as he always did when he found himself in a similar situation, he decided to be as direct as possible.

"An odd question, I know, but do you have any knowledge of witchcraft or devil worship in or around Penny-Deep?"

Father Fenton looked as if someone had just poked him with an electric cattle prod. Then his brow furrowed and his expression became dark.

He stepped closer to Adam and then asked in a low, conspiratorial voice, "Can I ask, is this in connection with the body found last night?"

"Possibly," said Adam. "It's by no means an official line of inquiry, more my own theorising about what could possibly have happened to that poor girl."

"Well, I know of nothing definite, but I do hear the odd snippet of gossip from time to time, and of course, Penny-Deep does have inextricable historical ties with witchcraft."

"Oh!" This came as news to Adam.

"Oh, yes. Penny-Deep held a witch trial, resulting in one of the last recorded executions of a witch in England. Sometime in the late sixteen hundreds, I think."

"Please, tell me more."

"Well the story goes that a local woman who had a reputation for practising the dark arts was arrested and tried after cattle and livestock belonging to local farmers began falling sick and dying." Father Fenton glanced around, wary of eavesdroppers.

Then he continued, "Her name was Elizabeth 'Lizzie' Dee. The local squire at the time, one of the O'Neil's, paid her a visit in order to confront her, and according to what he said, he caught her having sexual union with the devil."

Adam found all of this too hard to swallow.

It was obviously superstitious nonsense, but he let the vicar continue uninterrupted.

"When Lizzie Dee saw O'Neil standing there, she immediately put a curse on his wife. O'Neil ran home, only to find his poor wife had died of unknown causes. Needless to say, that when word got out about Squire O'Neil's wife, it was the straw that broke the camel's back in regard to Elizabeth Dee. A mob gathered, and Lizzie Dee was detained. The trial of Lizzie Dee was nothing more than a kangaroo court, set up hastily on the small farm where Lizzie lived. It lasted only minutes and resulted in Lizzie being hanged from a nearby tree."

"That sounds horrendous," said Adam. "But the history books are littered with such stories from hundreds of years ago. I was looking for something more recent, something pertaining to the present, here in Penny-Deep."

Father Fenton glanced around once again, obviously checking no one else was in earshot. Then he continued, "Well, what about this? The small farm where Lizzie lived has stood empty ever since her hanging. Over the years, I suppose it fell to ruin and ended up in a collapsed pile. No one knows because no one really goes up there. There have always been local stories of all manner of strange creatures wandering the area, preying on anyone foolish enough to go on the land. There are stories of villagers disappearing up there and tales of the ghost of Lizzie Dee being seen."

Adam had heard enough.

"Surely you don't believe in such things, do you, Father? Besides which, the suspects I'm interested in are more of the flesh and blood variety."

"I'm not saying I do believe in such things and I'm not saying I don't," said the vicar. “Either way, what I believe doesn't really matter. You see, the point of me telling you all of this is that over the last few years, a team of construction workers set up camp on the Dee land and rebuilt the farmhouse. However, I suspect it's much larger and grander than the original.

“Whenever anyone came into contact with the workmen, they naturally quizzed them about the new owner of the house. But if the workmen knew, they certainly weren't telling, and it was surmised that some wealthy out-of-town type, or incomer, as they are referred to locally, had bought the land to develop. Knowing something of the history and the stories surrounding that land, most locals began running a sweepstake as to how long the new resident would last.

“Most bets didn't give long and everyone was amused at the folly of whoever had purchased the old farm. But it turned out that the last laugh was at the local townfolks’ expense. The new occupant of old Lizzie's farm is a Katherine Dee, a descendant of old Lizzie. Now, what may be of interest to you, is that ever since Katherine moved in, I have been hearing things about the woman!"

Adam couldn't help noticing a slightly contemptuous tone to Father Fenton's voice when he said, "The woman!"

"What sorts of things?" asked Adam.

Father Fenton took his time to answer.

He appeared to be searching his memory and picking his words carefully. "Well just whispers really. But some of the townsfolk have encountered this Katherine Dee. They say she has a strange air about her, and some have said that she also practices the dark arts and all manner of witchcraft and satanism up at that farm. I don't know how they know this. I always dismissed it has idle gossip and nonsense. But now we have had this terrible event, with the girl's body being found, and you yourself asking me about black magic and the like... Well, it's making me start to wonder."

Adam was intrigued.

"Can you furnish me with any names of who said these things about this Katherine Dee?"

"No, not really. They were just odd snippets I heard here and there. As I said, I paid them no mind at first, so I really can't remember who said what. Besides, I have to treat such things in strict confidence, as you asked me to with our conversation. So I wouldn't feel comfortable passing on any names. Even if I could remember them."

Adam didn't know what to make of his conversation with Father Akers in the cold light of day, as he walked away from St Augustine's Church. It all seemed a little far-fetched.

But the vicar was right about one thing. He, himself, had asked about such things! As Adam walked up the path from the church to the lych-gate, he caught sight of Clive, the young curate who appeared to be hiding behind a tall gravestone, from behind which he occasionally peeked.

Adam followed the young man's gaze and realised that he was sneakily watching the two young women from the church. Adam had to agree with the vicar that the job of church curate and Clive probably did not constitute a match made in heaven!

On returning to the police station, Adam busied himself trying to carry out background checks on Katherine Dee. But his efforts were all to no avail. Ms Dee had no criminal record or any information markers, and a broader search of the internet brought back hundreds of women with the same name. But there was none that Adam could definitively link to the woman living in Penny-Deep. Of course, his efforts were hampered by not having details such as an exact date of birth, but even so, he thought he would have found some trace of information about her. It was all very puzzling. *But then, probably all a waste of time,* thought Adam.

Linking the murder to local witchcraft seemed very fanciful. Even he thought so, and it was his idea. Adam wouldn't dream of repeating his theory to the investigation team; he would be laughed out of the office.

Just then, Adam's thoughts were interrupted by the sound of his mobile phone. It was Mrs Chattox, and she had brought Sophia into town to do a bit of shopping, and Sophia was eager to visit Changes haberdashery to see if her dresses were ready. She wondered if that was alright.

Adam said it was fine by him. Then he added that he was about to finish work, and would meet them, and take 'little Miss Impatient' to the shop himself so that he could pay for the dresses on the off-chance they were ready.

***

Adam found Mrs Chattox and Sophia standing a couple of shops down from Changes. Mrs Chattox said she had a little more shopping to do and would see them both back home in time for tea. Then she hurried off with a shopping list in one hand and a large shopping bag in the other.

The ladies at Changes both greeted Adam and Sophia warmly, and much to Sophia's delight, Saffy informed them that she had just finished the dresses.

For the next twenty minutes, Adam had to watch Sophia conduct her own fashion show in front of a large standalone mirror. She tried on both dresses, marching up and down, viewing herself from every angle. Prim and Saffy stood cooing over her every move. Adam had to admit his daughter looked absolutely beautiful in the dresses, and they fitted her to perfection.

He thought of Diana and how proud she would have been of their daughter, and he wished with all his heart that she could have been there to see her.

Once Sophia's fashion show was over, the dresses were neatly wrapped and placed in a stylish bag that Sophia insisted on carrying all the way back to the police station car park, where Adam's car was waiting. The journey back home was an entertaining affair, involving Sophia asking Adam to describe to her how she looked in the dresses. These descriptions were something Sophia insisted he retold, over and over. Each time Adam complied, telling her how beautiful the dresses were, and how beautiful she looked in them, Sophia lapped it up.

***

On turning into the yard at Old Anna Farm, Adam saw the tall, dark figure of a man in a long black topcoat striding away from the front door of their home. Adam stopped the car and got out.

As the man neared, he recognised him as Frank Winter, the man he had just replaced at Penny-Deep Police Station.

"Can I help you?" Adam asked.

"I popped up to ask you the very same question," replied Winter. "I know I'm retired, and I shot off with haste, but when I heard about that poor young woman's body being found, I thought you might need a little help. You know, local knowledge and such."

Adam had taken an instant dislike to this man from the start.

He was sure his visit was just a 'fishing trip' for information regarding the murder investigation, either for his own titillation or the sake of gossip in the local pubs.

Adam was in no doubt. He just wanted to get rid of Winter as quickly as possible, and without telling him anything about the investigation.

Adam said, "That's very good of you, especially now that you're retired and presumably have far better things to be getting on with. Unfortunately, I know nothing. The major investigation team is handling the entire investigation down at headquarters, and they are playing their cards pretty close to their chests. I'm afraid I'm not in the loop on this case but if you are keen to help, perhaps you could contact the team directly."

Adam knew Winter would get zero information from the investigation team, and Winter gave Adam a look that made it clear he didn't believe him. Then Winter smirked and said, "Just thought I'd offer my services. By the way, I take it that's not your idea of exterior decorating."

Winter pointed towards their home.

By this time, Sophia had climbed out of the car. She followed Adam and Winter as they walked up to the front door of the barn. There was something large and black hanging across the door, and at first glance, it looked as if someone had smeared black paint across it.

But as they got closer, Adam and Sophia could see it was a large black crow with its wings outstretched. The crow, which was dead, was hanging from the door handle by a red cord.

Something else was also hanging down just below the crow. It was made up of twigs bound together in the shape of a five-pointed star suspended upside down.

Under his breath, Adam said, "What the—?"

"It was here when I arrived," said Winter, still smirking.

"I didn't know if it was something you had done for some reason. So I didn't touch it."

Adam ripped the crow and the pentagram down, then threw the dead bird over the garden wall into the bushes at that side of the barn. He kept hold of the twigs. "What is all this crap? Is it meant to spook me? 'Cause if it is, whoever did this certainly doesn't know me."

Winter studied Adam. Then he said, "Looks like some sort of black magic sign to me. No guessing who's responsible for that. Our resident witch would be my chief suspect."

Sophia's ears pricked up at the mention of a witch.

"I take it you are referring to this Katherine Dee woman," said Adam.

"So you have heard of her!" Winter exclaimed. "Well, for my money, I can't think of anyone else likely to have done it. We never had any of this sort of thing in Penny-Deep before she arrived."

"But why would she go out of her way to tie this to our front door!" Adam protested.

"Who knows what goes on in the minds of these Satanists?" Winter replied. "As for going out of her way, you do know that she is your neighbour, don't you?"

"Neighbour, what do you mean?"

"I thought you would have known." Winter could barely hide his delight at passing on the information. "Katherine Dee lives at the top of this hill. Just past the woods, up that track."

Winter nodded towards the trail that ran up the left side of the barn. Both Adam and Sophia turned and looked in unison, then looked at each other. "Well, I'll be off then," said Winter still smirking, and off he marched across the yard.

Adam looked down at Sophia and placed a reassuring hand on her shoulder. "The man is silly, Sophia," he said, "There are no such things as witches. Just very silly people."

Sophia said nothing, but she wasn't so sure that her father was right.

***

That evening, Mrs Chattox brought over their

evening meal, toad in the hole with lashings of gravy and vegetables. Sophia devoured the meal, once she had ascertained that the meal contained sausages and that no amphibians had been hurt during the preparation of the dish.

Adam had sworn Sophia to secrecy about the dead crow and the twigs attached to their door. He gave the excuse that it might frighten Mrs Chattox. Adam didn't think it would for one minute, but he had decided not to discuss Ms Dee with Mrs Chattox just yet.

He had a feeling that Mrs Chattox was a little economical with her knowledge of local goings-on, and he wasn't sure why. What Adam did know was that he wasn't ready to confront her just yet. Not until he had done a little more digging. As for Ms Dee, she was firmly on his radar and would be getting a visit at some stage in the very near future.

Chapter 11

The following morning, Adam was awake and out of bed early. He toyed with the idea of going around and pounding on the cockerel's hen house roof, to see how he liked being jarred out of his slumber. But these thoughts were quickly overtaken by far more pressing matters. He showered and dressed for work, then busied himself in the kitchen, making toast and scrambled eggs.

It wasn't long before he heard Sophia come padding into the kitchen.

She looked grumpy and still half asleep. When Adam asked if she'd had a good night's sleep, she said that she had, and then collected her breakfast before making her way into the living room, where Adam heard the TV switching on. Adam resigned himself to the fact that this morning, his daughter preferred breakfast with a series of cartoon characters rather than with her father.

By switching on the TV at that precise moment, Sophia caught the tail end of a news item about breast cancer. She listened to the early morning presenter, and all the memories of her mother's illness came flooding back. Sophia remembered how her mum had bravely fought but then, one day, her mum sat her down and told her, as gently as she could, that she wouldn't be able to win the battle. Her mum said to her that she would be going away sometime soon but would always watch over her. It didn't seem long after that conversation that her mother died.

Sophia had to fight back the tears that began to well up in her eyes as she recalled the memory. Once again, Sophia felt anger, especially towards the girls at her old school who had been cruel to her after her mum had died, and particularly the ones she had thought were her friends.

Sophia remembered how the girls at school had told her that cancer ran in families and that because her mum died young, she would too. These memories made her feel afraid, and as usual, when she had these terrible thoughts, she desperately wanted to ask her father if this was true. But as always, Sophia didn't want to upset him by talking about her mum's illness.

She also knew, her father loved her too much to tell her the truth anyway. He would say to her that everything was alright, and that she had nothing to worry about whatsoever. Sophia knew that this was what parents did. They would try and protect their children from anything that might upset or hurt them, even if what they were protecting them from was the truth.

Sophia turned the TV channel over to cartoons but sat eating her breakfast deep in thought, not really watching what was on the screen. Once she had eaten her breakfast and was satisfied that she no longer looked as though she was on the brink of crying, she turned off the TV and returned to the kitchen. Her father looked up, smiling.

"Hiya, princess! Don't tell me I've just overtaken Bugs Bunny in the popularity stakes."

"Bugs Bunny isn't on," murmured Sophia, absentmindedly pouring herself some fresh orange juice from the carton on the worktop. Adam noticed Sophia seemed to be in a low mood but wasn't sure if her grumpiness was just down to being up so early.

He smiled, reminiscing that her mother had never been a morning person either.

But then there was a knock at the door, and Mrs Chattox stepped in.

"That's my cue to go to work!" said Adam, “I'll tell you what, Sophia. I have to work another couple of days, but then, I'm going to take a couple of days off, and I'll take you somewhere nice. Somewhere that you can wear one of your new dresses. What do you think?"

He hoped that would cheer her up, but Sophia just nodded and remained subdued.

Adam informed Mrs Chattox that he would be home around six p.m., to which Mrs Chattox reminded him not to be late as hot food would be awaiting his return.

She would be cooking a nice dinner for them both.

Adam walked over to Sophia and gave her a hug and a quick kiss on the nose which she instantly wrinkled. Then he was off through the door.

During the remainder of the morning, Mrs Chattox cleared away the breakfast pots and then enlisted Sophia's help to pick blackberries from the hedgerows by her house. The elderly neighbour told Sophia she would teach her how to bake a blackberry pie.

But Sophia seemed less than enthusiastic, so Mrs Chattox came up with another suggestion. Sophia could play out in the yard for a while if that was what she preferred to do.

The fresh air would probably do her good, Mrs Chattox thought.

Sophia realised that she hadn't seen her friend, the silvery white horse, for a day or so. For that reason, the idea of being outside appealed to her. She asked Mrs Chattox for a few carrots just in case, and then waited patiently.

After a while, Sophia's patience wore thin.

She was hoping her new friend would appear to take her mind off things, and when the horse was a 'no show', she began to feel upset all over again. Sophia knew the horse usually came down the track at the side of their home, and so she had the idea of going to look for her.

Sophia took a couple of steps towards the track.

But then she remembered what the man had

said yesterday, about a witch living at the top of the hill. Sophia stopped dead in her tracks as she wondered what to do.

The horse would probably be on the grassland not too far up the path, and the man had said that the witch lived right at the top of the hill beyond the dark woods. After turning it over in her mind, she decided to walk up just as far as the grass meadow, to see if her friend, the horse, was there.

Sophia walked slowly up the track, looking carefully around her. But it was a bright sunny day, and witches probably only came out in the dark, she reassured herself. Eventually, Sophia came to a gap in the trees to her right, through which she saw the horse grazing on the lush green grass. Sophia pushed through the trees and walked towards the horse. It must have heard her because its head lifted and its ears pricked up. Sophia smiled, walking towards her new-found friend. But then she suddenly froze, and the smile fell from her face. The blood in Sophia's tiny body ran cold as a figure stepped out from behind the horse, draping an arm around its neck.

The figure stepped farther into view, and Sophia could see that it was a woman, tall and slender wearing a long emerald green dress that touched the grass.

Her hair was long and black, flowing down past her shoulders.

The woman looked beautiful with striking brown eyes, so dark they might even have been black. Sophia noticed the woman's eyes sparkle as she smiled in her direction.

Sophia had always thought that witches were old with pointed hats, and warts on their noses. But though this woman didn't fit her idea of what a witch should look like, Sophia couldn't help thinking this was the woman the man had told her father about, saying she was a witch.

"You must be Sophia!" the woman said, smiling.

Sophia gasped. The witch knew her name. Sophia hesitated, but then said, "Yes." Her mouth was dry with fear, and her reply barely audible.

"I'm Katherine Dee, and I live at the top of the hill."

Sophia knew it! This woman was the witch.

The woman stepped closer, her trailing dress covering her feet, somehow giving the impression she was gliding when she walked. Sophia had never been so afraid.

She didn't know what to say, and in her panic, she blurted out, "Are you a witch?"

The woman just laughed and then said, "So, is that what they say about me?"

"Yes, my father is a policeman, and a man came to our house yesterday and told him about you. The man said that you're a witch," said Sophia defiantly.

"Well, it must be true then." The woman

looked directly into Sophia's eyes.

Just then, a large black dog trotted out of the bushes, so large that its back came up to the woman's waist. The brutish-looking beast sat down by the woman, and stared at Sophia with unflinching eyes, licking its lips.

Sophia thought the dog looked as though it was about to pounce and devour her.

The woman stroked the top of the dog's head and said, "Don't be afraid, Sophia. My friend here won't hurt you." The woman instructed the beast to go and say hello to Sophia, who watched as the giant dog instantly jumped up and trotted towards her. Sophia couldn't move, rooted to the spot with terror. But the large dog stopped just in front of her and sat down. The hound then raised its large front, right paw towards her.

"He wants to shake your hand, Sophia. His name is Fancy."

Sophia took the dog's huge paw in both her hands and moved it up and down in a handshaking motion. Once she let go of the paw, the dog got up and walked around her, sniffing, before sitting by her left-hand side. "He likes you tickling behind his ears. Do that, and he'll love you forever."

Sophia reached out and began tickling the dog behind his two large, furry black ears. The dog that, when sitting, was about the same height as Sophia, then looked across at her and with a lash of a big wet, slobbery tongue, licked her face. Sophia couldn't help but let out a giggle.

"You see," said the woman. "New best friend for life and judging by the carrots you are carrying, you have come looking for Ruby."

“Is she your horse? Does she belong to you?” Sophia asked.

"No, Ruby is her own person. She belongs to no one. But we are very good friends."

“Why is she called Ruby?"

"That's a good question, Sophia," said the woman. "You see, when she was very young, her hair was a bright ruby red colour. But as she grew a little older, it changed to this silver-white."

The woman beckoned her over. "Come see. You can still see the odd fleck of her original colour in amongst her fur."

Sophia cautiously stepped up to the horse, and the woman ran her fingers through the animal's coarse hair, where she pointed out several flecks of red otherwise lost among the white.

Sophia looked puzzled, then asked, “Did you make her change in colour? Using magic?”

“No. It was all Ruby’s doing. All quite natural.”

Sophia fed the horse her carrots. Whilst she did so, her mind, again, began thinking about what had been troubling her all that morning. She thought about her mother’s cancer and if she too would get the disease, and about the strange woman standing by her side.

The woman still hadn't denied being a witch, but then again, she did seem nice and friendly. The swirling mixture of thoughts in Sophia's head prompted her to try her luck.

She asked, "Are you really a witch, and can you do magic?"

The woman, still smiling, said, "Why? Sophia, what do you have in mind?"

Sophia, unbeknown to even herself, had reached a point where she needed to talk to someone, and for some reason, it just felt right to let it all out and confide in this strange woman. Still feeding the horse, Sophia began to tell the woman about her mum dying young of something called cancer, and about how the girls at her old school said that it meant that she would die young, too.

Suddenly a whole year of pent-up emotion was released, and Sophia burst into tears, sobbing uncontrollably. "Can you help me?" she said. "I don't want to leave my dad. He'll be all alone."

The woman knelt and hugged her, comforting her until the crying stopped.

Both Ruby and Fancy added a bit of nuzzling too.

Once Sophia had regained some composure, the woman held her at arm's length, looking at her intently. She said, "The word *witch* originally meant wit or wise, or knowledgeable! Well, it just so happens I am very knowledgeable, Sophia. Firstly, I can tell you that the girls who said those things to you are stupid and know absolutely nothing. Now let me look at your right hand."

The woman gazed at the palm of Sophia's right hand, before saying, "Oh, Sophia!"

She traced a finger in a large arch around Sophia's right thumb.

"You see this long, deep line, Sophia?" Sophia nodded, and the woman continued. "It's your lifeline. See how long and deep it is? You are going to live a very long and exciting life. You will live to be a very old woman, Sophia."

Sophia's face lit up with a smile. "Are you sure?" she asked.

"I'm positive, Sophia, and you know witches always know these things. You will have good health and live long."

Sophia suddenly caught herself as she stumbled backwards, temporarily off balance. She had been listening to the woman's soft, soothing voice so intently, and staring into her large shiny dark eyes, that for a moment she seemed to have drifted off.

"Are you alright, Sophia?" the woman asked with concern.

Sophia smiled and nodded, then thanked the woman. She felt much better.

Finally, the woman said, "Never pay any attention to what silly people say, Sophia. I hope I will see you again, and that we can become friends. People call me Katherine, but my friends call me Kate." Katherine Dee then turned, and Sophia watched her walk towards the trees where she stepped through the foliage and disappeared, along with Fancy who followed in her wake.

Sophia liked Katherine; she was kind and caring, and that was plain to see.

There was also something unusual and exciting about her.

Was she really a witch?

And did she really want to be her friend?

Sophia suddenly felt a difference in herself after being around Katherine Dee.

It was hard to explain, but she felt as if a huge weight had been lifted from her, and she seemed to feel eight years old again. After saying goodbye to Ruby, Sophia headed back down the track to Old Anna Farm. She was deep in thought as she walked. Her father had always warned her against talking to strangers, and she wasn't sure whether Mrs Chattox would be angry or not that she had wandered so far away. Sophia decided that it was probably best not to mention walking up the track, or her meeting Katherine, to either Mrs Chattox or her father.

***

Adam had spent the last part of his working day making inquiries into the O'Neil estate and staff. Initially, Adam intended them to be cursory. It wasn't as if the estate were prime suspects regarding the missing girls. Granted, the woman's body had been transported in one of their vans. But the van had been stolen. There was nothing to implicate the O'Neil estate, and the theft of their vehicle certainly looked genuine. Still, it was a loose end, and Adam didn't like those at all.

The Scene of Crime Officer who attended the estate regarding the reported office burglary had telephoned earlier. According to him, the only fingerprints found had been those of estate workers. So on the face of it, the O'Neil Estates' role in the murder inquiry seemed something of a dead end.

But something kept gnawing at Adam. Something just didn't fit together well.

Transporting the body of a girl kidnapped from the city along the quiet country lanes of Penny-Deep was one thing. But to use a van stolen from a local country estate which was itself tucked out of the way? None of it made sense. No one would transport the body all the way out to Penny-Deep simply on the off-chance of stealing another vehicle, Adam reasoned.

Either the van was stolen to transport the body to Penny-Deep, from the city, or the body was already in Penny-Deep, and the van had been stolen to get it out.

Also, whoever broke into the O'Neil estate certainly had inside knowledge of both the estate and its workings. They obviously knew the availability of a van at that location, as well as where the keys for the vehicles were kept. Although far from conclusive in Adam's eyes, this last piece of the puzzle tipped the balance in favour of someone local being involved.

Could it be that the girls had been kept somewhere in Penny-Deep all along?

True to his word, Archie O'Neil had asked Ms Carfax to email a list of details for everyone employed on the estate. Adam noticed she had omitted her own details, but a phone call soon remedied that, and Adam couldn't help but smile at the thought of inconveniencing the obnoxious woman. Not to mention her feelings of impertinence at being lumped in with all the labourers and other employees as a possible criminal suspect.

Adam checked the backgrounds of the estate's staff. A couple had received minor public order convictions relating to drunkenness or criminal behaviour, but nothing serious. Maltravers, the estate manager, had also been questioned about domestic abuse, and also an allegation of threatening poachers with a loaded shotgun. But no formal charges had ever been brought against the man. Finally, despite Adam's hopes and wishes, Ms Carfax also checked out with a big fat zero.

After exhausting the list of estate employees, Adam decided he might as well check Archie

O'Neil. Interestingly, the checks on O'Neil came back with a couple of drunkenness and assault charges from when he was a young man. Nothing too serious, and the charges resulted in nothing more than small fines being issued by the courts. But it was enough to pique Adam's interest and give him the incentive to look further into O'Neil's background.

O'Neil was fifty years old and had never married or had children.

The elder of two brothers, this meant that he had inherited the family estate and money on the death of his father some twenty years ago. That said, O'Neil had managed to get kicked out of university for some undisclosed reason. But since then, he had already managed to accrue a small fortune through shrewd investments in the property market. Then, over the last ten years, O'Neil had set himself up as a hedge-fund manager, and this was now his primary source of wealth, offering investment opportunities for other wealthy individuals.

Adam carried on scouring the internet for more information on O'Neil, but there seemed to be very little else. On a whim, Adam sent a private email to an old army buddy, Kieron Jones.

After resigning his commission as Captain, Kieron had gone on to work in City Banking, down in London. Despite his commission and privileged background, Adam and Kieron had always gotten on like a house on fire and had developed a close bond based on mutual respect after being deployed in the Middle East together. They had always kept in touch. Not so much now, but directly after Diana had died, Kieron had called him every day and visited twice.

He was a good friend. Adam kept the email to Kieron brief, simply asking for any information on O'Neil and his hedge fund. Once the email was sent, Adam sat back in his chair and stretched.

He began thinking about heading home when his office phone rang.

It was Chief Superintendent Wise, and the Chief's opening sentence was all Adam needed to feel as if he had been beaten about his head and left stunned.

"We've got another missing girl!"

Chapter 12

The drive home was pretty much a blur for Adam. Some distant part of his brain was handling the business of driving, keeping his conscious mind out of the process. All other thoughts were crowded out of Adam's head by Chief Superintendent Wise's phone call playing over and over, like a looped recording. Adam listened to the Chief Super's grim voice playing in his head.

Each time, he extracted what he felt were the salient facts.

"The missing girl was sixteen-year-old Elizabeth Short," said Wise. "Last seen leaving college in the city, at eight p.m. last night, where she had been taking an evening class in speed typing and shorthand. Elizabeth was a very conscientious, family-oriented girl, who had never given her parents any cause for concern. She didn't have a boyfriend, and when she hadn't arrived home, her mother telephoned her known circle of friends, but to no avail. At two a.m., her parents finally reported her missing. Since that time, all available police resources were being used to search for Elizabeth. CCTV recordings show her leaving the college and walking en route to the bus station. Unfortunately, she took a shortcut over some waste ground off Bridge Street.

"Now, this land is used as an open-air car park and is ill-lit, and not covered by CCTV. After Elizabeth Short was seen to enter, she was not seen again. Officers are currently reviewing several hours of footage from cameras near to the car park, and all vehicular movements around that time are being logged, and the vehicle keepers checked."

By the time Adam was pulling up in the farmyard at Old Anna Farm, his mind had moved on to the parents of Elizabeth Short and the pain and anxiety they must now be experiencing.

Briefly, he thought about how he would feel if Sophia were to go missing, but then he quickly shut those thoughts out of his mind. Some thoughts were just too painful to confront.

Adam felt redundant stuck out here in Penny-Deep, and he felt guilty that he was not down at Central, helping find the girl. He had always been a man to take action, and even when the odds of success were insurmountably against him, he still felt better if he was actually doing something.

As Adam climbed from his car, he looked towards the track running up by the left side of his home. Perhaps there was one thing he could do. He had yet to speak to Katherine.

Adam set off at a brisk pace. The track varied in steepness from point to point as he passed the grazing land to his right, then the path skirted the dark woods. Previously, when he'd run up the track, he hadn't noticed just how large and dense the woodland was.

Every so often, he came upon a break in the trees that permitted him a glimpse into the woods. It wasn't difficult to see how they had got their name.

The interior of the woodland was so dark it seemed like a land of permanent night-time.

Eventually, Adam reached the plateau where once again, he could hear the rumbling of the waterfall, and he caught the odd glimpse of the large pond through the trees. After another short climb, Adam reached a second expanse of woodland, and to his left, the land rose severely into a steep rocky outcrop, the footpath being forced to veer off right, cutting through the dark woods.

The trees and undergrowth rustled with wildlife, some of which gave off the occasional scream or whoop. Adam could feel hundreds of pairs of eyes watching him. During his military service, he had cut through jungles much denser and darker, with far more wildlife, some of which was deadly to encounter. But something about these particular woods was somehow unnerving.

This small corner of the English countryside gave him an eerie feeling that he couldn't quite put his finger on. Once or twice, he thought he caught a fleeting glimpse of something from the corner of his eye, something large and black moving on all fours in the brush to his right, keeping pace with him, yet managing to keep just out of sight. Adam mentally admonished himself.

He was allowing his imagination to play tricks on him.

Adam walked on until the trees gave way to a large clearing, and there in front of him, Adam saw a large stone cottage with outbuildings.

The path he was taking led directly to the dwelling.

Adam's route to the cottage took him past a large and solitary tree that looked ancient and gnarled, standing in a clearing. He stopped momentarily, looking at its broad but oddly shaped trunk and then gazing up at its wide-spanning branches that creaked under a lush green canopy.

Suddenly, a soft voice broke his train of thought.

"Lovely, isn't it?

Adam was startled and turned suddenly to see who had spoken. He was surprised to see the same beautiful young woman with long black hair, the same one he had seen swimming in the nearby pond just the other day. Today, she wore a long, emerald green dress that caressed the curves of her body. "Wych Elm," the woman said. "That's what the tree is. The story goes that they hanged an ancestor of mine, Lizzie Dee, from its branches for practising witchcraft."

Suddenly, there was a cracking sound coming from the woods. Adam turned in the direction of the noise, to see something large and dark break from the cover of the dense woods behind him.

It was the large black mastiff dog, the same one he had seen with the woman at the pond.

It ran over and sat by the woman's side, staring at Adam.

"My name is Katherine Dee," said the woman. Then she said, "I've seen you before. You were up at the pond, watching me swimming the other day."

Adam could feel his cheeks begin to flush. So, she had seen him watching her swim naked!

"I was just having a look around," Adam stammered, feeling more than a little uncomfortable.

"Did you see everything that you wanted to see?" the woman asked with a flirtatious smile. She was toying with him, making him feel as if he had to explain himself when he was the one who was supposed to be questioning her and putting her under pressure. Adam decided to turn the tables.

"Well, I saw you swimming without a stitch of clothing. You should be aware that you may be committing offences against public decency and could find yourself in court."

"Yes, I like to swim sky-clad," Ms Dee replied, still smiling flirtatiously and laughing. "As for breaking the law. I believe I would have to be seen from a public place and to have intentionally caused someone alarm or distress. Is that not so?"

She stepped closer, tilting her head questioningly, her eyes boring into his own.

"As you were the only person watching me, Mr Policeman, did I cause *you* alarm or distress?"

"Well, er no. I, erm, can't say that you caused me... Well, never mind."

He was mortified! Adam could feel his cheeks flush even more.

Damn the woman, making him feel like some awkward adolescent schoolboy!

"I'm so pleased," she continued. "Also, the pond and all the land up here are privately owned, by me. So you see, technically, I also couldn't be seen in or from a public place. I could be viewed only from the place in which you quite clearly stood."

She was toying with him, playing with his embarrassment, and enjoying every second.

"Oh!" was all that Adam could say.

He was totally deflated and momentarily lost for what to say next.

"It's alright, though, Mr Policeman," she went on. "I do allow friends up here. So if you ever want to have a look around, to see what you can see, please do. That's assuming, of course, that you are my friend and that you won't be alarmed or distressed by seeing me naked."

Adam concluded that he was never going to win this game, so he decided just to be direct and ask his questions. "Ms Dee," Adam began but was interrupted by the woman.

"You can call me Katherine. Or Kate if we are to be good friends."

Again, the emphasis on *good friends* carried a lascivious undertone, and he felt a discomfort creeping along the back of his neck. Sure, most men would love for a woman to be so suggestive.

But this was neither the time nor the place.

“Ms Dee,” he continued, trying to keep a steady tone. “I’m Inspector Adam Cadman. Last night, someone tied a dead crow to the front door of my home along with an—Well, I don't know what you would call it but it was a circle containing a pentagram, made of twigs. Would you know anything about this?”

Ms Dee had to raise her hand to her mouth to stop herself bursting out laughing.

"I'm sorry," she said, "but did you come up here because you thought I would do such a thing? Is that it?

“As a matter of fact, I sincerely doubt that you would,” said Adam, quickly regaining his composure. "I think whoever left those items probably sought to unnerve me and was, in a very clumsy way, trying to cast suspicion in your direction."

"And why would that be?" asked Katherine Dee.

Adam had only just met Katherine and didn't know anything about her, other than she was extremely beautiful and extremely annoying. He had no reason to trust her and yet, for some strange reason, he felt as though he could. He also had a feeling that Katherine Dee may provide him with information that could be the key to cracking open the investigation into the missing girls.

So, all things considered, he decided to take a chance.

"I think you may be able to answer some questions I have relating to a major, and very serious, investigation."

Katherine now looked totally serious.

"Oh, really? Then come to the house," she said. "We can discuss it there."

On reaching the house, they walked through a gate and along a stone path that cut a winding way through a beautifully planted cottage garden. Adam looked at the front of the large stone cottage with interest. If he had not been told differently, he would have assumed that the house had stood in its present state for a couple of hundred years. They reached an oak and stone porch that sheltered a large oak door, and Katherine led the way inside. But as Adam turned to close the door, he saw the massive beast of a dog sitting at the gate as if posting guard duty.

Once inside, Adam followed Katherine through to a large but cosy living room, with a polished oak floor covered with several large Persian rugs. One wall of the room had a vast inglenook fireplace that housed a large wood-burning stove. Two long, plump sofas lined up either side of the inglenook. The rest of the furniture was antique and looked very expensive.

"Please take a seat," Katherine said.

Adam sat on one of the sofas and immediately sank into its comfortable caress.

Katherine sat on the sofa opposite. Adam began.

"You may have seen the news about the girls reported missing from the city over the past few weeks? You may also have heard about the girl whose body was found on one of the roads outside Penny-Deep."

Katherine nodded. "Yes, I am certainly aware of these things."

Adam continued.

"Some details regarding these events have not been made public. But before I tell you these, I need to be reassured that you will not tell another living soul."

Adam became aware that Katherine was staring directly at him with large, dark eyes that shone like pools of deep, black water. Just for a moment, he lost himself in them before regaining his concentration as Katherine spoke. "I give you my word. I will tell no one."

"All right," said Adam. "Well, the woman whose body was found just outside Penny-Deep, was one of those reported missing from the city. By the time I found the body, someone had set fire to it. But the post-mortem examination revealed that her heart was missing, along with her left hand."

"I see, but why do you wish to question me?"

"Well, I have a theory that this may be some sort of satanic symbolism, and every time I hear your name mentioned, it's usually accompanied by the words 'witch' and 'black magic,' or 'dark arts'." Ms Dee's lips give the smallest hint of a smile.

"And do you think I am involved in this?" she asked.

"No," said Adam. "And I am taking a huge risk confiding in you in this way. But if you do have any knowledge of this witchcraft stuff, then I could do with a little help understanding it, to work out whether I'm on the right track or not."

Once again, Adam became aware of the stare from the woman opposite.

Her gaze was quite hypnotic.

"You are not a religious man, Inspector Cadman, I take it. You were, I sense, a soldier?"

"That's right. I was in the Engineers."

"That may be true but only partly so. I sense there was much more to it."

Adam squirmed. How the hell did she know this stuff?

It was as if Ms Dee was looking deep inside his head and reading his mind.

He was just about to protest when she spoke again, quickly this time.

"Yes, I can help you," she said. "And from what you tell me, what was done to that poor girl has all the signs of satanic practice."

"Can you explain?"

"By taking the heart of a person, some believe that you are taking their very essence. This energy, they believe, can then be used to drive their magic and their intention out into the Universe, to bring about what they desire."

Adam felt disgusted at the thought.

"It all sounds pretty sick to me," he said.

"It is. Any taking of life is a sick and absurd thing," replied Katherine.

Adam had a flashback to his past life in the military. He quickly forced it out of his mind and wondered if Katherine was intentionally having a dig at it.

"What about you?" he asked. "How do you know all this? Are you somehow involved with this sort of stuff?"

Ms Dee shook her head.

"This sort of stuff? No! I value all life." Then she said, "Let me try and explain. We appear to live in a world of form, the material world. But behind this world of form is a world of forces. Some of those forces you will be aware of, such as electromagnetism and gravity to name but two. But there are many more, some known to science, some not. What you call magic involves many things. And sometimes, it involves the manipulation of these other forces."

Adam thought for a moment and then said, "So, the manipulation of these forces is what satanists do. So messing with these forces is evil, black magic?"

"Manipulating these forces is a little like manipulating electricity," said Katherine Dee. "Electricity can be utilized to power a baby's incubator or to complete a circuit that launches a nuclear missile. So tell me, is electricity good or bad?"

"Well, neither, I suppose," replied Adam.

"The same can be said for what you call magic. It depends on the intention behind its use. Whether it's good or bad intent, and also, it depends on what the practitioners are prepared to do to manipulate these forces. Needless to say, if they are removing people's hearts to this end, then there is nothing good about what they are doing."

Adam was silent whilst his mind tried to digest what he had just been told. Then he asked, "What about the missing left hand? Was that done for the same reason?"

"I believe that may have been done for symbolic reasons. A symbol that the practitioners involved follow, the left-hand path. What you would call black magic or satanism."

"But why?" Adam said, "Why on earth would anyone go to these lengths? Apart from being sick in the head."

Katherine Dee shook her head slowly.

"I don't know what the precise reason is, in this case. It could well be a bunch of sick individuals toying with things they don't understand. It's not unknown for people to dabble in things out of curiosity, fascination, and simply being misguided. Then it all goes wrong..."

She fell silent, and it was obvious she was contemplating what she was going to say next very carefully. "But I don't think that that is the case here. I believe that whoever is behind this is skilled in these practices. And that they knew exactly what they were doing."

"Oh. What makes you say that?" Adam asked.

"Because I can't see them."

"Well obviously, they're in hiding," said Adam. "No one would do this sort of thing out in the open." But Katherine cut him off. "No, I don't mean see them in the usual sense. I mean, I should be able to see them in my mind's eye. Psychically, if you will."

Adam wasn't sure where the conversation was heading; he didn't believe in all this witchy-woo and hocus pocus business. To him, it was all a load of codswallop.

But he didn't want to offend Katherine, and also, he considered the possibility that if she mixed in these types of circles, then maybe he could gain some valuable insight into the mind-set of the person committing these crimes. Assuming they all thought the same way regarding this rubbish, and assuming his theory was correct. So Adam decided to humour her.

"Go on," he said.

"Since the first girl was reported missing in the news, I have had a feeling that the girls were near. Somewhere in Penny-Deep or just outside. I tried using my abilities to locate them, to see where they were being taken and by whom," Katherine said.

She studied Adam carefully as she continued.

"I have seen the girls being held captive. They were held in a dark stone-walled room with an arched ceiling and large, solid wooden door. I get the feeling that this room is below ground level."

"A cellar," Adam cut in.

"Possibly. But possibly not. I don't know why, but I keep getting a feeling that it's got some religious connection. Something like a church or connected to one."

Adam wasn't buying any of this. He decided to get the conversation back to where he wanted it, where he could possibly gain an insight into the offender.

"You said you thought whoever was behind this might have some skill in these matters, as opposed to being an amateur. What makes you think this?"

Katherine looked frustrated.

"Well, that's what I was trying to explain. I should be able to see more. More detail of where the girls are being kept, and I should be getting some sense of who was holding them captive.

The fact that I can't leads me to believe that some form of magic is being woven to keep these details concealed. To work such magic would be well beyond some sick, misguided amateur. Also, it would require the energies of more than one person. It would require several."

None of this is of any help, thought Adam, crestfallen. The conversation had left earth, and was never coming back. He made one last attempt at gaining something useful.

"So, these magic practitioners. What do they look like? What should I look for, to tell them apart in a crowd?"

Katherine just smiled.

"You don't." She said, “You can’t. They look just like everyone else. Real adepts don't go in for occult jewellery or playing dress-up, certainly not out in public and certainly not if they are involved in this kind of dark magic. They come from many walks of life and many backgrounds. From doctors to manual workers, barristers to policemen, company directors to the unemployed. From the stranger in the street to the person next door. They are everywhere, among us."

"Actually, *you* are the person next door!" said Adam.

Katherine Dee smiled. "Oh, yes. I forgot."

Adam had the feeling that Katherine Dee didn't forget anything. Then he asked, more out of curiosity, "What's your take on those things left hanging on the door of my home?"

"The pentagram in the circle does have some symbolic meaning. But there's no harm in it by itself. The dead crow, well that's just a dead crow. I would say it's all just theatre dressing in order to frighten you a little, or as you said earlier, to try and mislead you into thinking I have some involvement, and in doing so, ultimately waste your time."

Adam eased himself from the comfort of the sofa.

"Thank you," he said. "That was most useful."

Though in truth, Adam thought it had been a complete waste of his time.

Katherine stood and looked directly into his eyes. She said, "No, you don't mean that! But that's because you don't see things at the moment. But you will. That's why I sent for you."

Adam looked confused. "You sent a message for me to come up here?" he asked.

Katherine Dee spoke as if addressing a child. "No. I sent for you to come here to Penny-Deep."

Adam had to stifle a laugh. Yet more claptrap.

"I'm sorry to disappoint but I came here for personal reasons to do with myself and my daughter mainly."

"That is what you believe. But you are here, just the same."

"So you are saying that you somehow sent for me?"

"Not for you specifically. I merely put an order in. But you do fit the requirements perfectly," she said, smiling flirtatiously once again.

Adam felt the need to be absolutely honest with this poor deluded woman.

"Ms Dee, I have to tell you that I don't buy into all of this magic nonsense. Perhaps I was wrong to come and see you. I think you are well-meaning but some of the things you say seem to be for effect and are just a little trite. Next, you'll be telling me there's a storm coming!"

Katherine looked him over, and then she said, "Then, just for effect and at the risk of being a little more trite, I will tell you that the storm is already here. You, Adam Cadman, are the storm!"

She smiled. "Unless, by storm, you are referring to a weather front. In which case, one of those is also on its way. I can feel it."

Adam turned on his heels and marched to the door, thanking Katherine for her time as he left. At the bottom of the garden path, the large mastiff still sat on sentry duty, eyeing him suspiciously as he passed. Adam turned once as he walked away, seeing the woman standing framed in her doorway. It was a shame, he thought, that such a beautiful woman should be so deranged.

***

By the time Adam had made his way down the track and back home, he found Sophia and Mrs

Chattox in the kitchen, the old lady about to dish out a delicious-looking fish pie.

"Sorry I'm late," he said. "I decided to pop up and see our neighbour, Ms Dee."

Adam watched Mrs Chattox for any sign of a reaction but saw none. Though Sophia was, for some reason, looking guilty about something. Adam decided on a more direct approach.

"Mrs Chattox, do you know Katherine Dee at all?"

She looked up distractedly from dishing out the food.

"Oh, yes, a little. We speak every now and again."

"Well if you ask me, the woman is stark-raving bonkers with all her talk of magic."

Mrs Chattox continued serving the food, saying, "You're not a believer then?"

"No, not at all. Do you know she tried to say that her magic was in some way the reason that I'm here in Penny-Deep?"

Mrs Chattox turned and looked directly at Adam. Then she said in quite a matter-of-fact way, "Well, you are here." Adam was momentarily startled by that; she had said precisely the same thing as the so-called witch! And she wasn't done yet, rambling on.

"I lost count of the number of people who tried to move here and rent this house, but the landlord wouldn't rent it to them," she said. "Not until you and Sophia came."

Well! Adam had expected better from Mrs Chattox.

"And I suppose you think that is in some way linked to Katherine Dee and her magic?" he said.

"No, but I do think it's linked to Katherine Dee owning all the land on this hill including Old Anna Farm. It means she's your landlord as well as mine."

Adam couldn't stop his mouth falling open in surprise.

"Mind you," Mrs Chattox went on, "when I asked her about why she kept turning potential tenants away, she did say something about waiting for the right person to arrive."

Chapter 13

Elizabeth Short was seventeen years of age. She was a slight girl with a boyish figure, pretty in her own way, with short black hair. But physically, she would never stand out in a crowd.

Elizabeth was a quiet girl with no boyfriend and very few female friends. Everyone described her as thoughtful, kind and gentle, a likeable girl who was quite homely, and who never caused her parents, or anyone else for that matter, an ounce of trouble or concern.

Elizabeth Short was, however, *different.* Below the surface, she didn't fit any of the descriptions attributed to her, by others. What no one knew, or suspected, was that Elizabeth Short would never let herself be one of life's victims. She had ambition, and behind her even-tempered facade was a core of steely determination, resilience, and a calculating mind. But what most people would find genuinely shocking, if they knew, was that Elizabeth possessed a temper of volcanic proportions. A temper which she constantly had to fight to keep in check.

Elizabeth had always wanted more from life and had worked hard to achieve it.

She did well at school, even though she found it a bore, and left as soon as she could. But she was studious by nature and excelled in anything that she found interesting, or anything she could see had a practical application in her life. Since leaving school, Elizabeth had been studying at college with hopes of eventually finding some secretarial work in the city. But that would only ever be a steppingstone for Elizabeth, a starting point from where she planned to advance herself further.

But during all of Elizabeth Short's careful planning for the future, she had never allowed for this contingency. She had awoken to find herself locked in a cold, dark room with only a candle for light. Unlike most who found themselves in such a predicament, Elizabeth Short was more angry than afraid. She had tried the only door once, and on finding it locked, she sat on the cold stone floor, without doing or saying anything further.

Elizabeth knew to conserve her energy. She didn't know who had taken her or why she had been taken and locked in the room, but she did know someone was going to pay for it.

Elizabeth, having taken stock of her surroundings, decided it was time to make use of some of her studies. Her martial arts studies to be more precise. Every weekend for the past four years, Elizabeth had visited a local gym where she'd trained in kickboxing. She was the smallest in the class, and at the start of her training, her instructor and fellow students regarded her as a small, quiet dormouse. But Elizabeth trained hard and enjoyed sparring, particularly with the larger men in the class. It was during these sparring sessions that she could unleash her temper, and it always felt so satisfying to her, like letting go of a tidal wave that she was forever struggling to hold back.

It didn't take long for Elizabeth and her ferocious temperament to gain the respect of her fellow students, who gave her the nicknames, Pocket Rocket and Psycho Short.

All alone and locked in this cold, dark space, Elizabeth fell back on what her instructor had told her.

"Fear is the biggest, hardest opponent you'll ever fight. Conquer fear, and no matter whoever or whatever stands before you, it will always be an even fight. Yours to win. Yours to lose."

Elizabeth sat perfectly still with crossed legs and a straight back. She concentrated on her breathing, letting what thoughts may come gently drift across her mind, but then always bringing her concentration back to her breathing. Once or twice, her thoughts turned to horrifying scenarios of what might happen to her. But she let those thoughts go without picking at them, paying them no attention. After all, they were just thoughts—and thoughts in themselves couldn't hurt her.

As she breathed gently, her mind drifted again, and Elizabeth remembered walking from college towards the bus station. She remembered walking across the open car park as a shortcut, so that she wouldn't miss her bus. A large man was wearing a baseball cap in front of her, and grumbling under his breath. He held a large, unfolded paper map, which he appeared to be trying to make sense of, locating where he was or where he needed to be.

The man stepped towards her and asked for directions.

But as she made to look at the map, someone grabbed her from behind. A cloth clamped over her nose and mouth, and Elizabeth remembered a strong, sweet chemical smell. But that was all she remembered. After that, everything was black until she woke on the cold stone floor.

Elizabeth continued to piece together her memory, noting what was important.

There were at least two people who had grabbed her, and at least one of them was a large male. Elizabeth focused her mind again, concentrating on her breathing.

She remained seated and meditating for what seemed like hours.

Eventually, Elizabeth broke from her meditation and stood up to stretch; she picked up the nearby candle to check her watch. But her wristwatch was missing, obviously taken.

Looking around, Elizabeth realised the satchel bag she used for her college work was also missing, as well as her jacket. Checking herself over, she saw she was still dressed in her black tee-shirt, black jeans and sneakers. Then, in one brief panicked moment, Elizabeth checked her underwear but that also seemed to be present and undisturbed. She relaxed again and sat back down on the floor with the candle beside her. Then another thought occurred to her, and rolling down the top of her left sock, she was relieved to see her silver ankle bracelet had not been taken.

Her grandmother had left her the trinket when she had passed away, and she had always treasured it. Elizabeth took comfort in how the candlelight glinted off the tiny silver charms that hung from the chain. Taking one last look around the room she was in, Elizabeth was satisfied there were no obvious means of escape that she had missed. She pulled her legs into a crossed lotus position, closed her eyes, and concentrated on her breathing once again.

Chapter 14

Adam Cadman returned to work early the next morning, having had a restless night's sleep. Several times, he had woken after having dreams about Katherine Dee. What was it about that damned woman that was plaguing his mind? Yes, he had to admit that she was stunningly beautiful and he usually would have felt quite attracted to her. But as beautiful as she was, she was also completely cuckoo, what with all her talk of hocus-pocus. Adam went over their conversation several times and still couldn't make any sense of it. Visiting Katherine Dee, he concluded, had been a complete waste of his time. Not to mention the fact that it was disturbing enough to have this nutcase as a neighbour—but finding out she was his landlady, no wonder he couldn't sleep!

Once in his office, Adam paced the floor; he always seemed to think better on his feet. Despite being sidetracked by the village nut job, he reasoned that his original hypothesis, about Victoria Timperley's mutilation being part of some occult ritual, was still a possibility.

Indeed, at the moment, he couldn't think of a better explanation.

Eventually, sounds began to emanate from downstairs, and Adam guessed that Angela had just arrived at work, and was unlocking the front doors, setting up for business at the front enquiry desk. Adam decided that he was going to look into his theory a little further to see if it had any credibility or not. This time he would try and find someone sensible, with whom to speak.

But who? Adam grabbed his tunic and hat and went to talk to Angela; perhaps her local knowledge could be of assistance. Angela was sitting drinking a cup of coffee and was clearly surprised to see Adam as he popped his head around the corner.

"Sorry, Inspector, I didn't know you were in the building, or I would have made you a cuppa," she said.

"That's alright, Angela. I may be going out if you can answer me this question."

Angela suddenly looked a little unsure and decidedly under pressure.

But Adam continued, "Who in Penny-Deep would be the best person to speak to regarding any local practices of the occult and black magic?"

Angela's face lit up but as she opened her mouth to answer, Adam cut in.

"Other than Katherine Dee!"

Angela's mouth closed again, and her look of unease returned. Then after a few seconds of thinking, she said, "Well, there's the church of course. Or you could try Professor Lo' Shell."

"Professor Lo' Shell. Who's he?" asked Adam.

"Well, he was an astrophysicist or something like that. He's retired now and has set himself up as a bit of a local amateur historian. He's a nice man. Everyone calls him Kip."

Adam pondered on whether it was worth visiting Professor Kip Lo' Shell, but then what had he got to lose? And it certainly couldn't be worse than his visit with Katherine Dee.

"Where do I find the Professor?" asked Adam.

"He lives in the big house on Swallow Hill Lane. You can't miss it."

"Thanks," said Adam. And with that, he was off.

***

At the end of Swallow Hill Lane, Adam saw the large white house with a flat roof and metal windows. The architecture was art deco and built, he guessed, sometime around the 1920s or '30s. Pushing through a blue painted gate, Adam walked around the side of the house to the rear garden.

The garden was large and well kept, and at the far end was a small round structure with a domed roof. "It's my observatory, Inspector, where I house my telescope and other optical hardware."

The voice was warm and jovial. Adam turned to see the smiling face of Professor Kip Lo' Shell standing in an open doorway. The professor was a man in his early sixties, who still possessed a full head of dark-brown hair in a buzz cut style, displaying a surprisingly small amount of grey. He was squarely built and of average height with a protruding belly. "How can I help you?" he asked.

"Well, I've come to pick your brains, if that's alright," said Adam.

"Oh! Not a long visit then." The professor laughed out loud at his own joke. "Please come inside. There's only Bob and me." Then he added. "Bob's my dog. I'm a bit of a Dylan fan."

Entering the house, Adam followed Lo' Shell along a narrow corridor to a much larger hexagonal hall. He then turned left into a reception room, elegantly furnished in keeping with the art deco style of the house. At Lo' Shell's bidding, Adam took a seat in a large brown leather club chair with large, sweeping leather arms. Adam heard a distant yap, and after the sound of much scurrying, they were joined by a small dog of indeterminate parentage.

Adam took this to be Bob, as the tiny dog sat in front of him.

"Now," said Lo' Shell. "How can I help you?"

Bob tilted his head to one side, looking at Adam with curiosity,

"I'm led to believe you're something of a local historian, and I wondered if you had ever come across any mention of the occult practices or black magic? That sort of thing."

Lo' Shell tilted his head and mirrored Bob's

look of curiosity.

"Well, I must say that it makes a change. I'm usually asked mundane genealogy questions by people trying to trace their family tree here in Penny-Deep. Can I ask, is this official police business or something you're are thinking of taking up?"

Lo' Shell's face broke out in a broad grin.

"It's official police business," said Adam who was about to add a brief explanation, when Lo' Shell held his hands up and stopped him.

"No, please don't feel you have to explain, I'm happy to tell you what I know."

Lo' Shell paused for thought, and then sat back in a matching club chair, facing Adam.

He continued.

"Almost every remote town and village in the country will have stories of witchcraft attached to them, somewhere in their history, and Penny-Deep is no exception. Usually, those accused of witchcraft were what is known as 'cunning folk,' people with a rudimentary knowledge of herbs and anatomy. They would act as midwives and even doctors for the poor. Occasionally, some would take it further and offer divination and the odd love potion."

Lo' Shell sat forward and clasped his hands as he went on.

"When we are talking about such cunning folk, Penny-Deep is, of course, famous, or rather infamous, for our very own Lizzie Dee who was hanged for being a witch."

"So you believe Lizzie Dee was one of these cunning folk?" asked Adam.

"Well, of course, I never knew her. A bit before my time," the professor snorted. "But from all the local historical records and writings, it would seem she was held in good standing by all the locals and was the first one they turned to if they had a problem either health-wise or with any matter where supernatural forces were thought to be at work."

The conversation was a little off track regarding Adam's inquiry but, after his visit with Katherine—old Lizzie's descendant—he found himself intrigued.

"If she was held in good standing by the locals, how come she ended up being hanged?"

"Well, my theory on this—and I have no direct evidence, I'm merely reading between the lines of the historical records—is that Lizzie Dee was the victim of Squire O'Neil's greed."

The professor went on to explain.

"You see, all was well until the good squire tried to purchase Lizzie's home and land. He offered a pittance, and she refused to sell. O'Neil then put the story around that Lizzie was angered by his offer and put a curse on his livestock. Shortly after this story started circulating, one of O'Neil's cows died, and then livestock belonging to other folks in the surrounding area started to die suddenly and inexplicably. I suspect that these livestock losses were down to poisoning by O'Neil, who was trying to turn public opinion against Lizzie. When the livestock deaths didn't tip the balance, O'Neil visited Lizzie on the pretext of asking her to lift the curse on local livestock. O'Neil then made an allegation that on calling at Lizzie's farm, he caught her having relations with the devil, and being so caught, Lizzie cursed O'Neil's wife.

"According to O'Neil, he then rushed home to find his wife dead. O'Neil ran around the town spreading this story and whipping up fear until he got what he was after. A lynch mob. O'Neil led the mob up to Lizzie's farm where she was hanged from the nearest tree."

"What do you make of O'Neil's wife suddenly dying like that?" said Adam.

"O'Neil was well known for his adultery with a constant string of mistresses. His wife was ageing and losing her looks. I think her death was either one heck of a coincidence or O'Neil decided to kill two birds with one stone, murdering his wife and blaming it on Lizzie Dee and her witchcraft."

"Did he get her land in the end?" asked Adam.

Lo' Shell gave a snort of derision.

"No. If I'm correct, poor old Lizzie Dee died for nothing. It seems that what O'Neil hadn't bargained on was that Lizzie actually came from a very well-connected and influential family who not only kept hold of the land but put the fear of

God into O'Neil. The O'Neils certainly went very quiet for several generations after that."

"Well if you are correct, it certainly sheds new light on Penny-Deep's history," said Adam. "But I was interested in more recent occurrences. I wondered if you knew of any occult practices being carried on presently, in the area."

Lo' Shell nodded.

"I appreciate that, but I thought it important to give you a little background on the Dee family before I went on to mention Katherine Dee."

Adam fought to stifle a deep sigh of despondency. He cut in.

"I have already had the pleasure of speaking to Katherine, and to be frank, I found her to be a little..." Adam struggled to find the best and politest way to describe how he thought of Katherine Dee. "... a little departed from reality."

The professor let out a little laugh.

"You may be right," he said, "but not in the way that you mean."

"Oh," said Adam. Once again, he found his curiosity piqued, as the professor continued.

"I have had the pleasure of spending some time with Ms Dee over the past couple of years. She is a beautiful and enchanting woman, who will take great satisfaction in winding you up if she thinks you are not taking her seriously."

"You don't mean to say you believe she has magical powers. Do you?" Adam asked.

"Believe? I am a person who neither believes

nor disbelieves. I only go on evidence, and when something can rack up enough evidence, then it may well provide me with enough interest to pursue it further."

"And in the case of Katherine Dee?"

"I have enjoyed many long and intellectually stimulating conversations with Katherine. Some of her views and insights on what you refer to as magic are not that far removed from what is now the cutting edge of physics. The scientific understanding of how our universe and this world we perceive as reality works."

Adam hadn't seen this coming! But he listened with interest as the professor continued talking.

"Of course, as interesting as I found my chats with Katherine, much of what she said could have been mere conjecture. I therefore asked if she would take part in some experiments where I could test her ability and her hypothesis regarding the inner workings of our reality."

"What happened?" asked Adam.

"Well, I set up several experiments to test Katherine's ESP—extrasensory perception. I tested her in areas of precognition and remote viewing, which means predicting events and outcomes before they happen and seeing randomly chosen objects and places from a distance. I set up these experiments to the best of my ability and ensured that each test was double-blind with little or no information given to the test subject. In every test, Ms Dee scored highly, way outside statistical probability. If these tests were conducted in any other field of research—a field which was deemed more acceptable to mainstream science—then the results would have been quite conclusive."

Adam sat stunned.

"So, what are you saying? That Katherine Dee possesses supernatural powers?"

The professor looked thoughtful, then said, "Supernatural? I don't believe in the supernatural. I believe only in the natural. But as the history of science keeps showing us, at any given point in time, we don't know the half of it. There was a time when electricity and the effects of bacteria were deemed supernatural. Hence, we say 'bless you' when someone sneezes, a throwback to when we thought the effects of viruses were, in fact, the work of the devil. No! Whatever abilities Katherine possesses, they are natural, just not fully understood as yet. Perhaps it's that these abilities are rare, or maybe she has managed to refine and hone them more than most other people. Who knows?"

The professor looked Adam squarely in the eyes, then said, "The most important thing I am trying to say, is this. If Katherine Dee ever sees fit to give you any information, no matter how bizarre it may seem, never dismiss it out of hand."

Adam sat, letting the professor's words sink in. Then the professor added, "Whilst you are trying to make sense of all that, I will add, in answer to your original question, that I don't know of anyone else in the locality who practices anything that could be described as the occult. But I wouldn't be surprised if there were someone I don't know about. Country folk have always had their own ways." The professor stood and turned to look out of the French doors.

Then turning back to Adam, he said, "I know it's a little early but do you fancy a beer? I only partake after dark or on the rare occasions that I have any company, and you certainly qualify as company. I have a mighty fine collection of craft ales, including some rather gorgeous Belgian blonds."

***

Adam left the professor without taking up the offer of a beer. He was after all, still on duty. Besides which, the professor had given him a lot to think over.

There was something about Professor Kip Lo' Shell that Adam took an instant liking to.

He was a knowledgeable man but not at all pompous. The truth was, Kip Lo' Shell didn't seem to take himself seriously at all. Adam felt comfortable in his company and found himself trusting what the professor had to say. However, he still couldn't fully reconcile what the professor said about Ms Dee with his own thoughts and feelings about her.

During the drive back to Penny-Deep, the sun was shining, and the quiet country lanes looked magnificent in full bloom. Adam allowed his thoughts to drift over what the professor had said, particularly with regard to not dismissing anything Katherine said out of hand.

As Adam approached Penny-Deep, the bell tower of the old church came into view. He was immediately reminded of what Katherine had said about the missing girls being kept beneath ground, possibly in a cellar, and that she had the feeling there was some religious connection.

On reaching the church, Adam pulled over on impulse and parked the police car.

Walking through the lychgate, he looked up at the tall, imposing bell tower, his eyes passing over the clock midway, then on to the arched belfry windows with the tired-looking oak louvres.

Adam followed the broad flagged stone path around the church, all the while scanning the bottom of the old building, looking for signs of a basement. At the rear end of the church was a huge stained-glass window below which the ground fell away, but only for about two to three feet.

Turning the next corner, Adam found something that piqued his interest. Several stone steps led down to a large oak door. He cast an eye around the churchyard and could see the two Armstrong brothers digging away at another grave some distance away. Neither of the two seemed to be paying him any attention, so Adam quickly ran down the steps to the oak door.

Turning a large steel ring handle, he applied his shoulder to the door but it wouldn't budge. Below the large metal ring was an equally large keyhole, and Adam concluded the door was locked.

He climbed the steps and continued to circumnavigate the church, looking for any other below-ground entrances—but he found no more. This time, it was Adam who was paying no attention to the two Armstrong brothers, their two shovels striking the soil in a soft alternating rhythm.

But though the brothers gave the impression that they were hard at work, with their heads down, their eyes had been following Adam all along.

Returning to the front of the church, Adam saw that the large doors were slightly ajar, and he decided to push his way inside and take a look around. The church appeared empty, and to Adam, it felt as though the silence and serenity of the old building created its own, palpable presence.

But in truth, there was another, more human, presence lurking just out of sight.

In the shadows that ran down one side of the church, behind the stone archways of the nave, stood Clive Brady, the church curate. As usual,

Clive was dressed entirely in black, and he knew full well he couldn't be seen from his vantage point. The spotty youth experienced a particular thrill in spying on the policeman, knowing that he had him at a disadvantage.

Just then, the silence was interrupted by the voice of Father Fenton, standing only a couple of feet behind Adam. "Can I help you, Inspector?" the vicar said.

Adam almost jumped out of his skin. Where had Fenton come from, and how had he managed to creep up without detection? *The man must move around on castors,* Adam thought.

"Hello again. Sorry to be a bother but I was passing by, and decided to pop in on the off chance," said Adam as casually as he could.

"Oh!" Fenton looked questioningly at Adam. "On the off chance of what exactly?"

"Well on my last visit, I was struck by the splendour of the church and wondered if I could have a proper look around. I have a fascination for ancient buildings, and it's not often you come across such fine examples of Norman architecture."

Father Fenton visibly puffed up with pride.

"Yes, she's a beautiful old building, Grade I listed, you know. There are records showing priests belonging to a church in Penny-Deep dating back to 1200. But there is masonry work in the church that indicates it's over a thousand years old. There are also the remains of a

Saxon cross built into the church walls, possibly indicating even older Christian involvement in the area. As you quite rightly stated, the architecture is Norman though the bell tower, some eighty feet in height, is a relatively new addition, having been built about five hundred years ago."

"Amazing," said Adam, who slowly followed Father Fenton around Saint Augustine's Church as the priest pointed out various architectural and historical points of interest.

"Are there any areas of the church below ground level?" asked Adam, when he felt that asking such a question wouldn't seem out of place.

Father Fenton looked slightly annoyed at being interrupted.

But then, clearly slightly flustered, he said, "Well, we don't have a crypt, if that's what you are wondering. Why is everyone so fascinated by bodies? It's what everyone always asks!"

"Crypt?" said Adam, who in truth knew nothing of architecture, Norman or otherwise—and even less about churches. But yes...he was interested in the mention of a crypt, apparently just like everyone else to whom the priest referred with disdain. Shame that there wasn't such a thing here.

"A crypt is a stone chamber beneath a church or other building. It's from the Latin 'crypta', meaning vault. These areas are traditionally blessed and typically contain coffins, sarcophagi or religious relics," said Father Fenton, as if leading a party of tourists on a rehearsed guided walk.

Adam could see that Father Fenton was just about to continue with his 'guided tour' of Saint Augustine's, so he pressed the matter a little further. "I'd love to see what's below the church," he said. "Particularly if it has Saxon or even older origins. The areas below ground level are always where you find the oldest and most interesting architectural gems."

Once again, Father Fenton became flustered, and Adam quickly came to the realisation that Fenton didn't want to show him the area below the church. "It really is a dark and musty area with nothing much to see," said Father Fenton "We tend to use it for storage, nothing more."

"Still, I am intrigued," Adam pushed, "I would be most grateful for even the briefest of viewings."

The two of them stood, momentarily, in the centre of the church, staring at each other in silence. Both realised they were in a 'stand-off', and as Adam stood his ground, smiling in a courteous manner, Father Fenton crumbled first.

He shuffled off towards the vestry, mumbling about finding the key for the door.

Minutes later, Father Fenton, brandishing a large key, returned and led Adam out of the church and down the stone path to the rear of the building, where the stone steps down to the oak door were located. Father Fenton descended the steps and unlocked the door.

Meanwhile, the Armstrong brothers were still digging in the lower graveyard.

They had been stealthily watching the scene at the rear of the church.

Once Father Fenton and the police inspector had descended the steps and entered the lower part of the building, the two brothers glanced at each other and then, they slowly ambled up to the rear of the church. Both men were large and muscular, and both walked purposefully, carrying their shovels in front of them like hunters stalking their prey would hold their rifles.

Father Fenton stepped to the edge of the last vestige of sunlight entering the basement. He reached into the darkness, and after some fumbling, clicked the light switch illuminating the cellar in dim orange light. The area was cold and musty with thick stone walls and stone flagged floor.

To his right, Adam could see an old coal boiler which had been decommissioned at some stage, probably when a new gas boiler had been installed in the church somewhere.

As his eyes adjusted to the light, Adam could make out a rusty dilapidated barbecue and an old raffle or tombola drum.

But then in the wall ahead of him, he saw a large arched doorway with an oak door.

Adam strode over to it, finding it locked. Father Fenton walked slowly forward, raising the key in his hand. He looked directly into Adam's eyes and said, "Are you sure you want to look behind this door, Inspector? Your life may never be the same once you enter."

Adam felt the hairs on the back of his neck stand on end. His mouth was dry, and he felt the cold shiver of adrenalin wash through his veins. He nodded to Fenton, who unlocked the door.

Adam leaned into the next chamber, and a bare bulb already lit that area.

The chamber was approximately twelve feet square and there, propped up against the right-hand wall, was an old ping-pong table. Along the left-hand wall were several stacks of plastic chairs, and in front, three piles of small plastic tables. Adam stepped inside and checked behind all the stored equipment, but there were no more doors or passageways. He made several comments regarding the old stonework, and when he was satisfied he had seen all there was to see, he followed the priest back out of the basement area and up the steps to the churchyard.

Adam thanked Fenton for indulging him and apologised for being a bother.

As he walked along the churchyard path, he spotted the Armstrong brothers now leaning against the headstone of a grave. They were obviously watching him but Adam paid them no attention. Once again, he felt he'd wasted his time, courtesy of Katherine Dee.

Chapter 15

All was still just before dawn at Katherine Dee's home, with darkness still draped over the house and its gardens. The large garden behind the house was a cornucopia of plants of all descriptions—flowers, vegetables, and herbs. Most were well known and easily recognisable but some were not so. Some plants hung their heads until the arrival of sunlight, as if sleeping, while others merely stood patiently, waiting for the start of a new day.

The stone-paved path that wound through this beautiful slumbering garden stopped abruptly at the rear gate, replaced by a freshly mown path that cut through the meadow grass, and led back into the dark woods at the rear of the house and grounds.

Only one person ever used this path. No one knew of its existence, and even if they had, very few would have had the nerve to follow it into the dark woods.

A short distance through the trees, the path came to another clearing, and there stood a stone circle of twelve standing stones, each no more than four feet tall.

The stones were old, worn and weathered over the millennia.

They took on a blue hue in the pre-dawn dew,

and in the centre of the stone circle stood a large oblong altar stone measuring in the region of six feet by three, and a good three feet in height.

On this stone stood a metal chalice, and in that chalice stood a long slim dagger, the handle of which stood proud of the chalice's rim, whilst the blade cut through the water contained within.

The tip of the blade touched on the silver pentagram pendant and chain that rested at the bottom of the cup. As the sun began to rise and the first rays of light hit the standing stones, forming shadows that stretched around the circle, Katherine felt the charges of power snake through the ground like electrical serpents. She felt their presence as they slithered towards the centre stone on which the chalice stood. Some passed beneath her as she sat cross-legged on the ground before the centre stone. The vibrant tingling sensation emanating from these lines of power would have surprised most people. But Katherine had been expecting them.

Indeed, she had been waiting for them. Now at this crucial time, she kept her eyes closed, and her mind focused on the chalice and its contents.

Once the sun had fully risen, and Katherine could feel its warmth on her face, she stood up and opened her eyes. She walked slowly over to the chalice and removed the dagger, which she tucked into the rope belt of her long green dress. Next, she reached in and removed the pentagram pendant whilst tossing the water to the ground. The pentagram shone brightly, more than silver should in the morning sunlight. There was a glow from the pentagram that Katherine could see, and a feeling of energy radiating from the pendant. Katherine smiled, pleased with her work. The pendant would serve her well.

***

Over in the Cadman household, Adam was up and getting ready to go into work. He was determined that today would be a Katherine-free day. He was not going to waste any more time on account of that woman and her strange beliefs.

Meanwhile, Sophia was up just for the exciting prospect of starting a new day.

She felt happy and was singing some catchy song she had heard on the radio.

Sophia's thoughts also involved Katherine.

She had thought about what Katherine had told her, about how she would live to be an old woman. Sophia no longer felt doomed to die young, like her mother. It felt as if a huge weight had been lifted from her. She was happier now than she had been for—well, for as long as she could remember.

After much internal debate, Sophia had come to the decision that she liked Katherine, even though she was dark and mysterious, and although people did call her a witch.

Katherine had been kind to her, and it was her words that had set her mind at ease. Her father said there were no such things as real witches; they were just silly people playing silly games. But Sophia hoped he was wrong and that Katherine *was* a real witch. It would mean that what she had said was correct about her growing old. Katherine didn't seem silly at all. In fact, she seemed to know what she was talking about, and she was incredibly beautiful. Sophia hoped she would become her friend, even though her father made it obvious that he didn't much like her. It was for this reason that Sophia decided that, for now, Katherine Dee would have to be her secret friend.

Sophia's newfound happiness had not escaped Adam's attention, and he took great delight in seeing his daughter acting like any other girl her age. Coming to Penny-Deep had been the right decision for her, and everything else was worth the compromise.

Father and daughter ate breakfast together, chatting about what their day would entail. Adam spoke about work but only in general terms; he tried never to bring his work home, and what with recent goings-on, he didn't want to give Sophia any cause for concern.

Sophia had decided it was much too nice a day to stay in all day, so she intended to play outdoors if that was alright with Mrs Chattox.

Adam promised he would have a word with their neighbour to clear this when he took Sophia over on his way to work.

With breakfast over, Adam cleared the pots, and Sophia collected her tennis racket and ball before they set off to start their respective days.

***

It was midday when the phone rang in Mrs Chattox' kitchen. Clapping the flour from her hands, she left her pastry-making and walked over to answer it. She had been expecting the call, and whilst checking through her kitchen window, she confirmed.

"Yes, she's outside in the yard now."

Mrs Chattox replaced the receiver and washed her hands, and quietly went on with her pastry.

Sophia was busy concentrating on bouncing her ball up and down on the tennis racket. She had gotten to seven hundred and eighty-three when something made her lose concentration and drop the ball. She felt as if someone was watching her, and when she turned, she saw Katherine Dee standing on the track at the end of the yard.

"Hello, Sophia, how are you today?" she said in a warm and friendly manner.

Sophia walked over, excited to see her.

"I'm good," she said, "I feel much better after talking with you."

Katherine Dee reached out and stroked Sophia's head.

"Good always remember what I told you and stop worrying; you are much too young to have an old worry head on your shoulders."

Sophia laughed, and Katherine said, "I was thinking about you and have brought you a small gift." Katherine held out her open right hand.

Sophia saw the silver pendant resting there, shining brightly.

"Do you know what it is?" asked Katherine.

Sophia looked closely then said confidently. "Yes it's a star necklace!"

It was good that the child didn't fully understand what the pendant represented or have any preconceived ideas about it. But Katherine thought a little explanation was only right.

"This is a special star necklace. This star represents you and the elements that you are made up of." Katherine delicately pointed to each of the points of the star in turn, whilst Sophia watched.

"This point is one arm and the element of water. Here below is a leg, and this represents fire. The next leg represents Earth, and the arm above it represents air."

"What about the top point; is that my head?" Sophia said, showing interest.

"Yes, that's right. The head point represents spirit or consciousness."

"Is it magical?" Sophia asked.

"Yes, it's especially magical. Whenever you wear it, it will give you protection and good luck!"

Sophia looked at Katherine with an expression that was a mix of excitement and awe.

Katherine hung the pendant around Sophia's neck and fastened the clasp.

"There you are. It looks beautiful on you! Now I must go, as I have things to do. But remember to always keep the pendant with you."

Katherine then walked back up the track towards the dark woods and her home. Sophia resumed playing with her tennis racket and ball, stopping every so often to examine her pendant. She loved it, and it made her feel very grown-up and special. But she decided it was probably best not to tell her father about it, due to his dislike of Katherine Dee. She couldn't understand why he was so grumpy about her as she seemed really nice. Just for an instant, Sophia thought of her mother. Her mum would have liked Katherine Dee, she thought; they would have become best friends.

***

Adam had just begun to read through a road traffic accident report when his mobile phone rang. The caller ID made Adam smile, and he took the call.

"Kieron Jones! How the devil are you?" he answered.

"I'm all the better for speaking to you, you old warhorse. I had to look Penny-Deep up. I'd never heard of the place before, and now I have, I want to know what's happened. Have you been put out to pasture?"

"It's a long story but basically, I'm here by my own choice. I loved working in the city, but the hours were long, and I was spending too much time away from Sophia. I could see it was taking a toll on her. So, here I am! It was either leave the job completely or move over into the slow lane."

Strangely, Adam found it hard to tell Kieron that he had opted for a slower, softer life.

After all the things they had been through together in the army, he somehow felt guilty, as though he had given up. But Kieron understood immediately, and with pure brotherly concern, he said, "Hey, I know you, that couldn't have been an easy decision. But it was absolutely the right thing to do. How's my little princess doing?"

"She is doing much better now. The move has done her a world of good. She's like a new girl, bright and happy, and full of life. The way a girl her age should be."

"And how are you finding life in Penny-Deep?" Kieron asked.

"Well, it's a beautiful town, surrounded by beautiful countryside. It has a reputation for being very quiet but then, as soon as I arrived, the body of an abducted young woman from the city turned up on the patch."

Kieron snorted.

"Typical! It could only happen to Adam Cadman. Are you on the case, or the main suspect?"

"Well, sort of on the case, or at least on the fringe of it. There's a good chance that the body was just dumped out here to get rid of it. All the other girls that have gone missing, four others in total, have all disappeared in the city. So that's where the main focus of the investigation is. I'm just doing a few routine inquiries up here to tie off loose ends."

Kieron sounded fascinated.

"Any possible suspects up in your neck of the woods?" he asked.

Adam wanted to make his reply sound more intriguing but couldn't think of a way.

"No, not really," he said. "There are only two people who ever so slightly raise my interest. There's nothing to warrant making them suspects. In fact, one of them is my landlady, it turns out!"

Kieron Jones burst out laughing.

"Oh, and why are you mildly interested in your landlady then?"

Adam wasn't sure if his reasoning would sound completely mad. But he explained to Kieron, trying not to sound too embarrassed.

"Well the body of the missing girl had the heart and left hand removed. It occurred to me that this could be some sort of a ritualistic thing like black magic or devil worship."

"So you think your old crone of a landlady is a witch!" said Kieron, sounding amused.

"I don't believe in that sort of stuff but half the town here thinks she's a witch, and not only that, but she also actually admits to being interested in the occult. As for her being an old crone! You should see her, Kieron. She's young and drop-dead gorgeous.

“On the downside, she's also as mad as a March hare. So whilst she's not an outright suspect, you can hopefully appreciate my mild interest in her."

"It's a pity she's crazy. A beautiful young maiden, to while away the hours in sleepy Penny-Deep, might have been just the ticket for you. Who's the other person of interest?" Kieron said.

"Well, that's why I emailed you! It's Archibald O'Neil. Again he's not a suspect as such. But the young woman's body had been transported in one of his estate's vans, which was abandoned at the scene. I visited O'Neil, and his estate office showed signs of a break-in, and the keys for the van had been kept in that office. I'm pretty sure everything is as it seems to be, but I'd just like to cover all angles before I close that lead down."

"I see," said Kieron. "Well, I did a bit of digging on O'Neil, but not so much as to attract attention. Bear in mind, I wasn't sure exactly what kind of information you wanted."

"To understand the man, it's perhaps best to look at where he came from. He has a colourful family history. Archibald O'Neil is the eldest of two brothers born into the wealthy and privileged O'Neil family who settled in England somewhere around the sixteenth century, having come over from Ireland. Or should I say, having been chased out of Ireland? The story goes that they were a pretty ruthless band of cutthroats, up to all sorts of thuggery and crime.

"It didn't take the O'Neils long to amass, quite a bit of property and wealth over here, as they took just about anything they wanted. With the wealth came influence, and the O'Neils cultivated theirs by throwing whoever they could under the cartwheels of the 1534 Treason Act, thus gaining favour with the King, Henry VIII. In return, the King granted them the land in Penny-Deep, where they built their manor house and estate. But becoming landed gentry didn't stop their criminal enterprises. Though they carefully maintained a facade of respectability, the O'Neils used any means they could to steadily build a property empire which they kept up until quite recently."

"Oh, what happened?" asked Adam.

"Archibald O'Neil happened! When you take the time to do a little bit of digging, it seems dear old Archie wasn't quite the financial property wizard that he likes to make out. On paper, he looked to be making great strides with his own property business, making big returns for his investors. But in truth, his business was teetering on being a 'Ponzi' scheme. Luckily for O'Neil, he inherited the reins of his family's property empire just before his own business came crashing down around his ears. For a couple of years, everything seemed fine, although he'd had to leverage the family business up to the hilt. Then the 2008 recession hit."

"What did he do?" asked Adam.

"He gathered together what capital he could get his hands on and set up a hedge fund. He surrounded himself with 'The Twelve,' as they are known, a group of so-called advisors who help manage the fund."

Adam was curious. Not so much with what his friend had said but more the way he'd said it.

"What do you mean by 'so-called' advisors?"

"Well, no one in the usual financial circles seems to know who these people are. We have heard a few names bandied about but none of them has even the remotest background in finance, though I must say they are a pretty well-heeled lot. They all come from old families with old money. Apparently, O'Neil mixed in the same circles as some of them in his youth, whilst experiencing a more bohemian lifestyle."

"It all sounds like a recipe for more financial disaster," said Adam, thinking out loud.

"You'd think so, wouldn't you? But the strange

thing is, the hedge fund has done remarkably well, bringing in huge returns for the investors. Even when they have bet against the market, they have come up trumps."

Adam knew little about the money markets but the little he did know prompted him to ask, "Could O'Neil be involved in some sort of insider trading?"

"It's always possible and would explain a great deal. But if he is, no one can find any evidence, and people have been looking very closely. You can't be as successful as O'Neil without attracting two things. Suspicion and jealousy, both guaranteed to bring scrutiny in the financial world."

"So how has this left O'Neil, on a personal footing?" Adam asked.

"He's doing just dandy! He's cleared off all his loans and other financial burdens whilst amassing a tidy fortune on top, and still he shows no sign of quitting. In fact, he's just in the middle of a huge but highly risky investment strategy, which if it pays off, will make him one of the richest men in Britain, if not the world." He paused, then went on. "But all of this seems a million miles away from the business you're investigating."

Adam thought over everything that had been said and then agreed with his friend.

It looked as though he could finally cross O'Neil's name off the suspect list.

With business out of the way, the two old friends carried on chatting, catching up with each other's lives and reminiscing about old times. Eventually, the time came to wish each other well and promise to keep in touch. When the call ended, Adam sat for a while, continuing to reminisce, and all the time smiling to himself.

***

Sally Bixby was just seventeen years old, and even without make-up, was strikingly beautiful. With long honey-blonde hair that fell to her waist, she had a slim but shapely body that turned most men's heads when passing. Despite her looks, Sally had always been a modest girl with a bright, outgoing personality. She had stayed on at school and was hoping to enter into university the following year, with the aim of becoming a veterinarian. Her father Mathew Bixby was the local vet in Penny-Deep, and Sally regularly helped him out during weekends. Sally was known by most people in the town and had a reputation for being community-spirited and willing to help in any way she could.

It was her love for helping out in the community that had brought her to St Augustine's Church to discuss preparations for the upcoming church fete. She and several other women of varying ages were sitting around giving progress reports to Father Akers.

Sally had volunteered to run a cake stall, and

she and her mother would be up baking some of the cakes the night before. Members of the Women's Institute would make the other cakes and buns, and she would collect them with her father the morning of the fete. Sally was the last one to give her progress report, and Father Akers seemed pleased with what she said.

As the meeting broke up, Sally stood and put on her long red coat and collected her handbag from beside her seat, before making her way over to Father Akers.

"Excuse me, Father," she said, “I was hoping to see Mrs Teesdale tonight. My dad said she hadn't returned to the surgery with Bert, her Yorkshire Terrier, and I was wondering if he was doing alright. My dad said he might need another course of tablets to see him through."

"I'm afraid Mrs Teesdale has badly sprained her ankle, that's why she is absent tonight."

"Oh, I'm sorry to hear that. I'll see if I can get out to see her, and take Bert his medication," Sally replied, wondering how she would find the time to visit Mrs Teesdale who lived a good couple of miles outside of the town.

"You are an angel, Sally! You really do too much. I'll tell you what. I'm planning on visiting Mrs Teesdale tomorrow evening. What if you drop Master Bert's medicine into the church here, and I'll make sure to take it with me," Father Akers said with a comforting smile.

"Would you? That's wonderful. I'll drop the

tablets in the day after tomorrow. Thank you."

Sally made her way off, out of the church and into the warm evening breeze.

As she made her way up the path to the lych-gate, Sally was unaware that someone had been waiting and watching for her to leave.

Sally had arranged to meet her father at his veterinary surgery on the aptly named Pad-Paw Lane so he could drive her home. She made her way from the church and along the High Street towards Crabtree's greengrocers. It was a lovely night for walking; the air was warm against her skin, and as Sally passed Beckett's florists, her nose became bombarded by the scents of all the beautiful flowers on display. The bright, multi-coloured blooms were so pretty to look at that she paid no attention to the reflection in the window. If she *had* paid attention, she might have spotted the figure standing across the road, and back a little.

He was clad in dark clothing, the face hidden by a black hoodie.

Though slim and with hidden facial features, it was apparent from the build that the figure was male. It would have also been blatantly clear, had Sally noticed the dark presence, that he was loitering on the other side of the street for only one reason. He was watching her.

Sally entered the florists and purchased a bouquet to take home for her mother.

Her mother loved flowers, particularly the

ones that had a strong scent.

She said that they 'always brightened up a happy home.'

Continuing her stroll along the High Street, flowers in hand, Sally reached the greengrocers and turned right down Henry Street. The narrow street was cobbled and sloped gently down towards George Street. Sally's high heels clattered on the cobbles as she walked, and she took a left turn to walk down the narrow back lane that had no name but ran between the rear of the High Street shops and terraced cottages that stood on George Street.

It was a shortcut that would ultimately bring her out onto Pad-Paw lane.

The dark figure stood at the top of Henry Street, looking down the tiny, cobbled road. He didn't arrive in time to see Sally turn left onto the small lane, but then he didn't have to. He could tell the direction she had taken by the sound of her heels.

Sally turned right onto another small alleyway, a split second before the dark figure appeared at the far end of the lane she had just walked. The dark figure took a leisurely walk through the alley, trying the back gates to all of the properties as he progressed. Most of the gates were locked but three or four were showing no signs of ever being secured.

Having found a back yard that suited his ugly and sinister purpose, the figure slowly pulled the gate back to a closed position before he made his way back along the lane.

Now, he headed up towards the High Street.

Down on Pad-Paw lane, Sally saw that her father had already locked up the surgery and was sitting in his Land Rover parked outside.

She made her way around to the front passenger door and climbed in.

"Hello, love," her father said, “The lift is free! You didn't have to buy me flowers."

Sally laughed. "They are for Mum. I thought they looked pretty."

"They are. I'm sure your mum will love them."

"While I remember," Sally said, “Mrs Teesdale’s badly sprained her ankle, and that's why she hasn't brought Bert to the surgery. But Father Akers is planning on visiting her tomorrow, so if you can give me a lift home, I said I'd drop Bert's tablets in at the church for him to take along."

"That's no problem at all," said Mathew Bixby. "Saves me a trip out to Bert and Mrs T."

The dark figure slinked back along the High Street, aroused and excited. Images of Sally Bixby and her long blonde hair ran through his mind as he tried to concentrate on the plan ahead.

Chapter 16

Adam spent the whole of the next day accompanying a couple of junior officers on their mobile patrols and finishing up what was left of the station's clerical work. He checked his watch.

It was seven p.m., and he'd had enough of the monotony that working at Penny-Deep proffered for one day. He decided to cut his evening shift a little short and head home. It was whilst he was removing his tunic and putting on his sweatshirt and jacket that the office phone rang. Adam looked at the phone and deliberated whether to answer it or not, but finally gave in to his guilty conscience.

"Inspector Cadman. Penny-Deep Police Station!" he answered.

"Adam. It's Chief Superintendent Wise here! I just wanted to catch up with you, and see if anything came from the inquiries up there, regarding the major incident we have running?"

"Unfortunately not a thing came out of it yet. There's no CCTV in Penny-Deep and none at Archibald O'Neil's estate. All the fingerprints found in the van and the estate office were attributable to estate workers who had legitimate access. The van did contain some smudges which would make it probable that someone, probably the person we are interested in, had been driving the van whilst wearing gloves," Adam went on. "The estate workers all finished work at around six p.m. that day, and O'Neil himself was hosting a dinner party. None of the guests at the party was local, as they were all up from London. The catering and serving staff were all supplied by Creme Catering, but they all alibi'd each other, and background checks turned up nothing remotely suspect. It all seems to be exactly how it looks. An opportunistic burglary, and theft of van. The big question is, why was the van, taken in the burglary, driving around the back lanes of Penny-Deep with the body of Victoria Timperley in the back?"

"It's a puzzle alright," said Wise, "the only obvious answer is that whoever is behind all of this is bringing the bodies into this area for disposal. It makes sense, I suppose. There's hundreds of acres of countryside and woodland around Penny-Deep. I'd have a search team up there straight away, but where do you start?"

There was a long pause, then Wise said with more than a hint of desperation, "I don't suppose there are any other leads up there that you could follow up?"

Adam almost felt sorry for his Chief Superintendent. He pondered, but only momentarily, on whether to tell Wise about his theory regarding some ritualistic murder and about Katherine Dee. But then he thought better of it and simply replied, "No, Sir."

"Okay, Adam, then I'll be off."

But then the Chief Superintendent remembered.

"Oh, by the way, I almost forgot! With regards to the CCTV footage from around the car park where Elizabeth Short was taken, there was only one vehicular movement in that area, at around that time. We couldn't make out the driver or the registration number, but the vehicle was a late model Range Rover. Dark, possibly black."

***

The temperature had noticeably dropped a couple of degrees when Adam stepped out of the front doors of the police station. A stiff breeze blew against him as he walked up the lane towards the High Street. Adam didn't feel like heading straight back home; he needed time to think and rid himself of the morose thoughts swimming around inside his head. Besides, Sophia and Mrs Chattox wouldn't be expecting him back home yet. So he decided to take a walk.

Adam felt more than a little disquieted after his conversation with Chief Superintendent Wise. He had always held the old man in high regard, and the Chief Super had certainly helped Adam advance his career over the years since he had first begun working for him. Now Adam couldn't help but feel he was letting his boss down in his time of most need.

Here he was, just idling his time away in this

sleepy backwater, instead of helping head up the major investigation team back in the city.

Once he was on the High Street, Adam walked along deep in thought, until his eyes were drawn to the lights coming from the Blacksmith's Arms public house.

As he drew level, he stepped over from the pavement to the cobbled forecourt of the pub, where a handful of cars were parked. Adam walked past the old stone horse trough that brimmed with water, and up to the black and white, Tudor-beamed building. Then he stepped inside.

This was Adam's first visit to the Blacksmith's Arms, and the interior echoed the Tudor facade with low ceilings and large wooden beams. At the far end was a large brick inglenook fireplace and dotted about were tables and chairs of varied descriptions. Some were occupied, some not.

Adam walked across the bare oak floor to the bar, where several people huddled around chatting in small groups. He ordered a pint of bitter, then stood alone, and to one side of the bar.

Adam was so deep in thought that he failed to notice the two Armstrong brothers at the far end, watching him keenly and muttering to one another. Several minutes passed before the two hulking figures alighted from their bar stools and walked over to Adam. The Armstrong brothers were heavily built, rough-looking individuals, so tall their heads almost scraped the pub ceiling.

The two men had enough similarities to mark them out as brothers, and both muscled in, invading Adam's personal space, causing him to step back and look up sharply.

"You that new policeman we got up here?" one of the brothers said through a cloud of beer breath.

"I'm the new district inspector, yes," said Adam, looking both men up and down.

"Me and my brother here, we don't like police," said the other hulk, leaning over, and prodding Adam in the chest with a gnarled forefinger the thickness of a Cumberland sausage.

"Well, so far, I have to say, I'm less than impressed with you two," Adam replied. "So, the feeling's mutual." It was obvious the two men were out for trouble. They were big hard men, undoubtedly strong and able to take some punishment, but untrained. They would fight in a wild style, relying on their size and strength. On most occasions, that would be enough to overpower and intimidate people in these parts, but they were big fish in a relatively small pond.

Adam's years in the army had made him a trained fighter, and he had already picked out the weaknesses and attack points on the two brothers. He was confident he could take at least one of them out, but two? Much depended on how fast they moved and how they worked as a unit.

He reached over to his right and sat his pint glass on the bar.

Adam could feel his heart beating quickly, and a shiver ran through his body. The untrained would mistake this as fear, but Adam knew it was just his body getting ready for the fight, the increased blood supply to his muscles and the release of adrenaline.

The two thugs wet their lips and grinned. They had wanted a fight, and it looked as though they had got one. The brother on the left, sporting a badly broken nose, stepped forward with both fists clenched as several other patrons of the bar jostled out of the way.

Suddenly, someone small and thin pushed between Adam and the two brothers. It was Father Fenton Akers. Turning to the two brothers, he snapped at them angrily. "Haven't you two got something more important to be doing? I know you have first thing in the morning, because I expect you both to be working in the churchyard bright and early. If you wish to keep your current employment, I suggest you go and finish your drinks and think about heading off home."

The two giants looked at each other and then sheepishly turned and walked off back to the far end of the bar. Father Fenton turned to Adam.

"I'm terribly sorry about that," he said. "The Armstrong brothers! The strength of a Silverback gorilla and the brain of a gerbil. The pair of them! They're not bad lads really, just none too bright."

"That's alright," said Adam, relieved that confrontation had come to nothing. "No harm done. Mainly thanks to you. I must owe you a drink for that intervention."

"It was nothing really. But I will take you up on your offer. I'll have an orange juice. Thank you."

Adam turned to the bar, ordered an orange juice and picked up his remaining half pint of beer in the process. He instinctively turned when he heard the main door of the bar opening, and was surprised to see Katherine Dee walk in. She was dressed in a smart black trouser suit and black blouse. As she walked through the bar, people moved aside and eyed her suspiciously.

She walked towards the far end of the bar, but as she passed Adam, she turned her head, nodded, and smiled. Adam nodded back in acknowledgement, but he didn't smile.

On collecting the vicar's orange juice, Adam returned to Father Fenton, but he couldn't help keeping an eye on Katherine. On being served what looked like a glass of red wine, she walked over to a table in the far corner of the bar and sat alone.

Father Fenton asked Adam about the murder investigation and the other abductions.

"Are there any breakthroughs or new leads? I was rather hoping the whole business could be brought to a close," he said.

Adam informed the vicar that nothing new had come to light and confided that the police were thus far stumped.

"What about your inquiries into the occult here in Penny-Deep? Did that amount to anything?"

"No. Another dead end I'm afraid," said Adam, "It was never more than a wild piece of speculation on my part. It wasn't a serious line of investigation."

Father Fenton smiled and sipped on his orange juice.

"Oh, I am pleased to hear that. One never knows. You do hear stories about such things as witchcraft still being practised in some far-flung rural places, just like Penny-Deep."

The priest stopped and thought, then leaning in, he said, "It may be less than charitable for me to say this but, if anything of that ilk were to be going on around here, I don't think you would have to look too far for the culprit." Father Fenton turned and looked in the direction of Katherine Dee.

Looking over, Adam saw that the two Armstrong brothers had now walked over to where Katherine Dee was seated. Adam also couldn't help noticing that she was smiling at the two brothers as she spoke to them. He watched as the two brutes pulled out seats and sat either side of her. Then all three leaned in, engaging in what appeared to be a deep conversation.

For some reason, Adam felt angry, and he had to admit it, there was probably a hint of jealousy there too. There was no denying Katherine was an incredibly beautiful woman.

Turning to Father Fenton, he said, "My summation of Katherine Dee is she's a harmless crack-pot. The only thing dubious about her seems to be the friends she makes."

"Hmm, I do hope you're right, Inspector. I'm sure you are, of course."

The two men chatted on, making small talk, with Father Fenton taking an interest in Adam's background and also in Sophia. Eventually, Adam was coming to the end of his pint, and Father Fenton, having finished his orange juice, made off back to the church, stating that he had a couple of his parishioners to visit. Adam watched as Katherine stood up and left the two Armstrong brothers still seated at the table.

She walked towards the main doors of the pub and again turned towards Adam and smiled.

"Goodnight, Inspector," she said as she walked out the door. Adam just nodded once again.

He stepped over to the bar and sat his empty pint glass down; then he stood thinking about Katherine Dee. He walked over to the main doors and stepped out into the cool evening breeze.

As he stepped onto the pub forecourt, he was just in time to see Katherine Dee drive away.

She was driving a new, black Range Rover.

Adam stood, trying to work out what Katherine was all about.

If witchcraft were real, he'd happily curse the woman.

Ever since he had first met her, she had had him in a state of turmoil; actually, he had done so even before he had met her, when he had seen her swimming naked at the pond, if he was honest. Katherine Dee was a misguided crackpot or at best a charlatan, and there was more than a hint that she may be mixed up with the missing women, he reminded himself.

But still, there was something about her that both deeply annoyed him and, at the same time, made him want to find reasons to believe her.

Adam looked back in the direction of the police station, but still, he didn't feel ready to head home. He looked back inside the pub but decided he didn't need company; he needed to be alone to sort out his thoughts, so turned to his right and paced along the High Street.

***

Sally Bixby had been waiting inside St Augustine's Church for a good twenty minutes when the side door opened, and Father Akers raced in.

"Sorry, my child," he said. "I was just talking to our new police inspector and lost track of time."

"That's alright," she replied. Though secretly, she was annoyed that her dad would be waiting to drive her home. She handed a small white box of tablets over to the vicar and said. "Please tell Mrs Teesdale that they are the same tablets as last time, so she should know how many to give Bert. But if there are any questions, tell her to call my dad at the veterinarian surgery tomorrow morning."

Sally walked quickly from the church, but she knew her father wouldn't be angry at being kept waiting. But it just didn't seem fair after he'd had a long day at work.

Emerging from the lychgate, she crossed the road and walked briskly along the High Street towards the greengrocers. There were still one or two people dotted about the town centre, but the shops were all starting to close up and the light beginning to fade.

As she reached the greengrocers, she saw that the shop was already in darkness as she stopped and looked down Henry Street. The narrow road was poorly lit, and she knew that the alleyway leading off there would be even darker. Sally contemplated walking the long route to Pad-Paw Lane, but then she was already late, and back alleys weren't that long.

She finally made her mind up. She had kept her father waiting too long already, so she set off down Henry Street and turned left into the small back alley that was her shortcut.

The figure crouched behind the green wooden gate waited patiently.

On hearing the clatter of high heels, his senses became alert, and he peered through a small knothole in the gate. It was her, Sally Bixby, the one he had been waiting for all this time.

He was so excited he could have easily sprung out into the alley at first sight of her, but he somehow restrained himself and watched as she walked by.

Sally didn't hear the creak of the gate or the rushed footsteps approaching from behind. Suddenly, a hand covered her mouth and an arm wrapped around her waist, dragging her backwards. Sally almost passed out with shock, but then she reached up with both hands, and just for a brief instant, managed to pull the hand away from her face. In that instant, Sally managed to let out one shrill, ear-splitting scream, before the hand clamped back, silencing her.

***

Adam was no nearer to making sense of his Katherine Dee conundrum than when he had first set off walking. Now, he realised that he had walked farther than he had intended and so stopped and turned around. Time had ticked by, and Sophia and Mrs Chattox would be expecting him home shortly. He had just walked past the unlit greengrocer's when a piercing scream brought him quickly to his senses, loud and nearby. Adam looked down the narrow cobbled road to his left and began running. He turned in the direction of the scream, down a small alley.

There, up in front, Adam saw a hooded male figure, dressed in black, struggling to hold onto a young woman, who was kicking and writhing, wildly. The figure hung on to the girl, desperately trying to subdue her, and drag her along the alley.

The male in the hood turned in the direction of Adam and then let go of the girl, and began sprinting away down the alley.

Adam ran to the girl and asked if she was alright; she was highly distressed but nodded. Adam saw the hooded male reach the corner of the far alley, but just as he turned right, he collided with a middle-aged man in a suit who came running around the corner in the opposite direction. The hooded figure turned the corner and continued running out of sight, but the man in the suit looked directly at Adam and the girl and shouted, "Get off her!" As the man ran towards them, the girl burst into tears.

Adam shouted. "Police Inspector Cadman! Take her to the police station. I'm going after him."

Adam sprinted down the alley, turning right then left, and then right again onto Pad-Paw Lane. Adam looked down the road and saw his quarry, the hooded figure had gained a good hundred metres on him, but as Adam began running, he purposely set a steady pace.

Adam knew that even at his current fitness

level, he could maintain that speed for several miles, all he had to do was keep the target in sight.

By the time the hooded figure had reached the first junction, Adam had gained a good thirty metres on him. At the corner, the suspect turned left, which meant that he'd be running uphill, back towards the High Street. Adam rounded the corner in time to see his quarry staggering the last few metres up to the next junction with the High Street. Adam smiled to himself; not only had he gained another twenty metres, but he could tell that the dark hooded figure was tiring.

The suspect turned left onto the High Street, and Adam gritted his teeth and powered up the hill.

Emerging onto the High Street, Adam peered down the street looking for the suspect. At first, he didn't see him and was just about to berate himself when he saw the figure up ahead; he had just crossed the main road and was running much slower with an ungainly gait, about forty metres ahead. Adam increased his pace now; he knew he had him.

By the time Adam was ten metres away, the figure had turned sharply into the lychgate at St Augustine's Church. Adam chased him down the church path, but the suspect managed to reach the side porch of the church and ran inside, closing the large oak door behind him. Adam pushed at the door, which gave a little, but something was blocking it from opening fully.

Adam put his shoulder to the door and pushed hard. There was a crashing sound, and the door gave a little more, just enough for Adam to squeeze his way into the church.

Inside the church, Adam saw that a stack of metal chairs had been pushed against the oak door. The chairs had toppled over as he had forced his way through. He stared into the gloomy corners of the church but could see no sign of the suspect, so he walked to the centre aisle and began heading towards the altar; he checked between all the rows of pews on either side as he moved.

Suddenly, there was the sound of a door opening and looking up past the altar, Adam saw Father Akers stepping out of his office and pulling on a tweed sports jacket.

"Hello again, Inspector!" he said. "Are you wanting something urgent? I was just on my way to visit a parishioner, Mrs Teesdale."

Adam sized the vicar up, but he was too short and breathing too evenly to have been the suspect. "Actually vicar, I wasn't after you at all. I was after a suspect who I saw run into the church after committing a serious sexual assault," Adam replied.

"Oh my!" said Father Akers, looking distractedly off to his right. "What does this suspect look like?"

"He's about six feet tall, slim build and dressed all in black with a black hoodie."

The vicar nodded towards the shadows under the stone arches, and roared, "Come out, Clive. I believe you have some explaining to do."

For a second or two, there was no movement, but then the dark hooded figure stepped out of the shadows and pulled down his hood. It was Clive Brady, the curate. Clive stood looking sheepish as Adam marched over and arrested him for the indecent assault.

Father Akers said in a sharp tone, "Is this true, Clive?"

Clive nodded his head.

"I'll pray for your soul, but your services will be, no longer required at St Augustine's!" said the vicar. Adam took out his phone and called the police station, requesting a patrol car be sent to meet him at the church.

***

Once back at Penny-Deep Police Station, Clive Brady was documented, searched, and placed in a holding room. Adam made his way through to the public area where he saw Mathew Bixby seated alone, looking upset and angry. Adam made his way over to speak to him, but Mr Bixby was on his feet as soon as he saw Adam. "Did you get him?" he demanded to know.

"Yes. He's under arrest and safely locked in a holding room."

Mathew Bixby let out a sigh of relief and slumped back down on his seat.

"Thank God for that," he said.

"Thank you for coming down to the station," said Adam. "Where is the girl now?"

"The girl is my daughter, Sally. One of your female officers took her off to make a statement."

"Your daughter!" said Adam. Now he understood why the man looked so upset and angry. Up until now, Adam had thought Bixby was just a passer-by. "How is Sally?" he asked.

"She's distraught but physically unharmed. At least that's what she's told me. It was fortunate we both arrived when we did."

"Yes, I was just walking along the High Street when I heard her scream. What about you?" Adam asked.

"I had arranged to meet her and give her a lift home. I was sitting waiting in my car on Pad-Paw Lane when I heard her scream. I knew it was Sally and came running to find her."

Adam offered Mathew Bixby a coffee which he declined.

Then Adam made his way to the interview suite.

The 'In Use' light above the door of the first interview room was lit, and Adam gave the door a quick knock before sticking his head inside. Sally Bixby was sitting at the table opposite PC Natalie Richardson who was busily writing down Sally's statement. "Sorry to interrupt,"

Adam said. "PC Richardson, could I have a quick word?"

Outside the interview room, Adam asked the officer for a quick precis of what Sally Bixby had said so far.

"Well, I only have the briefest of outlines so far, Sir," she said. "But Sally says that she took a shortcut to meet her father on Pad-Paw Lane. She says that the suspect appeared out of nowhere and grabbed her in the alleyway between High Street and George Street. She thinks he may have been hiding in one of the rear gardens of the houses on George Street, but she couldn't be sure."

"What happened next?" asked Adam.

"Well, she managed to scream, but he covered her mouth with his hand to stop her. He was trying to drag her away when you arrived, and he ran off. Fortunately, the assault ended there, but Sally is unsure what his intentions were."

"Okay. Thank you," said Adam. Please inform Sally that the man who assaulted her has been arrested and detained."

"I will, Sir."

Adam climbed the stairs up to his office and sat at his desk. He thought about Clive Brady; had this been a random, opportunistic attack or had he targeted Sally Bixby? Could Brady be responsible for the other missing girls? On the surface, the modus operandi was all wrong. Still, if the motive for the other abductions had been sexual, then Brady wouldn't be the first sexual predator to become more desperate and subsequently more audacious as he progressed.

Adam slowly reached for his mobile phone and searched his contacts list until he found Chief Superintendent Wise's mobile number. The phone rang three times before the Chief Superintendent answered it with a brusque, "Wise!"

"It's Adam Cadman, Sir. I wanted to make you aware that we have arrested a local male for a serious sexual assault. It appears that he was waiting for the victim in a back alley. Whether he targeted that particular girl or whether she was just unlucky enough to be the first one to walk by his location, we don't yet know."

"Did he try and abduct the girl?" asked Wise.

"We are not sure what his intentions were. Fortunately, the girl's father and I were nearby and managed to foil his attack at the outset." There was a long pause, and Adam could almost hear the Chief Superintendent's thoughts as he weighed up the information he had been given.

"What do we know about this person?" Wise asked.

"His name is Clive Brady. He is twenty-three years old and the curate at St Augustine's Church here in Penny-Deep. He currently resides in rented accommodation here in the town," Adam answered.

"Does he have a car or access to any transport?"

"He has an old ignition key in his possession, but he states it's for an old moped."

There was another long pause.

"Right then." Chief Superintendent Wise finally said, “I'm going to send the Major Incident Team up to search his accommodation, and then bring this chap down here to headquarters for an interview."

"Yes, Sir," said Adam, more than a little deflated at seemingly being cut from the rest of the investigation. The Chief Superintendent must have guessed what Adam was thinking, and added,

"No reflection on you, Adam. You know I would have been more than happy for you to head up this investigation. But you haven't been involved all the way through. The team are up to speed on all the evidential detail needed to interview this chap thoroughly. This is the first real lead we have had, and if there is any chance at all that this is our man, we have to get this right first time."

Of course, the Chief was right.

Adam knew he was but being cut out of the investigation still stung.

"Yes, Sir. I understand," Adam said. "I'll complete my statement before I head home and leave it for the Major Incident Team."

After completing the call to the Chief, Adam quickly called Mrs Chattox and asked her to keep his meal warm for him. He was going to be a little late.

Chapter 17

Adam was up and in to work early, keen to know what had happened with Clive Brady. What had he said about the assault on Sally Bixby, and could he be connected with the missing women?

Adam had no sooner reached his office, than the phone on his desk began to ring. He hung up his jacket and dashed over to answer it. The voice on the other end was Chief Superintendent Wise.

"Morning, Adam," said Wise. "I wanted to update you regarding Clive Brady. He was interviewed twice last night and made a full and frank admission to the offence of attempted sexual assault on Sally Bixby. He has been charged and remanded in custody to appear before the court on Monday morning. Apparently, he had seen the Bixby girl visit the church a few times and become infatuated with her. Brady admitted to following her and then lying in wait for her on one of her usual routes."

"I see," said Adam. "What about the other missing women? Can he be connected?"

"No. At least not at present. Brady flatly denied all knowledge of the missing women, although he did admit to knowing Victoria Timperley. It transpires that Brady went to school with her, and even went so far as to admit he had seen her in the wine bar the night she went missing."

"A bit of a coincidence," Adam replied.

"Yes, that's what we thought. But Brady offered up that bit of information when he really had no need. Unless he thought we knew more than we were letting on and was trying to cover his bases."

"What about his home address? Did anything turn up when it was searched?" asked Adam.

"No not a thing. Apart from a large stash of pornographic magazines, and that only seems unusual since Brady's a church curate! Or is that just me getting old?"

Adam wasn't sure how to answer that one and decided discretion was the better part of valour.

Then he asked, "What about the ignition key he had on him? Did he have a car or van of any description?"

"No. It was for an old moped, as Brady said it was. We found it in the backyard of the property, in a state of disrepair. We tried the key, and it fitted," said the Chief Superintendent.

Adam suddenly felt quite despondent. "So what do you think, Sir? Are you eliminating him from the investigation into the missing women?"

"No. Brady's not in the clear just yet, at least not in my mind. We know he's a sexual predator, and he's admitted to being in the same location as Victoria Timperley on the night she disappeared. So far, he is the best lead we have. We just don't have any solid evidence to link him with the other girls. He will probably be released on bail from the court on Monday. If that's the case, I intend to have a surveillance team on him night and day. In the meantime, I have sent you details of the last girl to go missing, Elizabeth Short. I'll keep you apprised of any developments at this end."

The Chief Superintendent rang off, and Adam had a shuffle through his in-tray and found a large brown folder in amongst the usual paperwork. The folder had a typed front sheet attached, that read:

SENT FROM CENTRAL FOR
YOUR INFORMATION

As the Chief had stated, the folder contained details of the last girl to go missing from central. Adam read through the folder.

Elizabeth Short aged seventeen. Born, Adam noted, on 25th December.

Adam looked at an attached, recent photograph that showed a happy, smiling girl with short black hair and an altogether androgynous appearance. The file went on to list the clothing she was last seen wearing. Black leather jacket. Black tee-shirt, black jeans, and black sneakers. She had been carrying a brown satchel bag which held her college things. The file also noted that Elizabeth was wearing a man's Seiko 5 automatic wristwatch, in gold stainless steel with a matching bracelet, and an antique silver ankle bracelet with several silver charms attached. Adam looked at photographs of these items that had been taken by the missing girl for insurance purposes.

Adam read on about Elizabeth's family, her friends, such as they were, and her routine.

He noted the absence of a boyfriend and her fondness for martial arts training.

Finally, Adam read about the night of her disappearance, including her last known whereabouts. Adam studied the two still photographs taken from CCTV. One was showing Elizabeth walking towards a large open car park, and the other showing a black, late model, Range Rover driving away from the same car park but on some other back road. The image wasn't at the right angle to make out either the driver or the registration plate of the vehicle. Adam's thoughts immediately flashed to Katherine Dee driving away in a Black Range Rover the night before.

Adam placed the Elizabeth Short folder on his desk and headed downstairs, in the hope that a decent cup of coffee could be found. Halfway down, he heard a familiar, yet out-of-place voice coming from the report writing room, and curiosity sent Adam that way.

The voice belonged to Brian Winter, in conversation with PC Newman and another constable. Both looked sheepish when Adam walked in. PC Newman, seated at a desk writing a report, put his head down and carried on typing away at the computer in front of him.

The other constable, PC Olivetti, sauntered out of the room. Adam sensed tension in the room and wondered what Winter was doing in the report-writing room. He was a civilian now and strictly speaking, had no right to be in any place except the public area of the front reception desk.

“Have you decided to come out of your retirement, Brian?" asked Adam lightheartedly, though inside he was far from amused.

"What? Oh, I was passing, and I thought I would pop in and see if I could find a scarf of mine. I've looked all over at home and can't find it. So I wondered if I had left it here," Winter replied.

Adam simply nodded and stepped out, making his way to the kitchen.

There, Adam found both coffee and Olivetti, busy pouring a fresh brew into several cups.

"Seems Brian Winter is missing the place," said Adam. "What was he talking about just then?"

"Nothing. Just chitchat, that's all," Olivetti replied, still looking a little sheepish.

Adam didn't know if the officer was telling the truth or not; he didn't know him well enough yet. But Adam had picked up on station gossip that hinted that Olivetti could always find some scope for flexibility in his reporting. Adam made his way back to his office, coffee cup in hand.

At his desk, Adam out took the Elizabeth Short folder and placed it in a secure drawer which he locked and removed the key. He didn't like or trust Winter and didn't like the idea of him being able to roam around the station unchecked.

A couple of minutes later, there was a knock on Adam's office door, and Winter breezed in.

"Well, I didn't find the scarf!" he announced. "So, I'll be off."

Good, thought Adam. *Don't let me stop you.*

"But before I go," Winter continued. "I've been giving some thought to all the strange happenings that seem to be taking place around here since you took over."

The dig at Adam was quite blatant, but he chose to let it go.

"You know, the dumped body of that girl and everything," Winter carried on. "Well, I can't help thinking that the Dee woman is somehow involved."

Winter was obviously snooping around hoping to get more information; he had been a crap police officer, and certainly didn't like Katherine Dee. But that didn't mean he was wrong, and at the mention of Katherine Dee, Adam was suddenly interested.

"Oh," said Adam. "Tell me more."

Winter visibly warmed to the interest being shown, and said, "Well, ever since she arrived in Penny-Deep, I have heard stories about her practising some sort of witchcraft, to the extent that some local folks are frightened to death of her. I did a lot of work, trying to trace her background and where she came from, but I couldn't find anything. Also, she has been seen out and about at all hours of the night. Sometimes travelling back from the city in the early hours."

"Well, having a late night in the city is not so strange, particularly for a young woman like Katherine Dee," said Adam.

"No, I agree," Winter came back. "But there have always been stories about that land on the hill, the land she occupies. Stories of people going missing up there and never being found again. These tales stretch back to when Dee's forebears occupied the place. For a long time, all was quiet, but then Katherine Dee arrives and starts living up there, not even denying that she's a witch. Add to that her frequent visits to the city, and what suddenly starts to happen? We begin to get reports of young women going missing and never being seen again. Except for the tone of course. And where does her body turn up? Penny-Deep!"

Adam contemplated what Winter was saying, in his muddled way, and in some sense, it mirrored his own suspicions. Especially with what he knew about the possible link between the car Katherine Dee was driving and the car seen near the abduction of Elizabeth Short.

But professionally speaking, everything Winter had said was circumstantial at best, and even as far as circumstantial went, it was as flimsy as a cobweb in a gale-force wind. But then again, it was a theory, in a case decidedly short of alternative ideas. It also fitted in with his theory about a ritualistic motive and his feeling that there was something not quite right about Katherine Dee.

Adam hated to pander to Winter, but the man just might be onto something. What's more, it occurred to Adam, that if he put up a reasoned argument against the theory, Winter would only hang around longer trying to convince him, when he just wanted to be rid of him.

"Well it's certainly interesting, Brian," Adam said, trying to sound sincere. "I'll look into it a bit more and maybe pass it on to the Major Incident Team."

"Oh! Would you? It would put my mind at rest, no end."

Adam walked Winter out of the police station and was relieved when he was gone.

Returning to his office, Adam crossed paths with PC Newman who volunteered some information that confirmed his suspicions about Winter.

"Sorry! I couldn't say anything before with

Brian Winter stood in the room," said the officer. "But I found him snooping in my clerical tray, reading a copy of my statement regarding the body we found. He was also asking a lot of questions about the investigation, though I told him nothing."

"Thank you, Jason. I rather suspected that was what he was up to."

***

The gravel drive crackled and popped beneath the tyres of the large catering vans that drove up to the front of the O'Neil manor house. Before the occupants of the vans could open a door and alight, Ms Carfax strode out of the front entrance of the big house, clipboard in hand, and began issuing orders in a loud voice. The catering staff were all aware that Archibald O'Neil was one of their company's best customers. He had held up to four lavish dinner parties a month over the last few years, bringing in thousands of pounds in revenue for Creme Bespoke Caterers.

It was for this reason, some of the staff told themselves, that they put up with Ms Carfax barking orders at them and generally talking to them like dogs. The truth, though, in many cases, was that she was the type of person you wouldn't want to cross.

Archibald O'Neil looked on from a first-floor window. He was pleased with how Carfax had got everything in hand with regard to arrangements for this weekend's event. He reached down and pulled a heavy gold pocket watch from his waistcoat pocket, and checking the time, he felt a tingle of anticipation; his guests would start arriving very soon.

Chapter 18

Elizabeth Short alternated her time between meditation and stretching exercises, all along keenly listening to the comings and goings outside her room. She could, with a little effort, hear when someone approached, and on those occasions, the door would open for someone to push in food and drinks with paper plates and cups. Although Elizabeth's wristwatch was missing, with a little concentration, her internal body clock could give her a rough idea of the times when somebody would bring her meals. Her captors, whoever they were, had made one mistake.

They had spaced these feedings at reasonably regular intervals.

Elizabeth could tell that one was due anytime now.

The drill was always the same. A key would turn in the heavy wooden door, that would then swing wide open. The room Elizabeth was kept in would be faintly illuminated by the light outside in the corridor. The woman who brought the food on a tray was of average height and build, and she would stand and wait at the door until she had located Elizabeth's position in the room.

When the woman was satisfied there was no

threat, she would step inside, and taking the paper plate and cup from the tray, she would place them on the floor before backing out of the room and closing the door. Twice whilst pretending to be asleep, Elizabeth had seen —through only partially closed eyes—a man standing outside in the corridor, glancing in. Elizabeth assumed that he was always there, whether she saw him or not. He was the backup there, if required.

Elizabeth had been stretching, warming her muscles and making them limber and ready.

She lay down on the floor directly in front of the wooden door and about ten feet away from it, positioning herself face down with her head resting on her left arm.

To the casual observer, she would appear sound asleep. But the truth was, her heart was racing, and her body was awash with adrenaline. She was ready!

First, Elizabeth heard the footsteps, then she listened to a short, murmured conversation before hearing the sound of the key turning, and the door swinging open. Through peeping eyes, she saw the silhouette of the woman with the tray, against the dim light in the corridor.

Elizabeth hoped that her eyes would adjust quickly enough to the light.

The woman paused a while, and then obviously under the impression that Elizabeth was sleeping, she stepped into the room. The woman focused on lifting the paper plate, bearing sandwiches, from the tray she was holding. She didn't see Elizabeth leap to her feet with all the stealth and grace of a panther, neither did she see Elizabeth's first two lightning-quick steps towards her. But when the woman did look up, it was in shock and disbelief.

She instinctively raised the tray to shield herself, exposing her midriff.

Elizabeth sent a quick and powerful maegeri, a front kick, plunging deep into the woman's soft solar-plexus, causing her to fall to her knees in agonising pain. As the woman went down, Elizabeth snatched the metal tray from her. With both hands, Elizabeth brought the tray down hard, striking the woman on the back of her head. The woman fell on her face, unconscious.

Suddenly, Elizabeth became aware of the man who had been standing, hitherto, out of sight in the corridor. He wasn't a big man, just average height and build, but even so, that made him bigger and stronger than Elizabeth. The man came through the doorway and rushed Elizabeth. But as he came into range, she punched the metal edge of the tray straight into the man's throat, putting her shoulder and every ounce of strength she possessed into the strike.

The man clutched at his throat, gasping for air.

Again, Elizabeth moved forward with a quick maegeri front kick. This time, the kick targeted the man's groin. As the man squirmed and writhed on the floor, Elizabeth stepped past him, and then turning on her left heel, she kicked her right leg up high, sending her right foot over her head. At the end of its upwards trajectory, Elizabeth's right foot came down in a swift arcing motion, her heel connecting with the crown of the man's head. Now, he too lay motionless and unconscious.

The corridor outside the room where she had been held was short and narrow with stone walls. To her left, the corridor was approximately twenty feet in length, before it reached a sharp right turn. Elizabeth was aware that every time she had been visited, the footsteps had come from this direction. She was uncertain who or what might lie in wait for her down this route, so Elizabeth took a chance and turned right. Following the corridor for a distance of only twelve feet, Elizabeth turned sharp right. Once around the corner, she saw a flight of five stone steps that reached up to a large, arched wooden door, similar to the one where she had been confined.

But, in the faint light, she could see that the large iron bolts securing the door were at her side. Elizabeth raced up the steps and tugged on the top bolt, that gave way and slid back.

Then Elizabeth crouched and grappled with the bottom bolt which refused to budge. Suddenly, she heard loud voices from behind, somewhere along the corridor. They were panicked and angry. With all her strength and weight, she heaved back on the bolt till it grudgingly gave way and drew back. Elizabeth held her breath as she pulled the door open; she could only hope that what was beyond was a better prospect than what was closing in from behind her.

As the door creaked open, a cold gust of air hit her face, and Elizabeth realised the door led to the outside world. Stepping through into the night, she found herself at the bottom of another flight of stone steps; these steps were steeper and took her up to ground level. Elizabeth did not turn to look back at the building that had been her prison. Instead, she let her eyes pick out the darkest part of the horizon, and with all the speed she could muster, ran towards it.

The dark jeans and top Elizabeth was wearing soon helped her to melt into the shadows, but now she could hear more voices gathering behind her. It sounded as if there were three or four or maybe more, it was hard to tell. She ran and ran until her lungs felt they would explode.

The field she was running across eventually turned to dense undergrowth, and she powered on, crashing through trees and bushes until she tripped and fell forward.

In the darkness, she braced herself, ready to impact the ground, but something caught her mid-fall, something springy and sharp. Something cut into the palms of her hands and the right side of her ribs. She heard the sound of her tee-shirt tearing, feeling a resistance at the same time.

Though the darkness, in the trees, was as black as ink, Elizabeth realised that she had stumbled against a barbed-wire fence. It wasn't high, only about three feet. The adrenaline coursing through her body made her impervious to the pain as she gripped the sharp, top strand of wire, and leapt over, accepting however it might rip and shred her clothing. Elizabeth stumbled again as she landed, but within a split second, she was back on her feet and running. She glanced over her shoulder and could see lights, and in amongst the many voices, she could hear the barking of dogs.

Elizabeth ran as fast as she could.

On and on she ran, never again looking back. She didn't have the slightest idea where she was. Some of the fields Elizabeth ran through were planted with crops of wheat or barley that were waist high and made running difficult, the long strands of crop grabbing at her legs and ankles.

After running for what Elizabeth thought were twenty to thirty minutes, she estimated she had run approximately three miles. She continued running until she arrived at a small embankment, at the top of which was a drystone wall. Climbing the embankment, Elizabeth leaned over the stone wall and saw a road. Leaping over onto the road, she pondered which way to run. Then she heard the distant sound of a car engine coming from her right, and looking along the road, she could now see approaching headlights. Elizabeth began running towards the vehicle. She positioned herself in the centre of the narrow lane, waving both her arms up and down as she ran.

Within seconds, the headlights blazed over Elizabeth, and there was a screech of brakes as the blue Toyota 4x4 skidded to a halt. Elizabeth ran to the driver's side as the door window lowered with a powered hum. "Please help me," she screamed.

The man in the car was small and slight, his beady eyes shocked and frightened through the wire spectacles he wore. "Are you alright, my child?" he asked in a high pitched voice.

It was then that Elizabeth noticed that he was wearing a black shirt with a white dog collar under his grey jacket. He was a vicar!

"Please, you have to help me! Some people are chasing me. They kidnapped me and kept me locked in a building somewhere."

"Goodness!" said the vicar looking incredulous, "I'm Father Fenton Akers! You had better jump in, and I'll seek help."

Elizabeth ran around the front of the vehicle and clambered into the front passenger seat.

The Father put the car in gear and drove them away, though not nearly fast enough for Elizabeth's liking. "Now tell me all about what has happened to you, my dear," the vicar said.

Elizabeth began trying to explain in a quick, panic-stricken way. The vicar didn't interrupt. He just listened intently, nodding his head as he drove. Eventually, Elizabeth came to the end of her story and slumped back in the car seat, shivering more from shock than the cold.

"Is your name Elizabeth Short?" asked Father Fenton.

"Yes. How do you know that?" asked Elizabeth with some concern.

"The local news has been talking about nothing else. The police have been searching high and low for you."

Elizabeth felt relief. Father Akers reached into his jacket pocket and produced a mobile phone and began keying in numbers.

"I think I had better call the local police station and see what they want us to do. Are you alright if I keep driving, or would you prefer it if I stopped while I speak to them?"

"No! Just keep driving! In fact, drive faster if you can," said Elizabeth, hastily and in frustration.

A few moments later, someone clearly answered the Father's phone call, though Elizabeth could only hear Father Akers' side of the conversation.

"Father Fenton Akers here from Penny-Deep Church. I have just found a young lady whom I believe you are looking for. Elizabeth Short!"

He paused, listening, and then said, "Yes, she said she had escaped and some people are now chasing her. Where do you want me to take her?" Again there was a pause. "And I take it you will arrange for someone to meet us there. Splendid. Thank you."

The vicar terminated the call. Turning to Elizabeth, he said, "Penny-Deep Police Station. They are going to have someone meet us."

Elizabeth began to relax, and they drove on in silence for the next few minutes. Then Father Fenton asked. "Do you know Penny-Deep at all?"

Elizabeth thought how sweet the vicar was.

He was obviously trying to keep her calm by making inane chit-chat. She really didn't feel like talking but made an effort so as not to hurt Father Fenton's feelings.

"No. I have only visited once, and that was when I was very young. My parents brought me out here for a picnic."

At that moment, they came to a fork in the road, and the vicar took the left turn.

They travelled on for only a couple more minutes before the vicar took another left turn. This time, they turned down a single-track road between two dry stone walls that were barely one car in width. Elizabeth suddenly became alert. They seemed to be heading roughly back in the same direction from which they had travelled.

"Where are you going?" she said anxiously.

"It's a short cut I know. I want to get you to the police station as quickly as possible. I don't mind telling you that all of this and the things you told me have quite shaken me."

Elizabeth began to relax a little but was still concerned about their direction and fearful that they might come across the people who were looking for her. She scanned the fields on either side, but they were in darkness, and partially obscured by the dry stone walls. As they turned a slight right-hand bend, Elizabeth's worst fears came true; there, blocking the lane was a group of about ten to twelve figures, standing, holding torches, and some had dogs on long leads.

"Stop!" she yelled. "Reverse quickly! It's the people who are after me."

Father Fenton braked sharply. Elizabeth turned in her seat to look out the rear windscreen at their only escape route, but she could see several figures leaping over the dry stone walls at either side and blocking the lane behind them.

Elizabeth released her seatbelt and began clawing at the door catch. She partially opened the door when a vice-like grip seized her right arm. She turned to see a snarling angry face barely recognisable as Father Fenton Akers. The vicar had removed his spectacles.

"No, you don't, girly," he spat.

The point of Elizabeth's right elbow hit the vicar in the left eye, and he yelled out in pain, clutching at his face. Elizabeth pushed the car door open, but it was too late she was immediately grabbed by a large, bearded monster, whose immense strength almost crushed her.

She clawed at the man's eyes, and he retaliated by headbutting her in the face, breaking her nose and dazing her. The giant threw her to the ground, and as she fell in a semi-unconscious state, the back of her head collided with the hard road surface with a loud crack.

A large pool of blood immediately began to fan out on the grey tarmac.

Father Fenton was out of the car and was down examining Elizabeth Short within seconds. Turning to the giant who had thrown the girl down, he snapped, "She's dead, you fool. You've killed her. Do you know what this means? Have you any idea of the trouble this will cause?"

Chapter 19

Adam Cadman had had a fitful night of sleep, or to be more accurate, he'd had a fitful night of lying awake. His mind had been continually turning over the details of the missing women from the city division, and the discovery of Victoria Timperley's mutilated body in Penny-Deep. Also, and for some reason that he found incredibly annoying, he couldn't help thinking about Katherine Dee.

He had a growing suspicion that she was involved up to her neck in the disappearance of the women and in the murder of Victoria Timperley; the trouble was, he had no evidence, nor did he have any real reason for thinking this way, other than that she was certainly strange and everyone else thought so too. Even more disturbing was that when he did manage to catch brief snatches of sleep, his slumber was invaded by dreams of Katherine Dee.

This time, he dreamt she was telling him there was a storm coming. And to be prepared!

Eventually, Adam gave up on any hope of sleep, and with the first traces of daybreak, he got out of bed and dressed in his running gear. Quietly, so as not to wake Sophia, he made his way downstairs and wrote a brief note, explaining that he had gone for a run and would return shortly, just in case Sophia was up before he returned.

Even at such an early hour, Adam found the air warm and still. There was a muggy heaviness all around that made him sweat all the more whilst running. He ran up the track towards the dark woods, glancing briefly at the pool where he had seen Katherine Dee swimming, but this time, the water was empty. He couldn't help but feel a little disappointed.

At the top of the track, he ran through the dark woods until he came to the clearing where he could see Katherine Dee's house. Slightly to the left, he saw the old Wych Elm and recalled his conversation with Ms Dee by the tree. He felt an urge to be near her again, though he tried to fight this inexplicable emotion. Once again, he glanced at her home, which was in darkness—and then he forced himself to turn around and run back through the woods.

By the time he exited the dark woods and ran down the track, daylight had broken through in earnest. Unlocking the back door, he entered the kitchen and made his way straight upstairs to shower. He could hear the sound of water already and concluded that Sophia was already up and showering in her en-suite.

Father and daughter eventually met in the kitchen.

Adam had dressed in his uniform ready for work and took care not to splatter his clean shirt whilst he rustled up scrambled eggs on toast for Sophia and himself.

They sat and chatted while eating breakfast.

Sophia was bright and cheerful and said that she was enjoying their new home in Penny-Deep. She looked thoughtful and then said, “I wish Mum could have lived here with us. I think she would have liked it here. Do *you* think she would have liked it?”

The surprising turn in the conversation caught Adam off guard. He thought for a second, and then answered honestly. "Yes, I think she would have loved it here, sweetheart."

Adam felt a momentary pang for what might have been.

Then he shook himself from his thoughts.

Clearing the dishes, Adam informed Sophia that Mrs Chattox would be over shortly and instructed her to watch cartoons till then. Slipping on his jacket, he leaned over and kissed his daughter on the forehead. Suddenly, a flash of something bright caught his eye, and he reached over and tugged at something below Sophia's collar.

It was a silver chain. "What's this?" he asked.

Sophia suddenly looked sullen and concerned. Adam pulled on the chain some more, and the pentagram pendant came into sight.

"Sophia, where did you get this?"

Sophia hung her head. She just knew her father would disapprove.

"I was talking to Katherine Dee, and she gave it to me," she said.

Adam was furious. The pendant looked like some sort of witchcraft jewellery, and he didn't like the idea of Katherine Dee hanging such things around his daughter's neck. Adam was so enraged, he felt like ripping the necklace off. Thankfully, he managed to control his anger, instead, reaching around and unfastening the clasp so as not to hurt Sophia.

On removing the pendant, Adam placed it in his shirt pocket.

He intended to take this matter up with Katherine Dee at the first opportunity.

How dare she hang such things around his daughter's neck!

Sophia began to protest, saying that the necklace was a gift and it was hers to keep. But Adam was having none of it. He told Sophia that she shouldn't accept gifts from strangers and that he would hand the necklace back to Katherine Dee and speak to her about it.

Sophia was about to explain that she had spoken to Katherine Dee more than once, and that she liked her and considered her a friend! But then she thought better of it and remained silent. Her father was clearly angry and clearly didn't like Katherine Dee for some reason that she couldn't understand. Sophia decided that her father didn't need to know she had spent more time with Katherine. It was better that way. He was angry enough.

Sophia watched as her father marched off, mumbling under his breath.

***

Adam was in a bad mood for his entire journey into work. Who the hell did Katherine Dee think she was, giving his daughter such things? By the time he parked his car in the car park and headed into the police station, he had begun to calm down. Adam entered through the main public entrance so he could have a quick word with Angela at the front desk.

However, he could see she was busy dealing with a middle-aged gent, who looked fit and strong, dressed in loose work shirt and trousers.

As Adam made his way to the stairs leading up to his office, he could hear the man protesting.

"It's never taken seriously, and I'm fed up with it. It's criminal damage I tell you, and it's my livelihood!"

Adam sat at his desk and looked at the mountain of paperwork that had accumulated. He was looking for an excuse not to do it when there was a sudden knock on the door, and Angela stepped into the office.

"Sorry to bother you!" she said, "But I've got a Mr Rusby downstairs. He's one of the local farmers, complaining about damage that's been caused to his crops. He's demanding that someone go out and see it and take a formal complaint, but everyone is tied up at the moment."

"Is there no sergeant on duty?" Adam asked.

"Not until six this evening, and Mr Rusby is refusing to leave until something is done."

Angela looked flustered

"Okay," said Adam, slipping on his tunic. "I'll come down and speak to him."

Downstairs, Adam saw that Mr Rusby was the same man he had passed earlier at the enquiry desk, as he had entered the building. Adam walked over and introduced himself. He continued, "I believe you have had some crops damaged. Can you tell me what's happened?"

"I was passing the fields this morning when I saw that a whole lot of my wheat field had been trampled into the ground. Totally destroyed."

"Kids?" asked Adam.

"Kids! More like a bloody battalion of stormtroopers. You should see the mess. This damage is going to cost me good and proper." He grumbled. "Well, I'm not having it. I want to lodge a complaint!"

***

Adam agreed to visit the field with Rusby and arranged to follow the farmer in his old Land Rover, to the scene. Whilst driving the marked police car past St Augustine Church, Adam saw Father Fenton speaking to the two Armstrong brothers.

They were both holding shovels and towered

over the vicar who looked to be enraged about something and was giving the two men a piece of his mind. Still, thought Adam, it was good to see the two thugs being meaningfully employed in tidying up the old graves.

A couple of miles out of town, Adam followed Mr Rusby as he turned right down a narrow lane. Eventually, they came to a stop, and both men alighted from their vehicles. Adam immediately saw the damage in the wheat field to his right. A large swath of wheat, approximately twenty feet in width, was trampled flat in a long diagonal line across the field. Well, at least he wasn't being called to investigate a crop circle, he thought to himself with humour.

"See what I mean!" said the farmer. "If this is allowed to keep happening, I'll be out of business before you know it."

Adam took out his pocketbook and began taking some details. The crop had been seen intact around ten o'clock last night and had been found in its current state at five o'clock this morning.

Adam looked down the field following the trail of devastation.

Then he asked, "Where does that lead to?"

"Depends," said Rusby. There are more fields down that way, some mine, and some belonging to others. There are multiple ways in and out."

Adam was only slightly curious. There was little he could do in real terms, but whilst he was up here, he thought he might as well show some interest; perhaps he could get an idea of which direction the vandals had come from.

"Do you mind if I have a walk down there?" he asked.

"Not at all. If you stick to what's already been trampled, you can't cause any more damage. It's all been trodden into the dirt, and it's never coming back. Not this season."

Adam leapt over the drystone wall whilst the farmer asked if he could leave and get on with other work. There wasn't any point in the two of them walking down the wide corridor of flattened wheat, and Adam dismissed him and walked on. Adam allowed himself to unbutton his tunic whilst out of public view. The air was still warm and close, causing him to sweat, even though the sky was slate grey and heavy. *There's a storm coming.*

He was suddenly struck by this thought and by how those same words kept cropping up.

As he reached the bottom left corner of the wheat field, something glinting in the down-trodden wheat caught his eye, and for a brief moment, he was reminded of the pentagram necklace around Sophia's neck. He bent down and reached for the shining object.

Holding it up and inspecting it, he saw that it was a tiny silver horse trinket. No. On closer inspection, he noted the fine silver horn on the horse's head. It was a unicorn. Hadn't he seen something like this recently? He wasn't sure, but a tingle of nervous excitement ran up his spine.

Taking out his mobile phone, he called Angela back at the station and asked her to go to his office, as quickly as possible, and look in the brown folder regarding the missing girl.

He also asked her to take a snap of the photograph in the file that showed the silver charm anklet, then send the photo to his phone.

Adam waited for what seemed like hours before his phone finally pinged. Looking at the screen, he used his fingers to expand the photo until he could clearly see the charms on the ankle chain. The first charm was a leaf, and the second was a letter E. The next charm along was a heart, but then his eyes saw the fourth charm—and sure enough, this was a silver unicorn.

Adam rested the charm he had found on the phone screen, comparing it to the picture. It was identical, even down to the unicorn's tail where it appeared a tiny piece had broken away at some point. Adam's first reaction was to phone Chief Superintendent Winter and the major incident team and get them up there. But checking his watch, it was, ten a.m., and from experience, he knew they would still be in a briefing. He decided to give it another hour and then call.

Who knew, he might have discovered more evidence by then.

Adam marked the spot he had found the charm. Taking his white handkerchief out, he pinned it to the ground using a ballpoint pen. Then he walked on. In the bottom corner of the field, the trampled wheat came to an abrupt end and he was unsure which way to go. A broken-down wooden fence leading into a field of pastureland seemed to offer the route of least resistance. Though there were no obvious signs of disturbance in the field, it seemed to be the most obvious way for a group of people to have easily entered the wheat field. The other edge of the field was lined with bushes, trees, and dense undergrowth, not to mention a barbed-wire fence.

Adam was just about to head into the pastureland when he decided to make a cursory check of the barbed-wire fence. The top strand of wire seemed a little slack and bowed down slightly, as though some weight had been applied. Perhaps someone had climbed over, he thought, as the fence was old and rusty and had probably been straddled many times.

But then something caught Adam's eye, something small and dark attached to the top strand of wire. Adam walked over and inspected the appendage.

It was a piece of black material, approximately two inches long and roughly torn at the edges. Although he couldn't remember the exact details, he recalled that Elizabeth Short's clothing had been black. A short distance away from the material, Adam also noticed something else dark and coated on a section of the wire around a barb, if he wasn't mistaken it was dried blood.

Adam knew the correct thing to do was to stop and preserve the evidence at the scene until assistance arrived, but curiosity drove him onwards. Steadying himself, with his left hand on top of a fence post away from the evidence, Adam leapt over the barbed wire fence, pushing through the undergrowth and the bushes. Once on the other side of the planted boundary, Adam looked to the top of the field. There, he saw the unmistakable form of a small spire attached to what appeared to be a small chapel or church. Suddenly, the words of Katherine Dee echoed around his head. "Some religious connection. Something like a church or connected to a church."

Adam tried to get his bearings, but being new to the area, he wasn't sure exactly where he was. He knew the chapel must be near to the O'Neil estate if it wasn't, in fact, part of it.

Gingerly, Adam began walking up to the building that appeared to be stuck out in the middle of nowhere, standing in seclusion. As he walked, a few raindrops began to hit his head and shoulders. Adam kept both his eyes and his ears alert to any sight or sound that would indicate he was not alone. He circled the building but could see no one. Making his way to the front, Adam pushed gently on the large oak doors. To Adam's surprise, the door on the right swung open.

Just in time, he thought as the rain began to fall in earnest.

Inside the chapel looked pretty much like most old churches, but a little smaller. There was a central aisle with several rows of fixed wooden pews, and at the head of the aisle was an altar and a raised pulpit to the left-hand side. To the right was what appeared to be a stone christening font.

As silently as he could, Adam walked around the chapel but could see nothing unusual.

He checked the pulpit and around the font before stepping behind the altar and towards a large red velvet curtain that hung on the rear wall. Pulling the curtain to one side, Adam saw a small doorway leading to some stone steps. Adam made sure the curtain hung neatly behind him before he made his way down the steps to a large arch-topped oak door. Turning the iron ring handle, the door opened, and Adam stepped into what had once been a crypt.

The air was cooler in the crypt, but there was something else, something he couldn't quite put his finger on, a strange atmosphere.

It was heavy and menacing, something that told him he wasn't welcome here.

Adam saw a steel light switch mounted on the wall to his left and reaching over, he switched on the small wall lights that chased out some, but not all, of the darkness.

The crypt was still foreboding, and as his eyes became adjusted to the gloom and shadows, he could see a large stone table or altar in the centre with symbols of what he took to be black magic practice adorning the walls and floor all around it. At the far end at the top of several stone steps, was a large wooden chair reminiscent of a throne. There was another oak door too, to the left-hand side, and pushing through it, Adam found himself in a narrow stone corridor.

He followed the corridor, already illuminated by small wall lights, around to the left.

Then halfway along the next section, he discovered another room to the right.

The oak door was locked, but a huge metal key was in the lock which turned with surprising ease. The room, on the other side, was in darkness, but Adam located a light switch in the corridor outside. With the light on, he checked inside. At first sight, there was little to see, just four bare stone walls with no windows, a stone floor and a low arched ceiling. The room's only contents were a plastic bucket, a loo roll and the stump of a burnt-down candle in a holder.

It occurred to Adam that these items were the minimum requirements for someone held prisoner.

Adam stood in the centre of the room, turning slowly and looking for anything he might be missing. Then on the wall, to the right of the door, something caught his eye, scratched into the stone. Crouching, he read the graffiti.

MILLY CANARY HELP ME PLEASE

Adam recognised the name it was one of the girls who had been abducted in the city a few weeks earlier. Amelia Canary. Taking out his phone, he opened the camera app and focused on the scratched message. Adam was too busy trying to capture the best image he could, to notice the ever-so-gentle footsteps creeping up behind him.

As Adam plunged headlong into a swirling vortex of darkness, his last thought was of Sophia growing up without him.

***

Back in the graveyard at St Augustine's Church, the Armstrong brothers were neatly replacing the last shovels full of soil on an old grave that they had been tidying. According to the inscription on the headstone, Mary Barkley had died in 1912 and had been a loving wife and mother.

The two brothers stood back and admired their handiwork.

The headstone that had subsided a little at one side, was now standing straight and erect. The errant grass and weeds were all removed, and the soil freshly turned and set with bulbs and flowers.

The Armstrong brothers' appreciation of their own labours was interrupted by Father

Fenton, who hurried over to them with his phone still in his hand. He raised the phone for them both to see, intimating that he had received a call, and he spoke excitedly.

"I have just received word. There has been a development and your fat may just have been dragged from the fire."

The two large men looked at each other, and their dour expressions began taking on a more optimistic appearance.

Chapter 20

As the day wore on, the torrential rain that battered Penny-Deep was joined by high winds, and the dark clouds overhead became darker. Both of the on-duty constables at Penny-Deep were busily running around from one emergency call to the next.

The storm had brought about several road accidents and incidents of flooding in some low-lying areas, causing many vehicles to have to be abandoned. The public enquiry desk area at the police station was now crowded with people who were either stranded and seeking shelter or making reports of various catastrophes brought about by the storm.

At six p.m., Sergeant Pete Johnson started his shift along with two more constables to cover the evening period. The sergeant thought it best to keep the two morning officers on duty, working overtime, but when he asked Angela where the inspector was, so he could okay the overtime spend, she told him that no one knew the his whereabouts. In the back office, Angela told Pete Johnson about the inspector leaving the station that morning with the farmer, Mr Rusby, to inspect some damage in a field. That was a short time before nine-thirty a.m.

Angela went on to say that no one had heard

from him all day.

The last contact had been a phone call he had made to the front desk. He had phoned her and asked for images of a missing girl's ankle bracelet sending to his mobile phone. Angela checked the time of the call, and that was at nine-fifty-five a.m.

Pete Johnson grew more and more concerned, as Angela told him that she had tried to raise the inspector numerous times, both by radio and mobile phone.

Pete Johnson had taken an instant liking to the new inspector. He had heard all the glowing reports about him and his capability as both a detective and a leader. But the sergeant always preferred to go by his own observations and instincts, rather than the reports of others.

And in all his dealings with Adam Cadman, so far, his instincts told him that he was a good man and a keen, conscientious police officer. Going missing or remaining out of contact was not something he would intentionally do. The sergeant tried to think of all the logical possibilities but came up with none. Perhaps there had been a breakdown in communication or some misunderstanding, and Inspector Cadman was at home. Pete Johnson knew this was highly unlikely, but he decided to telephone the inspector's home, just on the off-chance, and check if he was there.

***

Mrs Chattox had taken Sophia over to the converted barn to await the return of her father. They had baked a large gooseberry pie together with fresh gooseberries from the garden and brought it over to enjoy after dinner. Tonight's main course was a lamb stew, already warming in the oven.

With the chores all done, Mrs Chattox and Sophia had flopped down on the sofa, watching some American comedy programme about a group of friends.

It was one of Sophia's favourite shows, and she enthusiastically informed an indifferent Mrs Chattox about the lives of the characters and who was going out with whom.

Despite Sophia's chatter, the elderly woman was struggling to keep her eyes open in the cosy warmth of the living room, following the activities of the day.

The sound of the phone came as a welcome distraction, and she sauntered over to where it stood on small side table to answer the call. Hopefully, it wasn't going to be Mr Cadman calling to say he was held up at work; the lamb stew was almost done.

Mrs Chattox didn't recognise the voice on the phone line and listened as he introduced himself as the sergeant from Penny-Deep Police Station.

When he asked for the inspector, she told him

that Mr Cadman hadn't arrived home yet, and if she could pass on a message when he did return. There was a pause, and then the sergeant asked if she had seen the inspector during the day at all or knew where he might be.

These questions concerned Mrs Chattox more than a little.

"I haven't seen him since he left for work this morning," she said. "I was expecting him home anytime now!"

Sergeant Pete Johnson detected the worry in Mrs Chattox' voice and said, "I'm so sorry to bother you and please don't worry. We are rushed off our feet down here with the storm. We are all working overtime and we'll all be late home! Also, the storm is affecting our communications."

He lied, however, not wanting to panic the elderly lady.

"We are having a hard time reaching anybody. He's probably tied up with some job or other. Please just ask him to call the station when he drops in."

The phone call ended, and Mrs Chattox walked over and flopped back down next to Sophia, telling her that her father would be late home because of the storm.

Sophia silently accepted what was said and carried on watching the programme.

But Mrs Chattox now had a very uneasy feeling. Her stomach was churning.

Back at Penny-Deep Police Station, Sergeant Johnson dug out the phone number for Mr Rusby. The phone took several rings, but it was finally answered. Mr Rusby sounded as if he had just been woken from a deep sleep, and the conversation was short and to the point.

The farmer stated that he had left the inspector in the field leading off Cross Lane and hadn't seen him again. When asked if he could still be there, the farmer answered categorically, "No!" He had driven down Cross Lane several hours ago, and the inspector's police car had gone.

The sergeant put down the phone just as a drenched and windswept PC Newman clattered through the front doors to announce that the river Lethe had burst its banks, and the ford was under several feet of water. Penny-Deep was totally cut off! As if the day hadn't already been bad enough.

By ten p.m., Mrs Chattox was growing increasingly anxious.

She had given Sophia her dinner by now, and stayed with her, watching TV.

Outside, the sky repeatedly cracked open with flashes of lightning, quickly followed by low and loud rumbles of thunder. The electrical storm sounded to be directly above Penny-Deep, and though Mrs Chattox listened intently, she could discern no sign that it was moving on.

Sophia had eaten her dinner and was now in

her dressing gown, ready for bed. Mrs Chattox could tell that Sophia was now starting to become worried too.

The little girl's face was flushed with anxiety, and she constantly walked to the window, looking out. But she said nothing, plainly keeping all her thoughts and anxieties to herself.

She was beginning to feel terrified, in fact, both by her father's failure to return home from work, and by the loud crashing of the thunderstorm that made her visibly flinch each time it shook the house. And to make matters worse, strong winds were now blowing the heavy rain horizontally, causing it to forcefully strike the windows and door like a constant spray of machine-gun bullets.

Twice, now, Mrs Chattox had called the police station to be told that Inspector Cadman was still out of contact. Each time, she made a follow-up call to Adam Cadman's mobile phone, only to reach his voicemail message. As calmly as she could, so as not to worry Sophia any more than necessary, Mrs Chattox sidled over towards the phone to check-in with the police station once again.

She was only a few feet away from the side table when lightning flashed so brightly through the sky, that it raised the illumination in the brightly lit living room, before disappearing again, taking the house lights and TV picture with it. Now in total darkness, Mrs Chattox fumbled until she found the phone, but on lifting the receiver to her ear, she heard no dial tone.

At that moment, there was a loud knock at the door, and before Mrs Chattox could stop her, Sophia excitedly shouted, "It's my dad!" Sophia ran over, unlocking the sturdy oak door in time for the lightning to flash overhead, showing two giants with broken noses and huge, bushy beards.

Sophia let out a scream and jumped back, but the two men came charging into the house.

The first man through the door grabbed Sophia by the arms. Mrs Chattox ran over, shouting at both men to leave the girl alone and to get out. But as she tried to intervene, the second giant lashed out, his flat hand hitting her across the face, sending her sprawling to the floor.

Sophia managed to break free and ran, crouching over the elderly woman, but Mrs Chattox didn't move. Suddenly, two powerful arms grabbed Sophia, almost squeezing the life from her tiny body, lifting her into the air and carrying her outside, screaming.

Outside, in the farmyard, Sophia saw a large black Range Rover to which the giant was carrying her. Her young mind tried to make sense of what was happening, but she couldn't.

She only knew these two monsters meant her harm, and she saw what they had done to Mrs Chattox, but why? Sophia was terrified. If only her father were here, she thought.

Where was he?

Had these two monsters hurt her father like they had hurt Mrs Chattox?

Though very much in the grip of terror, these thoughts made Sophia angry and blind with rage. Both her arms were pinned in a vice-like grip, and her continual kicking and screaming were doing no good, but as they reached the Range Rover, Sophia tilted her head forward, and without thinking, clamped her teeth either side of the giant's broken nose and bit down as hard as she could.

Corrigan Armstrong was a brute who had experienced more than a little pain in his time.

He had fought all who dared stand before him, including his brother, and had brushed off all the hurt and damage ever inflicted on him. But at that moment, Corrigan Armstrong thought he had been struck by the same lightning that flashed above. Indeed, it felt like millions of volts of electricity had shot through his face and into his head.

The world began to spin a little faster on its axis and his legs buckled under him.

Instinctively, Corrigan reached his arms out to steady himself against the Range Rover, and in doing so, dropped Sophia. She hit the ground running. She wanted to get back to Mrs Chattox and lock the door of her home on these men, but the second giant blocked her path to the front door, so she just ran. Once across the yard, she turned right on the track, hoping that if she could get to the dark woods, she could hide from the two monsters. But after running only fifty feet up the path, Clancy Armstrong was right behind her, his bloodstained brother also catching up.

Sophia was about to scream when something loomed up from the track in front of her. She stopped running and stood perfectly still, as did the two Armstrong brothers.

For a moment, all three had trouble trying to work out what stood before them.

It was tall and thin and glistened in the rain.

Dressed all in black, the head of the thing tilted backwards, causing the long black hair that hung lank in the rain to part, and Sophia saw the face of Katherine Dee.

"Come to me, Sophia," she said, and Sophia ran to her side and felt an arm wrap around her shoulders. The two brutes began to advance, and Clancy Armstrong said, “Give her here, witch, and we'll not hurt you."

"I'm in the mood to kill both of em," snarled Corrigan through the blood streaming over his lower face.

"That's not going to happen," said Katherine Dee with a confidence that made the two large men falter a little. "Leave now, and I will have no reason to harm you," Katherine Dee continued, holding both brutes in a fixed stare with her large, dark eyes.

Sophia watched as her protector reached out her right arm, pointing her finger to the ground. Then she turned as if drawing an imaginary circle around Sophia and herself, whilst speaking in a strange language. Both men immediately jumped back as if something had frightened them.

But, for the life of her, Sophia couldn't see what it could be.

The two brothers watched as the flames burned high and fierce, forming a circle that surrounded the girl and the witch. The brothers could feel the intensity of the heat, and both looked on incredulously at how the occupants of the circle could tolerate it.

Corrigan Armstrong pushed by his brother.

He knew only too well what fate would befall them both if they did not return with the girl.

If a woman and a young girl could survive the flames, then so could he.

Reaching out, he moved towards the ring of fire, intending to grab the girl and drag her out. If the brat got a little singed, then so be it, he reasoned. But as soon as he was in reach, the right sleeve of his jacket erupted with flames, causing him to scream out and jump back, colliding with his brother Clancy. The contact spread the fire from one brother to the other. Now both were alight. Both men scrambled out of their burning jackets, but still, their bodies were alight.

Sophia watched the giants hop up and down, screaming and patting themselves down. Still, she could see no apparent cause or reason for their actions as she stood with Katherine Dee on the dark track. If she hadn't been so terrified by the two men and afraid of what they might have done to her father, she would have found their behaviour hilarious. Especially as they now threw themselves on the muddy ground and rolled around, begging Katherine Dee to make it stop.

Katherine Dee finally spoke. "Only lying in water will put out the flames."

Both men jumped to their feet and began running down the track, careering wildly from side to side. They continued to scream and ran straight past the farmyard, down towards the main road to Penny-Deep, not even bothering to try and take the Range Rover in which they had arrived.

Katherine Dee looked down at Sophia and smiled. "Are you alright, Sophia?" she asked.

Sophia nodded, then she remembered Mrs Chattox.

She told Katherine what had happened, and they walked quickly down to the house.

The front door was still wide open and inside, Mrs Chattox still lay on the floor, although she had started to stir and move a little. Katherine Dee crouched down and held her in her arms.

The elderly woman then yelled out, "The

girl!"

"It's alright, Sophia is safe. She is here with me. I will look after her."

Mr Chattox visibly relaxed and Katherine Dee helped her to her feet. The old woman had a nasty cut and swollen welt to the right side of her face, and Katherine examined her carefully while Mrs Chattox told her about the disappearance of Sophia's father.

Completing her examination of Mrs Chattox, Katherine Dee said, "Nothing serious. Nothing that won't mend. Now, you know what to put on this?"

Mrs Chattox nodded. Then Katherine said, "I must go and take Sophia to where I can best protect her. Will you be alright?"

Mrs Chattox replied, "Go! Just look after Sophia."

Katherine Dee took Sophia back outside into the wind and rain.

As the lightning lit the yard, something white and large shot up into sight. Sophia almost screamed but realised, in time, that it was Ruby the horse, rearing up on her hind legs.

As the thunder clapped, the horse walked calmly over to them, and Katherine picked Sophia up and placed her on the bare back of the white mare. Katherine Dee then hitched up the soaking, long black dress that she was wearing, and stepped up onto the drystone wall at the front of the house, before also climbing onto the horse's back. She sat behind Sophia and held her tight.

Ruby galloped out of the farmyard and turned right, up the track, eventually running through the dark woods where she instinctively cut a path through the trees till they came to the clearing where Katherine Dee's house stood. Katherine jumped down, and Sophia watched as she turned to the woods and—raising both arms out wide—she once again began to speak in a strange language.

Nothing seemed to be happening, but Katherine continued to speak, before turning back to Ruby and leading her over to the house. "Come with me," Katherine Dee said, lifting Sophia down to the ground. Katherine Dee then led the way into the large stone house.

Sophia stood at the gate, not moving, but then a gentle push to her backside came from the soft muzzle of Ruby, and Sophia followed Katherine Dee into the house.

By the time Sophia entered the living area, Katherine Dee was just returning from another room somewhere in the property. She handed Sophia a large towel and a big black wool jumper and tee-shirt. She told the wet and shivering little girl to dry off and change into the dry clothes, pointing her to a cloakroom off the kitchen.

Then taking advantage of Sophia being out of the room, Katherine telephoned Penny-Deep Police Station and asked for Inspector Cadman.

The officer on the phone sounded harassed—and too young to be doing the job.

When Katherine told him she was a neighbour and looking after the inspector's daughter, the officer confided that the inspector had been missing since early that morning and officers were out searching for him, the best they could, in the storm.

Still, they were by now very concerned for his welfare.

Katherine Dee put down the phone.

She too was now worried about the police inspector's safety and tried to think of all the possible places he could be. She could try and locate him psychically, but if he were being held in the same place as the missing girls, then she wouldn't be able to break through the magical obfuscation.

Just then, Sophia returned to the living room. The black tee-shirt and jumper were far too large for her small frame. They fit her like a below-the-knee dress, but at least she was warm and dry, and now Katherine Dee had to ensure the little girl's safety while she also attended to urgent matters.

When she'd had the house rebuilt, Katherine Dee had taken the opportunity to have one or two small additions put in. Walking over to the bookcase, Katherine reached behind the beading on one of the shelves, releasing a catch that caused a section of the bookcase to open like a door.

She reached inside the tiny room and turned on a small light.

"Here, Sophia. I need you to hide in this secret room, just for a short while," she said.

Sophia looked inside.

The room was tiny, with just enough room for a single bed that fit snugly end to end a few feet back from the door. As Sophia was stepping inside, Katherine Dee stopped her and felt around her neck, checking. “Sophia!” she said. Where is the pendant I gave you?”

Sophia suddenly felt embarrassed and ashamed. “My dad took it from me. He didn’t like me wearing it.” She looked crestfallen, as if she was about to cry.

"Don't worry about that, Sophia, it's okay. But tell me what did your father do with the pendant when he took it from you?"

Katherine Dee silently hoped for luck. Sophia had to think back, trying to remember the events of that morning. "Well, he took it from me this morning and put it in his shirt pocket before he left for work. He said he would speak to you about it later."

Katherine Dee crouched down and looked Sophia directly in the eyes. "This is very important, Sophia. Do you think your father will still have the pendant in his shirt pocket?"

"I think so," said Sophia, a little baffled about the sudden interest in the pendant, at what seemed like a time when other matters were far more important.

Katherine Dee ushered the young girl into the secret room.

"There is a handle here, Sophia, that will open the door from the inside. But under no circumstance open it unless I tell you to. Do you understand?"

Sophia nodded, fully aware that she may face more danger. Then she asked sheepishly if Katherine was going to leave her alone.

"I have things I must do, Sophia, but don't worry. You won't be alone. You'll be with a friend."

Just then, the huge black mastiff trotted into the small room, and as Sophia sat on the bed, the hound sat on the floor beside her. "I must go, Sophia. Don't be afraid. Fancy will protect you," Katherine said, and with that, she closed the door in the bookcase.

Katherine turned out all the lights in her home. She gave a cursory glance at the bookcase to check for any signs of light escaping and giving away the location of the secret room. There was no light, and Katherine, still in her soaking, long black dress, sat cross-legged on the floor and closed her eyes. The pendant she had given little Sophia possessed an energetic charge that would make it glow like a psychic beacon, showing its location, even in places protected by obfuscation spells.

Katherine had given the pendant to Sophia for her own peace of mind, just in case the unthinkable happened and Sophia ended up being taken. If her father still had the pendant in his shirt pocket, it would be the best—and possibly only—way of locating him.

***

Father Akers paced nervously up and down the aisle of St Augustine's. Taking out his mobile phone, he tried calling Corrigan Armstrong but the call cut to Corrigan's voicemail.

Akers cursed the two brothers; they should have collected him by now, en route to O'Neil's estate. The girl they had been sent to capture was only eight years old, and in the care of an old woman. What could possibly go wrong?

Just then, the side door of the nave sprang open, and an elderly man, whom Akers recognised but whose name he couldn't recollect, stepped inside.

The man was soaking wet but seemed in good spirits as he shouted over to the vicar.

"Here, Father! Those two brothers you have to do work for you! They're causing a right ruckus out in front of the Blacksmith's Arms."

Now, what have those two stupid lummoxes done? thought Akers, ignoring the man and marching angrily out of the church and towards the public house.

Despite the howling wind and lashing rain, a

small group of people had gathered in front of the Blacksmith's Arms, and as Akers drew near, he could see the two Armstrong brothers thrashing about, screaming and shouting, immersed in the water in the large stone horse trough.

Striding directly up to Corrigan Armstrong, Akers grabbed the large head by its ears and pulled him close so no one else could hear. "What the hell are you two idiots doing? Where's the girl?"

"What do you mean, what are we doing?" spluttered Corrigan. "You can see what we're doing! We're trying to put out the flames. That witch Katherine Dee set us on fire and she's taken the girl."

Akers flung Corrigan's head backwards, causing it to splash down under the water.

As he began to march back to the church, Akers called out to the assembled onlookers.

"It's alright, folks! They're either drunk or on drugs. I'll call the police."

Once back at St Augustine's, Akers took out his mobile phone and made a call, but it wasn't to the police. The first was to Archibald O'Neil.

Chapter 21

The twelve important guests had been arriving at the O'Neil estate in ones and twos throughout the day. Each had a room designated to them by Carfax, so on arrival, each one had made their way directly to their quarters to freshen up and change. By early evening, all twelve guests had made their way down to one of the main reception rooms, wearing their ceremonial gowns and mingling with a crowd of other guests similarly attired.

Soft drinks and nibbles were served, but it was understood by all present that no alcohol would be consumed until after the completion of the ceremony at midnight. It was vital for their success that everyone would keep a clear and focused mind. Even ex-inspector Brian Winter, who was not a part of the 'twelve', and therefore not taking part in the ceremony, refrained from alcohol.

Archibald O'Neil enjoyed playing the bon viveur, particularly to such distinguished and eminent guests. He mingled amongst them, making time to chat to each, except for Brian Winter, of course.

O'Neil eyed Winter, studying him, and his 'fish out of water' demeanour. Winter had only really been of any use to him as the local police inspector. But now Winter had been forced to retire, O'Neil was unsure what to do with such a sycophant. True, he had been useful when trying to divert attention by trimming the new inspector's home with a dead crow and occult paraphernalia, as well as maligning Katherine Dee. But one thing was clear: Winter knew too much, and when the time came to cut ties, the threat would probably have to be eliminated. Permanently!

However, now was not the time, O'Neil comforted himself.

There was no rush, no need for a rash decision just yet; he should concentrate on the ceremony and then enjoy the meal and festivities that always followed such events.

Two of O'Neil's guests casually walked over to him, one male, one female, and both members of the 'twelve'. They were both powerful individuals in their own right; both were enormously wealthy and came from well-connected and extremely influential families. The man spoke.

"We understand there has been a complication with tonight's offering."

The man spoke softly, but with an unmistakable intensity in his tone.

O'Neil was keen to allay their concerns.

"We indeed had a little drama, but that has all been sorted out. Actually, I think the loss was fated as a great blessing. Because with the loss arrived great fortuity. We have come by another offering, very young and very innocent, and the power we release will be unbridled."

"How young?" said the man.

"I'm told she is eight years old."

The woman licked her lips.

Then both the man and woman walked away to chat with other guests.

O'Neil stood alone, watching his guests, pleased with how he had finessed the man and woman who had shown concern about the night's offering. They didn't show it outwardly, but O'Neil knew he had impressed them, and his stock was definitely on the rise with these people. They listened to him now and respected him. He was becoming one of them, and after tonight, he would join them in another way, by becoming one of the richest men in Britain, if not the world.

Could the night get any better? He seriously doubted it.

Just then, Carfax tugged at the sleeve of his gown. O'Neil looked at her with annoyance.

"What is the problem, woman?" he snapped.

"There's a phone call for you in the study," Carfax said, red-faced and flustered.

"Well, tell them I'm busy and take their details. I'll call them back when I'm good and ready."

"No, "said Carfax. "It's a call you really need to take now."

O'Neil really couldn't imagine what could be so critical, but whatever it was, he could tell it was worrying Carfax.

Stepping into his office, O'Neil closed the doors behind himself and walked over to the phone, the receiver of which was lying on his desk.

"O'Neil here!" he said.

"We've got a problem. The girl's got away!"

O'Neil recognised the voice. It was Akers.

"What do you mean, the girl's got away? She's eight years old, and you sent those two gorillas after her. I'm pretty sure we held the advantage unless there was going to be an IQ test," spat O'Neil contemptuously.

"Well, it's the Dee woman," said Akers. "She's gone and got herself involved. Corrigan Armstrong's saying Katherine Dee has taken the girl."

O'Neil couldn't believe his ears; just like that, his perfect night was being ruined and his rightful destiny snatched from his hands.

"What do you want me to do?" asked Akers.

"Just get yourself up here. You can help Carfax with the final preparations as usual, while I get the girl."

O'Neil slammed down the telephone receiver.

"Idiots!" he hissed. O'Neil stood, trying to think about what to do as the phone rang again.

He was going to ignore it, but then hoped beyond hope that it was going to be good news.

Perhaps they had managed to get the girl back. He grabbed the phone.

"O'Neil."

"Hello, Archie boy! Charles Dutton here."

Just when O'Neil thought his luck had plunged as low as it could go, he felt the ground crack beneath his feet. "I've just received information that you've gone ahead with that highly risky investment strategy," said Dutton.

"That's correct, Charles; keep your fingers crossed for me, won't you," O'Neil replied, trying his best to sound upbeat and confident, at the same time wondering where Dutton got his information.

"Oh, I will, Archie. I wish you all the luck in the world with this one. I was merely curious as to how you still managed to go ahead with the scheme, seeing as I instructed you to remove my portfolio from the pot." Then he asked, "You *have* removed my stock and made sure that it is perfectly safe, haven't you, Archie?"

What exactly did Dutton know, thought O'Neil? Could he still bluff him?

"Oh, don't worry," said O'Neil in full bluster. "Yes, your portfolio was removed from the pot. Your stock is perfectly safe. Of course, it was a tremendous blow to us, you pulling out like that, but fortunately, we had no end of investors wanting to fill your seat. So you see, we were able to go ahead without you," O'Neil lied.

"That's good to know, Archie. I apologise if I'm

becoming a little paranoid in my old age. Fifty million is a large sum of money, and I'd hate to think about what I would do to anyone who parted me from it, especially if they did so by doing something stupid. But then, that might be a good mental exercise for me to wrap my brain around."

Dutton paused, the silence thick with menace.

"You know, just hypothetically, like." Another pause. Then, "I tell you what, Archie. If I come up with any ideas around the matter, I'll tell you on Wednesday when I pop around to sign my stock over. Bye, Archie."

Dutton terminated the call, but O'Neil stood motionless, the phone receiver still to his ear.

Archie O'Neil was afraid.

He was worried he'd let down the powerful people in the other room, the ones he admired and with whom he wanted to be associated. If this all went wrong, those people would laugh and pour scorn on him. He would forever be shunned from their orbit. O'Neil was afraid that if everything went wrong tonight, he would lose his wealth and position. But worse still, he was terrified at the thought of what Dutton would do to him if everything went pear-shaped.

O'Neil slammed the handset back onto the phone cradle. He couldn't allow tonight to fail; he needed that girl. She was to be the offering that would make his dreams come true. Damn that Katherine Dee woman!

If she insisted on interfering with his plans, she would get what was coming to her.

Archie O'Neil marched over to the doors of his study and flung them wide open, clapping his hands loudly.

"Ladies and gentlemen," he shouted. "Before tonight's offering, I have arranged a little sport just to get us in the mood!"

Chapter 22

Adam Cadman stirred on the ground, his mind desperately trying to make sense of what had happened. His last memory was that of a sweet, chemical smell.

Chloroform! He was examining a scratched message on the wall when someone had crept up behind him and put him out with a cloth soaked in the stuff.

Adam could see from the flickering candle-light that he was in the same room, but as he dragged himself to his feet, he saw the large oak door was closed. He tried the handle, pulling with all the strength he had, but still the wretched door wouldn't budge. He heard a shuffle and a creak outside in the corridor, and knew someone was on the other side of the door.

Adam shouted to whoever it was, but they ignored him.

Realising the futility of calling to be let out —which would only burn up all his energy and mark him out as a troublemaker they might just want to get rid of—Adam stopped and began taking stock of his predicament. He was still dressed in his police uniform, but his radio and mobile phone had been taken. So too had his keys, including the one to the police car he'd been driving.

He wondered how long he had been unconscious, but a check of the time was impossible, as his Omega wristwatch had also gone.

Adam sat on the ground, thinking. Surely, someone at the station would have realised he was missing by now. They must have been looking for him.

Suddenly, there was a low rumbling sound and Adam's muscles tensed in readiness, before realising that the noise came from outside and was the sound of thunder. He knew his current situation was useless, and that it was pointless wasting his energy. So he sat back, resting against the cold stone wall, eyes closed and waiting for an opportunity to escape to present itself.

***

Back at Penny-Deep Police Station, Sergeant Pete Johnson had informed headquarters about the inspector's disappearance and asked for a trace to be put on both his mobile phone and radio. The call eventually came back to report that neither the radio nor the phone was responding, and while there was a faint chance that this could be down to the thunderstorm, it could equally be a terrible sign that the devices had been either broken or destroyed. The last call made on the mobile had been triangulated and was roughly in the location of the inspector's last-known whereabouts.

Officers had thoroughly searched this area, and neither the inspector nor his patrol car was anywhere to be found. The officers had even crossed the fields right onto the O'Neil estate, where they spoke to the estate foreman Maltravers, carrying out minor repairs at the old chapel. Maltravers stated that he had been there all day, from early morning, and that he had unfortunately seen no one.

The sergeant went into the back office and stirred the three officers who were partaking in a hot pot of tea and a bite to eat. All three were already soaked to the skin and exhausted, but none seemed to mind. They were far too worried about the inspector. But before the sergeant could give them new search instructions, the patrol room phone rang and Pete Johnson answered it.

It was Father Akers from St Augustine's, reporting the two Armstrong brothers thrashing around in the stone water trough in front of the Blacksmith's Arms pub. He said that they appeared to be high on drugs or something when he spoke to them, and he was worried they might drown themselves. Pete Johnson thanked the caller for the intel but it looked as though the continued search for the inspector would have to be put on hold. The Armstrong brothers were always a handful. The sergeant told one of the officers to get the police van. Surely, three officers and a sergeant would be able to cope with the Armstrongs. Hopefully!

***

At first, Adam Cadman thought he imagined the sound, but it came again and again, each time slightly louder, more piercing. It sounded like a scurrying, a rustling across the floor in the far corner of the room. He opened his eyes, peering into the shadows cast by the last vestiges of the flickering candle. At first glance, the darkness in the far corner seemed to move, and Adam dismissed it as a trick of the candlelight. He closed his eyes, but once again, he was disturbed by the rustling. Adam's eyes sprang open, and this time, Adam was sure something was moving in the shadows. He watched as the dark shape emerged from the blackness into the dim light of the candle.

Whatever it was seemed tall and slender, with what appeared to be a pale face curtained by long black hair. At first, he thought it was Katherine Dee! He was sure it was her, but as the figure glided ever closer, he noticed the candlelight was still visible through the spectral image —and the face, what little he could see, was lacking any discernible features.

Adam felt a cold shiver run down his spine.

He was a man whose courage had been tested many times, but now he sat still and unnerved, watching the strange apparition glide over to the oak door, before passing straight through it. Adam jumped to his feet and pressed against the door that was still solidly locked. Next, he grabbed the candle and inspected the dark shadowy corner of the room, from which the figure had emerged. But there was nothing there except the cold stone walls, and they were hard and unyielding to his touch.

Maltravers, the O'Neil estate foreman, was sitting on a hard straight-backed chair in the corridor. He had been there for what seemed like an age. The copper could never get out of the storeroom, as the door was too solid and securely locked. But after finding and subduing the policeman, Maltravers had been ordered to guard him. So far, his only entertainment had been telling the police search party that he hadn't seen their precious inspector.

Besides, he was only supposed to be guarding the police inspector for a while, just until those two thugs, the Armstrong brothers, returned with the policeman's daughter. Then they were to take care of the inspector and dispose of whatever was left.

The light in the corridor was dim, and the constant strain on Maltravers' eyes made them feel heavy, gritty, and sore. Trying the best he could to get comfortable on the hard chair, he allowed his head to loll back, and let his eyes close just a little, to rest them.

The voice was soft and playful, telling Maltravers how hard he had been working and how tired he must be. Was he too tired to indulge in some pleasure? The voice now became flirtatious. The woman before him was incredibly beautiful. Really, he knew he should have been alarmed by her presence, but she laughed and teased him some more, telling him not to spoil their fun.

It would be their secret; no one would know! He could have her right here, right now. She held out her arms and stepped backwards into the storeroom. Maltravers left his seat and followed, but then something got in his way. He stood momentarily while the voice playfully told him how cold she was now she was naked. The soft voice told him to unlock the door and hurry to her, to take her, right here and right now before their chance was gone.

Maltravers unlocked the door and was about to step in and embrace this seductress when he suddenly awoke. Had he been dreaming? Where was the beautiful, naked woman?

Adam Cadman's fist hit Maltravers squarely on the chin, sending him crashing back against the wooden chair that smashed into kindling. The estate foreman lay prostrate on his back, unconscious, and Adam knew he wouldn't be any further problem for quite some time.

He checked the man's clothing for his possessions but found only his Omega watch, which he took back. Annoyingly, Maltravers didn't even have a phone of his own about him, so Adam left him sprawled on the ground. Once out of the chapel, Adam decided not to take the route back across the fields where he had left the police car. Instead, he followed the well-trodden meadow path up the hill until he eventually saw the large O'Neil manor house.

At the rear of the manor house was a garage block with one of the doors standing wide open. Adam checked inside and saw several vehicles, but there were no keys for any of them.

Keeping close to the tree line, Adam edged up to the main house, arriving just in time to see a large crowd of people dressed in what seemed to be ceremonial cloaks and hoods, bursting out of the front of the house and running to several parked cars.

Archie O'Neil's voice bellowed out over the ensuing racket, shouting, "Follow me!"

Archibald O'Neil climbed into his silver-coloured Rolls Royce and drove off at speed, followed by numerous other cars that had been parked at the front of the manor house.

After the last vehicle had disappeared up the long driveway, Adam tentatively made his way to the front of the house. The main doors were open, and he stopped and listened but couldn't hear any signs of life. As quickly and as quietly as Adam could, he made his way inside to find a telephone and contact the station. Adam looked around the large hallway, and there, on an antique side table, he spotted what he was looking for. The phone rang a couple of times before Angela answered it.

As soon as she heard his voice, she blurted out, almost in tears, "Inspector! Thank God. We have been worried stiff about you."

"Angela. I'm okay as you can hear but send two officers immediately to the O'Neil Manor house. Right now. I've been held prisoner but managed to escape."

Adam would dearly have liked to surround the place, but Penny-Deep had limited police resources and the storm would, no doubt, be keeping many of his team tied up with other emergencies. Adam heard a noise behind him, turning in time to see Father Fenton Akers walk in through the front doors. The vicar looked bemused, and said, "Inspector, is Mr O'Neil about?"

Adam put down the phone and stepped closer to the vicar, wondering what he was doing there.

"He left a short time ago. Can I ask why you want to see him?"

"Oh, by all means. I have been in talks with Mr O'Neil about making a sizeable donation to St Augustine's Church, for the usual upkeep and repairs. He invited me over to collect a cheque. I'm sure he said to come tonight as he was having a bit of a party.

The vicar smiled and added, " Between you and me, I think our Mr O'Neil likes a crowd, to make sure his philanthropic endeavours don't go unnoticed."

Adam was just beginning to relax again when a shrill scream cut through the air behind him. Suddenly, someone hit him from behind, and through the large hall mirror, he saw that Ms Carfax had jumped on his back, wailing like a banshee and trying to scratch his eyes out.

Adam grabbed both of the woman's wrists and pulled her nails away from his face.

He turned to the vicar for assistance, but then he saw the vicar had removed a long thin dagger from beneath his topcoat, and was running towards him, thrusting the blade at his chest.

Without thinking, Adam twisted his body away to avoid the knife.

There was a thud, and suddenly, Ms Carfax stopped screaming and slipped heavily from his back, down to the ground, a dagger handle sticking out between her shoulder blades. Adam saw it, recoiling in horror. From the blank look on her face, Adam knew Carfax was dead.

Yet there was no time or opportunity for sentiment.

The vicar was red with rage, but as Adam took a step towards him, he turned and ran through the front doors. Adam ran after him, but the Akers managed to get to the vicar's car and lock the doors before he could catch up.

The vicar just turned and smiled at Adam, before putting the car in gear and thrusting his foot down on the accelerator pedal. Adam watched Akers disappear down the drive of the estate.

The sound of a police siren arrived only a short time before the police car itself; such was the speed at which it was being driven. Adam, who had been sitting on the front steps of the manor house, jumped to his feet. He ran over to greet the two constables, and told them about the body in the hall, giving a brief explanation of what had happened. PC Foster seemed particularly shocked and commented, “Father Akers! Well, I never! He’s the one who married the wife and me!"

Adam ordered the officers to seal off the house, as it was now a crime scene.

PC Barden quickly filled Adam in on what had been happening back at Penny-Deep and how they were cut off, with resources stretched to the limit due to the storm.

"Right then. I'll go get Akers!" said Adam, and with that, he took the officer’s patrol car keys and one of their radios.

***

Mrs Chattox kept her house in darkness. She was expecting unwanted visitors, and sure enough, they arrived. As she peered through the net curtains of her home, she saw Archie O'Neil drive into the farmyard in his silver Rolls Royce, followed by six other vehicles.

The farmyard was now swarming with people, and she heard O'Neil address them.

"The girl we seek has been taken. The men I

sent to collect her have told brother Akers that Ms Dee took her. In fact, my men saw Katherine Dee and the girl heading in the direction of Dee's home. I know the name Katherine Dee will be familiar with many of you, but worry not, we are many, and she is but one."

Mrs Chattox didn't like what she was hearing.

She liked it even less when O'Neil announced, "Now follow me! We'll walk up to Katherine Dee's house, kill us a witch and take the girl!"

The crowd gave up a cheer and followed O'Neil out of the farmyard.

They followed O'Neil up the track towards the dark woods.

Mrs Chattox knew better than to call Katherine Dee and warn her. She would already know they were coming for her and Sophia, and she would be busy preparing for them.

Chapter 23

Fenton Akers fumbled with the combination dial on the safe in the church vestry, then held his breath as he tried the handle. The combination lock had always seemed temperamental to him, and he couldn't afford the time if it wanted to mess him about now.

The safe door opened and Akers breathed a sigh of relief. Taking the large strong-box from the safe floor, he placed it on the carpet and, with the key from his shirt pocket, he unlocked it and began lifting out the cash which he placed in the large holdall by his side.

Then Akers took out a passport from the top shelf which he pushed inside jacket pocket. Reaching into the safe one last time, his groping right hand finally found what it was searching for under the top of the safe, and he pulled hard against the sticking tapes holding it in place.

The revolver came free, and after removing several redundant strands of tape, Akers opened the chamber to check it had a full complement of bullets.

That done, he stashed the gun in the right-hand pocket of his coat.

Akers' mind had been racing ever since he had left the manor house. He knew that he had to get away from Penny-Deep as soon as possible, and then he could arrange to slip out of the country.

Akers walked through the church nave and back out into the storm.

The wind and rain almost bowling his slight frame over, he walked as quickly as he could towards the shadows of the lychgate. Akers had decided he would walk, sticking to the back streets and leaving his car until he could find one to steal. No doubt the description of his vehicle would have been passed out by the police in connection with the murder of Carfax.

Reaching the lychgate, Akers began walking through the dark, roofed structure when a voice from the shadows caught him by surprise, making him jump. "Going somewhere, Father?"

A bolt of lightning pierced the night sky, lighting up the interior of the lychgate, and, in that momentary revelation, Akers saw the face of Adam Cadman.

Akers panicked and swung the holdall into the police inspector's face. The weight of the bag crashed against Adam's head as the thunder rumbled angrily above, knocking him backwards.

As the bag fell to the ground, Adam saw Akers running off across the front of the church.

The police inspector gave chase. Turning right, past the front of the church tower, Adam expected to see Akers a short distance ahead, but the man had disappeared.

Calculating that Akers couldn't have gone far in the seconds he was out of sight, Adam began checking around the graveyard, carefully looking around the nearest headstones.

Minutes passed, but Adam just couldn't find the man.

He was retracing his steps, about to give up when he noticed a tall, narrow wooden door on the side of the clock tower.

It was only a couple of feet in width, and when he pushed it, the door gave way and opened.

Inside was a set of steep stone steps equally as narrow as the door and spiralling up towards the top of the church tower. The stairway was so tight that Adam had to turn his body sideways to climb it. He didn't have a torch or his phone to help guide him in the pitch darkness. Instead, he reached his left hand down to touch the cold, worn stone steps and steadily felt his way ahead.

It was difficult for Adam to work out how far he had climbed on the continually spiralling stairway. But eventually, he saw a beam of light that shone from below a wooden door.

Pushing the door gently, Adam found himself in a large wooden box of a room, a number of thick and aged ropes draping from the ceiling and attached to the wall.

It was obviously where the St Augustine bell ringers came to do their thing, Adam noted.

Outside, the thunder crashed once again while Adam looked around. To his right, he noticed another small wooden door, and passing through, he stepped into a short stone corridor housing the workings of the church clock. Following the passage, Adam turned into an open space that appeared to be another room, but as the lightning flickered through the old and broken wooden shutters on the bell tower windows, Adam had a brief view of a long drop below him. Just above, he saw the large church bells, and to his left was what passed as another flight of stairs.

This stairway, however, consisted only of large stones jutting out from the wall.

These stone steps were severely worn, with no backs or risers and no handrail.

To climb the steps would be tricky and dangerous in daylight, but to climb them in the dark would be foolhardy. Besides which, Adam had seen no sign that Akers had passed that way, so he turned and began to walk back towards the bell ringers' room.

But then he heard something, a noise above him.

Adam stopped and listened but heard nothing more. He was starting to think he had imagined the noise when he heard it again. It was faint against the sound of the storm, but now he was sure he could hear footsteps, someone walking around above him.

***

The followers of Archie O'Neil fanned out as

they entered the dark woods. The trees were whipped around wildly by the storm, but still, the group pressed onwards through the thicket and undergrowth. Though the thunder clapped and shouted its protest through the trees, the lightning barely managed to shine through the dense foliage. But O'Neil and the crowd accompanying him all carried flashlights of various descriptions. O'Neil himself had a large handheld Dragon T12 searchlight producing 200,000 candlepower, and the beam from that lamp alone was sufficient to illuminate the woods for several hundred yards. O'Neil and the others had clawed their way through the unforgiving undergrowth for what seemed like hours, when O'Neil's lamp picked out the figure of Katherine Dee standing before a large oak tree. She stood slim and shapely in a long black dress. The rain had slicked down her long black hair that cascaded past her shoulders.

O'Neil and the others stopped a distance of thirty feet away from the solitary young woman. O'Neil licked his lips. He had heard all about Katherine Dee, and knew he was going to have a reckoning with her. She didn't seem all that powerful now, standing out there, all alone.

"Where's the girl!" shouted O'Neil. "Give her to us."

Katherine Dee crossed her arms over her chest, placing her hands on top of her shoulders.

Then standing firm, she began to speak, her

voice deep and guttural and so unnaturally powerful, it immediately unnerved several of O'Neil's weaker followers.

"The girl is under my protection. Leave this place or suffer the consequences."

O'Neil smiled a sadistic smile and yelled, "Take her."

There was a moment of hesitation, and this time it was Katherine Dee who smiled. But O'Neil barked the command again, and eventually, four individuals cut ranks and moved towards the lone figure. The two women and two men marched straight towards Katherine Dee but, as O'Neil and the others watched, Katherine seemed to fall apart somehow. Her entire body collapsed into a large black mass that shot forward. Through the powerful torchlight, they saw the black shape was, in fact, a flock of large black ravens that attacked the four individuals who were the closest, scratching and pecking at their faces and heads. The group of four flailed their arms around to ward off the birds while trying to run back to the rest of the group. But eventually, all four succumbed to the relentless attack and fell to the ground, their hands and faces badly cut and bleeding.

"Leave them!" shouted O'Neil as he waved the other followers onward.

O'Neil did a quick headcount, determining that he had enough people with him to do what needed doing. He made sure the members of 'the twelve' held back and didn't get too involved. He couldn't afford to let any of them become incapacitated before the ceremony, and there was a sufficient number of ancillary followers to tackle Katherine Dee.

Onward they crashed, through woodland.

Parts of the undergrowth were too dense to pass, and the group split into ones and twos as they tried to negotiate paths of least resistance. Two of the women began to panic as they found themselves alone, but then felt relief as they re-united with three of the men. "This way!" said one of the men, pointing to a clearing ahead. The five made for the patch of short open grass extending only a short distance beyond. All four were relieved to be out of the thick under-growth that scratched and pulled at their legs. The ground here felt soft, like walking on a cush-ion. There was a comforting warmth too, that seemed to rise around their legs, giving them a strange but pleasant experience. They waded on as the warmth seeped around their chests like a warm bath.

It was one of the women in this group who first realised something was wrong.

She was indeed up to her chest in water—water, and mud.

Lightning flashed overhead, and all five saw Katherine Dee standing there, staring down at them. They weren't in a clearing at all, trees and brambles still surrounding them. Worse still was that they were all sinking in a stinking, sludgy bog. The woman screamed, and all five tried to pull themselves free as they realised the reality of their situation.

But it was useless; the bog was too thick and the more effort they exerted, the more life it sucked from their arms and legs. Archie O'Neil was alone now.

He had lost all of his followers somewhere in the dark woods.

He had seen some of the weaker ones turn and run, including some members of 'the twelve'. They believed shadowy beasts were stalking them with red and yellow glowing eyes, and a loud growling could be heard among the trees, gradually closing in on them, causing the others to bolt.

As for the rest of his group, O'Neil had no idea what had happened to them.

Katherine Dee appeared at various locations, and the fools had given chase, never to be seen again. O'Neil himself felt fear, like the others, but he was able to brace himself, knowing, or at least suspecting, that whatever was stalking them wasn't real. They were being glamoured, fooled by the use of magic, and their only real adversary was one lone woman.

Bursting out from the tree line, Archie O'Neil had reached the clearing where he could see the house of Katherine Dee. It stood in darkness, and as he strode towards it, the rain beat against him, having now foregone the shelter of the trees. Again, the lightning flashed above, momentarily turning the night into daylight. In that instant, he saw Katherine Dee walk out of the front door of her home. She walked out into the clearing, and O'Neil reached to his hip and pulled a large hunting knife from its sheath.

***

Fenton Akers looked down on Penny-Deep from the roof of the church tower. Leaning over the parapet, he surveyed the churchyard but could see no sign of the police inspector who had chased him. Akers knew there were only two possibilities. Either the idiot policeman had given up, and left the churchyard, perhaps widening his search, or he had spotted the bell tower door and found it unlocked. If that were the case, he might be on his way up to try and arrest him.

Akers eyed the hatch in the roof and considered what would be the best position for him to confront the officer and get a clear shot. Akers tugged at the revolver in his coat. The gun had got caught in the wet lining of his pocket, but eventually, it pulled free.

Adam inched his way up the worn steppingstones that led up to the roof hatch. He moved carefully on all fours in the darkness, a flash of lightning illuminating the colossal church bells that now hung just below him. The bright flash also gave him another glimpse of the long drop that awaited him if he slipped. Now on the last couple of stones,

Adam manoeuvred himself onto his back before reaching up and pushing the hatch open. He waited in case Akers was by the trap door waiting to attack him, but there was no sign of him. The thunder rumbled so loudly, Adam thought for a moment that it would shake the whole tower to rubble. He reached up again and carefully pulled himself up onto the roof.

He stood, bracing himself against the driving wind and rain, looking around for Akers.

The roof itself gently sloped from all four sides, forming a low pyramidal shape, surrounded by a three-feet-high parapet wall. From the mid-point of the roof, a large metal weathervane with a fish design stood reaching into the night sky.

As Adam scanned the roof, for a moment, he thought he had been mistaken as there was no sign of Akers, but then he caught sight of him crouching in the corner of the parapet.

Then he heard Akers hiss.

"Seems like it's my turn to skulk in the shadows now, Inspector."

Adam began to step towards the small thin man, but froze as Akers stood up, and the revolver became visible.

"That's right, Inspector. It regrettably all ends here for you."

Akers pointed the revolver directly at Adam and moved slowly towards him. This action told Adam that there was a good chance Akers was unfamiliar with using a firearm and was probably not a good shot, thus he was getting as close as he could to his target.

"Give me the gun, Father. It's no use; I reported what you did to Carfax. One way or another, you're going to be caught, so don't make your situation any worse than it already is."

Adam was trying to appeal to the man's better judgement, but Akers just laughed.

"You can drop the 'Father', as that's not who I am. As for my situation, you really have no idea what I have done. You would be the last to know anything about me."

"This is the end," Adam replied firmly.

"For you, most definitely! Unfortunately, not for your daughter who, even as we speak, will be having the most depraved things done to her before her death."

Adam saw red. He had never for one moment suspected that Sophia could be in any sort of danger. With rage overcoming his rational mind, Adam charged forward, his right hand grabbing Akers by the throat, his left trying to take the gun.

Akers yanked wildly at the trigger, and the gun fired. Adam felt a searing pain burn into his left shoulder, causing him to slip on the wet, sloping roof and fall to his knees. As Adam looked up, Akers kicked him in the head, sending him sprawling face down.

While kicking out at Adam, Akers too lost his footing, falling on his backside.

By the time Adam lifted his head, Akers had reached out, and taking a firm grasp of the weathervane with his left hand, he pulled himself to his feet, still holding the gun in his right hand. Adam got to his knees. He should have been afraid of dying, but all he could think about was Sophia and what was happening to her.

His only hope was to rush Akers and beat the whereabouts of his daughter out of him.

Akers wrapped his left arm around the weathervane to steady himself, and raised the gun; this time, he would hit his target square on if it took every bullet in the gun.

Adam knew he was going to take some shots; it was unavoidable but also unimportant.

He just needed to survive as long as it took to get Sophia's location and pass it on. Adam readied himself and took a deep breath. He watched as Akers smiled cruelly and took aim.

Adam began to rise to his feet and move towards Akers.

The ink-black sky ripped open with a blinding flash, and Adam saw a huge dancing arch of electrical energy reach down and grab the weathervane. An enormously powerful white light engulfed Akers, who stood bolt upright. Then a cloud of pinkish-orange smoke rose around him.

Adam waited for the smoke to clear before he walked over to Akers who had slumped to his knees, still clinging to the weathervane. What was left of Akers was a charred crisp of a body, in burnt and tattered clothing still smouldering and steaming in the rain.

Adam didn't even try to remove the revolver, as it appeared welded to Akers' hand. Akers was dead, there was no doubt about it. And the sky suddenly let out thunderous applause.

Adam's relief at not being killed was short-lived.

His thoughts were now frantically consumed by saving Sophia.

Making his way down the church tower and across the churchyard, Adam leapt over the wall of the graveyard. He ran to the police car parked nearby, trying to contact despatch via the radio. But all Adam could raise was static and dead air, probably due to the storm, he thought.

For a split second, he toyed with the idea of returning to Penny-Deep Police Station. Adam examined the wound to his shoulder and concluded it looked worse than it was. The bullet had torn a path across the surface of his skin, taking out a gouge of flesh, but not penetrating to any depth.

It was painful, and bled a lot, but that was the extent of it. Adam made his mind up.

He put the car in gear and raced off towards

Old Anna Farm.

***

Driving into the farmyard was impossible due to the number of empty cars parked there. Adam jumped from the police car and ran towards his home.

Both houses were in darkness, and Adam first shouted Sophia and then Mrs Chattox.

But there was no reply.

On reaching his front door, he found it slightly ajar, and his heart sank. It felt as though all the air had been knocked out of him.

He was about to enter his home when he heard someone calling his name. Adam turned to see Mrs Chattox standing at her door, and he ran across the yard to speak to her.

Adam could see that the elderly neighbour was injured as he neared. The right side of her face was now swollen in colours of blue and violet, intersected by a nasty cut.

"Mr Cadman, I'm sorry. I tried to stop them. Truly, I did," the old lady blurted out amid tears.

"I know, I can see that," Adam said, trying to comfort her. "Do you know where Sophia is?"

"Yes, Katherine Dee took her."

Adam snapped. "I knew it. I *knew* she was involved in all of this."

Mrs Chattox took Adam's arm, saying, "You don't understand. When the men came to take Sophia, Katherine Dee came to protect her. She scared the two brutes away, but we knew that wouldn't be the end of it, so she took Sophia up to her house to keep her safe."

"Did you call the police?" he said, horrified.

"No, I couldn't. The phone lines are down, and I can't get a mobile phone signal."

Adam turned and looked around the yard.

"Who do all these cars belong to?"

"They came not long ago, a gang of them. That Archibald O'Neil, he's leading them. They all went up the track after Katherine Dee, to get Sophia."

"Right, I'm going up there," said Adam.

"Be careful going through the dark woods, Mr Cadman."

Adam snorted and growled. "Don't worry, if any of them get in my way, they'll regret it!"

Mrs Chattox shook her head.

"It's not them folks you need to be careful of. Katherine Dee knew they were coming, and she will have made sure something is waiting for them."

Adam heard what the elderly woman said but discarded it.

The only thing that mattered was saving Sophia.

***

Katherine Dee slowly walked across the clearing until she drew level with the Wych Elm. The old tree was being battered one way and then the other, by the gale-force winds, and Katherine took what shelter she could at the base of the tree. She watched Archie O'Neil walk purposefully toward her. And as the lightning flashed, Katherine saw the glint of the long blade he carried in his right hand, but she stood fast and shouted at O'Neil.

"Come no further."

But O'Neil strode on. He was going to teach this witch one last lesson. Reaching Katherine Dee, he lunged forward with the hunting knife, causing her to jump backwards.

Adam Cadman emerged from the dark woods, into the clearing. Though some distance away, he could see both Katherine Dee and O'Neil. He could also see the large knife O'Neil was wielding. Adam shouted out for O'Neil to stop, but the thunder drowned out his voice.

Adam began running to try and save Katherine.

O'Neil made a long, arching swing with the knife, the blade just missing Katherine Dee's face as she leaned back. Again, O'Neil stepped forward and shouted.

"Nice of you to have waited here for me, witch."

But Katherine Dee just looked bemused and replied.

"Oh, but I'm not the one that's been waiting here for you."

As the lightning flashed, something pale

caught O'Neil's eye in the tree above him.

He jerked his head up to take a better look, immediately wishing he hadn't. There, hanging from a thick branch by a rope around her neck, was a pale, old, bag of bones—an old hag, dressed in rags. While O'Neil stared at her in disbelief, her eyes blinked wide open and her mouth gaped in a silent scream, baring her broken teeth. O'Neil knew it was old Lizzie Dee.

As the lightning flashed again, Lizzie's facial features vanished.

And all that O'Neil saw illuminated was the face of a skull. He screamed out in shock. A loud cracking sound drowned out the scream, but this time, the sound wasn't thunder. The large, old branch gave way under the wind's constant barrage and came crashing down.

Rooted to the spot with fear, O'Neil raised his arms to try and shield himself, but it was a futile gesture. The weight of the branch took him to the ground and crushed him.

Adam saw the massive branch fall on O'Neil; why the fool didn't try to get out of the way, he didn't know. By the time Adam reached the body, he could see a small amount of blood coming from both of O'Neil's ears and his nose. For a moment, he thought about moving the branch now resting across O'Neil's chest, but it was too big and far too heavy.

Adam felt for a pulse, but there was none. Archibald O'Neil was dead.

Katherine Dee stood to one side, casually watching the scene like some passer-by, but without the usual concern. Adam asked if she was alright, and she simply nodded.

"I know he came to get Sophia, and I saw him trying to stab you!" said Adam.

"He was just keeping a long overdue appointment," Katherine Dee said nonchalantly, before turning and walking towards her house. Adam walked after her.

"Where's Sophia?"

"She's perfectly safe. Come with me. I'll reunite father and daughter," she said.

***

They reached the large house, and once inside, Katherine Dee closed the door on the storm and tried the light switch but there was no light.

The thunder and lightning had now taken her electricity supply out.

"Must be a power outage due to the weather," she said, lighting several large candles dotted around the living room.

Adam was feeling impatient.

He couldn't see Sophia anywhere, and his impatience almost boiled over when it appeared that Katherine Dee had stopped at her bookcase to select a book, but then there was a clicking sound. Adam saw the door in the bookcase pop open, and he started to walk over, but Katherine Dee stopped him. "Wait there, Adam. Sophia isn't alone. A friend is guarding her."

As Katherine Dee opened the door wider, Adam swore he could see two demonic red eyes staring back at him. But as the candlelight reached further into the tiny room, he saw Sophia sitting with her thin arms wrapped around the neck of the enormous black mastiff.

"Was she safe in there with that animal?" Adam asked.

Katherine Dee smiled.

"Perfectly! Both Sophia and I are perfectly safe with our friend here. It's your safety I have my doubts about."

Adam wasn't sure whether Katherine Dee was joking or not.

But he stood perfectly still just to be on the safe side.

"Besides which," Katherine Dee continued. "If O'Neil or any of his followers had managed to get past me and found Sophia, there would have been carnage; whoever tried to get to her would have been ripped apart before our friend here would have let them take her. Sophia was as safe as I could possibly have made her, given the circumstances".

"Can we keep him, Dad?" Sophia said excitedly.

Katherine just smiled as Adam spluttered some reply about how the huge beast belonged to Ms Dee, and that she would miss him if they took him away from her.

"I guess so!" Sophia said, enthused—as if she had only asked the question to test her father. Adam was secretly pleased that that particular conversation had ended before it really began.

The giant dog softly padded out of the tiny room, and eyed Adam suspiciously before trotting off into another part of the house. Sophia stepped out and ran to her father. Adam picked her up and held her tightly, never wanting to let go again. But eventually, he knew he would have to.

Outside the house, the storm was still raging.

Adam turned to Katherine Dee and said, "Thank you. I'm still not completely sure what's been happening tonight, but I know I owe you a huge debt of gratitude. And by the way, I'm sorry..."

"About what?" Katherine asked, sincerely. She was a little perplexed.

"I was even angry...about the pendant you gave to my girl. I was being stupid..."

Katherine simply smiled, and the warmth spread across the space between them.

Nothing more needed saying. All was good.

Then after a moment's thought, Adam said, "With the phones and radios being out of commission, I need to get back to Penny-Deep Police Station and organise the team to start clearing up this mess and try and make some sense of it. I don't want to take Sophia out in this weather, so I wonder if she could stay here, till I can collect her."

Adam paused.

"Truth is," he said, “I would feel a lot happier if I knew Sophia was safe while I make sure the danger to her is over. I've come to realise this is probably the safest place she could be right now!"

Katherine Dee smiled. "I'd be glad of the company."

Then she reached over and handed a set of car keys to Adam.

"Take my Range Rover. There's a hidden back way out of here, down to Penny-Deep. Just follow the track leading down from the garage over to the left side of the clearing.”

Chapter 24

By five a.m., the storm had cleared, leaving the air fresh and light.

The sun had risen over Penny-Deep.

And even at that early hour, there was a warm and soothing glow over the town. In the stillness before the morning bustle, it was difficult to see the night's events as being anything other than a bad dream. Adam knew it would be difficult for many of the residents to wake up that morning, and on hearing the news, to come to terms with what had happened in their beautiful little town.

Adam had busied himself mustering as many officers as he could to guard and protect the crime scenes. The officers already guarding O'Neil's manor house were relieved by fresh ones.

Also, officers were posted at the small chapel.

Maltravers had disappeared by then, but his details and description had been circulated as wanted, and he would, no doubt, be arrested in due course.

The church, along with the graveyard, was now completely sealed off, and Akers' holdall was full of recovered cash. Two further officers were also sent to stand by and protect the body of Archie O'Neil until it could be photographed in situ and removed. No doubt the coroner's court would class his death as an accident after Adam gave his account of what he saw happen.

Radio communications with force headquarters had eventually returned, and at six a.m., Adam, with the aid of a borrowed mobile phone, contacted Chief Superintendent Wise.

"Good morning Sir. I'm sorry I'm late contacting you, but the storm knocked out all communications in Penny-Deep."

"No problem, Adam. Anything to report?"

"As a matter of fact, there's a lot to report."

Adam took a deep breath. "During the night, we’ve had three deaths, one of which was murder. And all, I believe, are connected to the girls missing from the city."

The Chief Superintendent sat stunned on the other end of the phone as Adam continued.

"Yesterday, I stumbled upon an old chapel on the O'Neil estate, where I believe the girls had been held captive. I found a scratched message in a basement room, from Amelia Canary, no less."

"My God. Have you any idea who was holding them there?"

"Yes it was Archibald O'Neil and some of his estate staff, along with the local vicar and an assortment of O'Neil's friends," said Adam. "Oh, and two local brothers who were used as hired muscle by this group."

"But why?" demanded the Chief Super.

"I have a bad feeling that those poor girls

were taken and killed in some perverse satanic ritual."

Chief Superintendent Wise listened sombrely, then asked. "If that's the case, have you any idea where they could have hidden the bodies?"

"Yes, I believe so," said Adam. "The local vicar Akers had the Armstrong brothers endlessly digging in old graves, supposedly to tidy them up and reset the headstones. If I'm right, we need to check those graves, and see who's actually in them."

The Chief Superintendent agreed with Adam.

The old graves would have made a smart hiding place for the bodies, and until these revelations, no one would have thought to look there. Wise said, "I'll arrange to get some ground-penetrating radar equipment up there, plus a forensic team and a team of officers with shovels."

Then he asked, "What about this O'Neil and company; have any arrests been made yet?"

"O'Neil is dead. A falling branch killed him during the storm. But not before he and his cronies imprisoned me and tried to abduct my daughter."

"Good Lord!" said Wise.

Adam continued, "The local vicar, Akers, tried to stab me when I escaped, but inadvertently stabbed Ms Carfax, O'Neil's secretary, killing her outright. I followed Akers to the top of Penny-Deep Church tower where he shot me in the shoulder before being struck by lightning and killed."

"Bloody hell!" exclaimed Wise. "Is anybody left alive? It sounds like Armageddon up there."

"The two Armstrong brothers are locked in the detention rooms here at Penny-Deep Police Station, along with several of O'Neil's friends who are implicated. Five more have been discovered stuck in a bog in the woods, would you believe! One of them is retired Police Inspector Winter. A guard has been posted over them, and they will be arrested as soon as they can be winched out."

"Winter! Well, I can't say I'm shocked he was up to no good. I never did like the man."

At that point, Adam could hear the Chief Superintendent start to bark orders at others on the other end of the phone. Returning to Adam, Wise said, “I will be moving the whole Major Incident Team up to Penny-Deep, to look into what's been happening. Do you have enough space for them?"

"I can arrange for them to set up in the local primary school while the children are on their long summer break. I’ve been told the water level at the river crossing is subsiding, so getting up here should no longer be a problem," said Adam, thankful that help was on its way.

The Chief Superintendent was satisfied that Adam had taken care of everything needing to be done for the present. Adam had informed him that officers were preserving all the relevant scenes, and Wise thought how fortunate it had been that his best detective had just moved up to Penny-Deep. Then pointing out the irony, he said to Adam, "My God! What a night you have had. To think you moved up there for a quiet life and to spend more time with your daughter!"

The Chief Superintendent's words reminded Adam about prioritising what was important. He had moved here for Sophia, yet the events of the last days had left him isolated from her and had placed her in direct danger. Now, she was more important than everything in the world put together.

"Actually, Sir," he cut in. "If it's alright with you, I'd like to clock off duty now and get my shoulder seen by a doctor before collecting Sophia. She's had one hell of a night, too, and I just want to be with her more than anything else."

"Of course," said the Chief Superintendent. "You do what you need to do. Take some time off if you need it. If we need anything, we'll call you as things progress."

Then he added, "Thank you, Adam. I don't know where we would have been, or how this would have ended, without you."

***

In the days that followed, Adam and Sophia grew to be inseparable. He had been worried that she might have suffered psychologically, but there was no sign of it. Fortunately, she seemed to regard the whole incident as one big adventure and talked about it excitedly.

In all honesty, what had occurred was perhaps less of a trauma than the loss of her mother had been. Katherine Dee popped by every day to see how Sophia was feeling, and simply to chat. She still seemed a touch strange to Adam, but now he saw in her a good heart and a beauty that was no longer about her outward appearance.

Katherine always brought the white horse called Ruby with her, as well as Fancy the large mastiff, or the *hound from hell* as Adam called him under his breath.

Adam always felt nervous around the beast, but in fairness, he knew the dog had protected Sophia, and whenever Sophia played with the hound from hell, he was putty in her hands.

It was a warm, sunny, Saturday afternoon when Katherine Dee next called at Old Anna Farm. She spoke to Mrs Chattox, and on hearing her voice in the yard, Sophia ran out to greet her.

Adam was just completing his written statement. He sat up from the kitchen work surface that he was using as a desk and rotated his left arm, easing the stiffness in his shoulder.

The bullet had cut through only surface tissue, across the top of the muscle. The damage was minimal, and Penny-Deep's Doctor Percival had done an excellent job of stitching it.

The wound was healing nicely, with no sign of

infection.

While writing his statement, there were certain things Adam omitted. Not that they would have any bearing in a court of law anyway. But it was just that these things he left out were the things he had difficulty understanding. On a whim, he decided to have a chat with Katherine about them.

Out in the sunshine, Sophia was playing fetch the ball with the giant mastiff, who would always drop the ball at her feet, then sit and lick Sophia's face until she threw the ball again.

Sophia's giggling filled the air.

Katherine Dee looked radiant in a brightly flowered dress. Every time Adam saw her, he was stunned by just how beautiful she was. She smiled and walked over to him.

"Hello, Inspector Cadman! How's the shoulder today?

"Much better thank you. And please call me Adam."

For a while, they exchanged pleasantries and chatted about Sophia.

Then when the time seemed right, Adam said, "I owe you an apology. In fact, I probably owe you several. I mean, in addition to the one I gave you before, about the pendant."

"Oh!"

"You told me that the missing girls were being held below ground in some sort of a religious building, and I didn't listen to you. Actually, I scoffed at what you said, but you turned out to be right."

Katherine smiled at him.

"Yes I was, wasn't I," she said with a mock smugness that teased him.

Then she said in a more serious tone, "But whatever they were doing there, whatever dark magic they were using, it made it impossible for me to see the exact location. And no one outside O'Neil and his circle of friends knew the old chapel existed on the estate. So don't you go guilt-tripping, thinking that you could have done more to save those poor women if you had listened to me."

In truth, those thoughts had been haunting Adam. Katherine continued.

"Besides," she said, "You're a policeman, used to dealing in cold, hard facts. You belong to a logical, ordered world. I suppose some of the things I told you must have seemed strange to the point of being unbelievable."

"While we are on the topic," Adam said, now starting to feel a little uncomfortable but continuing anyway. "When I was locked in that place, it was dark except for some failing candlelight. During that time, I saw something cross the room where I was held captive. At first, I thought it was you, but as it passed me, it seemed more like a ghost that glided through the solid door. How would you explain that?"

Katherine looked thoughtful, then said,

"There are two possible explanations. The first one involves me locating you astrally, then creating a Tulpa, which was able to glamour the guard outside the room to open the door so you could escape."

Adam thought about what she had said, then he asked, "You mentioned two possible explanations, what is the second one?"

Katherine gave him a serious look, then answered, "You were just missing me and fantasising about yours truly." She burst out laughing, almost as if she couldn't stop.

Adam felt embarrassed and failed terribly at hiding it.

When Katherine had stopped laughing at his expense, he pressed on.

"Okay, Okay! Going with the first explanation, then how did you find me—astrally?

"I had previously been able to travel to some of the missing girls, astrally. But as I told you, the magic cast around the chapel had always stopped me from being able to pinpoint the location. Those visitations had taken many hours of concentration, and unfortunately, despite the effort, I gained little except a feeling for the place."

"Then I was lucky you were able to find me so quickly," said Adam.

"Luck had nothing to do with it. It was the pendant I gave to Sophia. I charged it with an energy I could easily see, even through a thick wall of obfuscation magic. The charm was always meant as insurance for Sophia, so I could keep her safe. But then, when you had gone missing, I checked that she was still wearing the charm and she told me you'd taken it and put it in your pocket. Finding you was easy; the pendant lit up like a beacon. Astrally, that is."

Adam felt small and even more stupid now, having taken the pendant from Sophia and made such a big issue of it. His prejudice and arrogance could have cost Sophia her life. He said, sheepishly, "Will the pendant still work, Katherine? I... I mean, I'll make sure she wears it. Like I said before, I was stupid."

"Well, it works but the charge runs down over time, like a battery. But if ever we think it's necessary, I can charge it again. In the meantime, just let Sophia wear it. It was a gift from me to her, and she did seem to like it." Adam nodded wholeheartedly. "She does. She *loves* it."

They sat on the wooden bench in the front garden, soaking up the sun and watching Sophia and Fancy play. But after a while, Adam broke the silence.

"The Armstrong brothers fully admitted their part in everything," he said. "They admitted abducting the girls in the city, and then taking them to O'Neil and Akers, at the chapel. They even mention your name when they're interviewed."

"Really?"

"According to the detectives that interviewed the brothers, both were absolutely terrified of you. They were happy to admit everything, apparently, so long as you were kept away from them."

"Well, I never!" Katherine said innocently.

Sophia and the mastiff seemingly tired of playing ball, and they came over to sit on the grass, next to the bench. Adam and Fancy had a stare-off, but there was only ever going to be one winner. Adam shifted slightly on the seat to avoid the big dog's gaze.

Then Adam, still deep in thought about the Armstrong brothers, said, "The night I saw you drinking with the Armstrongs in the pub, I thought you were all friends."

Katherine laughed and snorted derisively.

"I had a feeling those two were somehow involved with the missing girls. I had a vision of them taking one of the girls' bodies in a van and tried to stop them but couldn't. So I decided to spend a little time with them and get inside their heads. It was easy enough. they came over and clumsily tried to chat me up."

"What did you find out? "

"Well, there wasn't a lot going on inside those two heads, I can tell you that for starters. But I was left with no doubt that they were involved in the abductions."

"Why didn't you come over and just tell me!" said Adam.

"Would you have believed me? Besides, I had no tangible evidence. Only vague images as I read them both." Adam knew she was right, of course.

There was no way he would have believed her then.

He puzzled about events a little more and then asked, "What did you do to the Armstrong brothers? Sophia told me what happened when they tried to take her, and she told me how you scared them away. But how was that possible with those two gorillas?"

"They were both feeble-minded, and while I was inside their heads at the pub, I decided to do a little gardening. Just in case."

"Gardening?" Adam was confused.

But Sophia turned and suddenly interjected, "You mean you planted some seeds, don't you?"

Katherine Dee smiled at Sophia and then said, "Yes, Sophia, that's right! My, you are clever! I planted some seeds in their minds that lay dormant, ready to burst forth if and when I needed them to." Adam assumed she was talking about some sort of hypnotic suggestion.

He was happy to let the matter drop. Then Katherine said, "My turn to ask a question! Assuming you know the answer. The black magic rituals O'Neil and his followers were performing... What was so important that they thought it necessary to sacrifice young women?"

"The major incident team are still digging

into the background, but some of O'Neil's group, who have been arrested, have admitted they were harnessing dark forces, so they had an edge while conducting lucrative, but very risky, hedge fund deals."

"I see," Katherine said thoughtfully. "What an utterly twisted and wicked thing to do."

Then she said, "The love of money is the root of all kinds of evil."

Adam looked surprised. "Are you quoting the Bible?"

"Yes, Timothy 6:10. Speaking of holy things, where did Father Akers fit into all this?

"The real Father Fenton Akers was found hidden, buried in one of the old graves like the missing girls. As far as the major incident team and forensic people can work out, he was murdered a couple of years ago. Probably as soon as he arrived in Penny-Deep, after spending years working in Africa, he was replaced by the man we knew as Akers. The replacement bore a passing resemblance by all accounts. All he had to do was dye his hair ginger. The church bishops for this area didn't know the real Father Akers, him being out of the country for so long. The fake vicar stepped into his shoes without raising suspicion."

"So, who was the man we all thought was Father Akers?"

"No one knows. I've had to sit PC Foster down and tell him he isn't legally married!"

Both Adam and Katherine laughed.

"As far as we have been able to trace, the only documentation for Akers was a passport that melted along with his false teeth. His hands were too badly burnt to obtain fingerprints, and his DNA didn't match any on record. All the arrested co-conspirators thought he was Fenton Akers."

Adam continued, "Even my predecessor, ex-Inspector Winter couldn't shed any light on who Akers was. Winter was dragged from the bog with four others in full ceremonial costume and had obviously been in with O'Neil from the beginning. Although he won't admit it, I suspect it was Winter who told O'Neil I had a daughter who could be taken."

For a moment, Adam's mind relived the horror of what might have been. Katherine put a hand on his arm to comfort him. She said, "Adam, they are all now paying the price for dabbling with forces outside their understanding. They should have known that whatever you put out there has a habit of returning to you three-fold or more."

Then Adam remembered something.

"When O'Neil was killed, you said he was keeping an overdue appointment or something. What did you mean?"

"His ancestor hanged Old Lizzie Dee from the Wych Elm tree. When O'Neil tried to kill me under the same tree, it was the same branch that

Old Lizzie was hanged from that came down and killed him. I think perhaps Old Lizzie had been waiting to exact revenge on the next O'Neil who tried to harm a Dee."

For the next hour, they talked on about happier, more normal, things. Mrs Chattox came over and began cooking dinner to which Katherine was invited, while Adam took his statement down to Penny-Deep Police Station. Katherine Dee took Sophia and Fancy for a walk up the track where they visited the pond by the waterfall. They sat talking on a large rock by the water, chatting. Katherine said, "Do you know how Penny-Deep got its name, Sophia? Not many people do."

Sophia shook her head.

"It all started here, a long, long time ago, when people would toss a penny into the deep water and make a wish. It's said that all the wishes came true."

Sophia was enthralled.

"Do you have a wish you would like to make?"

Sophia was about to speak when Katherine handed her a large, old copper penny.

"Don't tell," Katherine said. "Not anyone. Not even me, or the wish won't come true. Now close your eyes and make the wish to yourself, before tossing the penny into the deep."

Sophia thought carefully about what she should wish for, and how to word it just right. She looked at Katherine carefully, smiled, and then

—closing her eyes—she tossed the coin into the air while making her wish. She heard a loud *plop!*

Printed in Great Britain
by Amazon

54046264R00188